M
HUGGINS   Hug

D042900+

T.

DATE DUE

MY 18 '98			
MY 30 '98			
JE 11 '98			
JE 23 '98			
JY 1 '98			
JY 27 '98			

the big kiss

the big kiss

DAVID HUGGINS

AN ARCADE MYSTERY

 ARCADE PUBLISHING - NEW YORK

FIRST U.S. EDITION 1997

This is a work of fiction. Names, places, characters, and incidents are either the products of the author's imagination or used fictitiously.

Library of Congress Cataloging-in-Publication Data

Huggins, David.
    The big kiss / by David Huggins. —1st U.S. ed.
        p.   cm.
    ISBN 1-55970-409-8
    I. Title.
  PR6058.U335B54 1996b
  823'.914—dc21   97–24383

Published in the United States by Arcade Publishing, Inc., New York

Distributed by Little, Brown and Company

10 9 8 7 6 5 4 3 2 1

the big kiss

1

London Tap

THERE WAS A CHIP OF BONE BEHIND HER LEFT EYE that was pressing up against her brain and they were going to take it out later that afternoon. The doctor said I could sit with her for a few minutes so a male nurse with a rockabilly haircut led me down the corridor to her glassed-off room. She lay asleep surrounded by machines that were taking readings and piping medicine into her wrist. When I took her hand in mine it felt so cold that I was glad when her mouth twitched and told me that she was alive. Her good eye opened for a second and when she smiled at me I felt love for her, the unconditional kind you hear about.

The nurse changed the dressing on her other eye. My heart shrank. The eye was horribly contused, a slit plum swollen out beyond her brow. I squeezed her hand. This was my fault and I felt the weight of karma bear down until I could barely breathe. If I hadn't gone back to Alan's mews that night, none of this would have been happening.

I asked the nurse for some water to swallow my lithium tablet. He filled a paper cup at a tiny sink. With the force of an hallucination, I remembered her laughing at the news that an average glass of London tap water had already passed through seven people. I took the pill, brushed a strand of hair from her forehead and began to cry. As I wiped away the tears I wondered how many pairs of eyes they'd been through before they got to me.

The nurse told me that it was time to go and showed me to an empty waiting-room. I couldn't face going home alone. A window faced south towards Putney and I looked out at high-rises sparkling against the dark sky. Storm clouds were gathering to the south-west, just as they had on the night it all began.

2

Car Trouble

IT HAD BEEN RAINING HEAVILY THAT NIGHT when the taxi dropped me back at the mews to collect my car. Lightning flickered on-and-off like a dud strip-light. The thunder followed as I paid the driver.

All the lights were on in Alan's house and the blue Mini that I'd seen earlier was now parked by his front door. I needed some coffee before the drive home. I struck the brass door-knocker twice. Music was playing inside. Marvin Gaye. When I knocked again I heard a loud thump that seemed to come from upstairs, the sound of something heavy falling. The impact rattled the windows. I dropped to my knees on the wet cobbles to shout Alan's name through the letter-box.

I peered through the slit to see the back of a sofa and part of the open-plan kitchen beyond. A green wine bottle stood by the sink. It hadn't been there when I'd left thirty minutes earlier. In a break between tracks there was a sharp cracking sound. I thought I heard a moan from upstairs.

I hammered the door-knocker, shouting to make myself heard above the storm. It was a small house on two floors. I couldn't understand why nobody came to the door. At the bay window I looked through a gap in the curtains but all I could see was the neat stack of books on the coffee-table and the abstract print framed on the far wall. I wanted to call the police but my mobile phone had a flat battery. I looked round to see if there were any lights on in the other houses but it was one a.m. They were all dark.

As I ran to look for a phone box on the main road, I twisted my ankle on the slick cobblestones. I hobbled a hundred yards down the road before I found a steel British Telecom unit clouted into the pavement, a giant tack that offered no shelter from the rain.

I was about to dial 999 for the first time in my life when I had second thoughts. If I called the police I knew I wouldn't get home for hours. I was feeling exhausted. I wiped the rain from my eyes, telling myself that I had overreacted. What if Claire and Alan were just having a row, a fight?

In the end I decided to dial Alan's number. I rang five times before it was picked up.

'Alan? Is that you? It's Steve,' I said.

I heard Marvin Gaye in the background and then someone dropped the phone. There was the sound of a struggle before the line went dead.

When I re-dialled the number it was engaged. Even then I couldn't bring myself to call the police. I limped back to Alan's place just in time to see his BMW CSi pulling out of the mews, the headlights sweeping over me through the warp of falling rain as the car turned onto the street. I couldn't see the driver. The lights were still burning upstairs at Alan's house but the ground floor was in darkness. The blue Mini was still parked outside. There was no response when I hit the door-knocker.

Streetlight reflected off the wet cobbles but the doorstep was dry. I noticed two spots glittering on the pale stone. They were perfectly round, serrated at the circumference like cog-wheels. I knelt down to touch one with my finger. It smelt metallic like fresh blood. I banged on the front door, calling Alan's name. A window opened across the mews and a man shouted that I should clear off or he'd call the police. I dawdled for a couple of minutes to wind him up before I climbed into my Mitsubishi Shōgun.

I knew I was over the limit from the drinks as I pulled out of the mews. I had to concentrate on the road and drive with due care and attention, keeping an eye out for flashing blue lights. I was arrested for vandalism as a teenager and I felt an echo of police paranoia when a white van appeared in my rear-view mirror. Fortunately it turned off towards Olympia.

My windscreen wipers had difficulty clearing the vol-ume of rain but when I reached Hammersmith the downpour eased a little. I began to wrestle with my conscience, guilty that I hadn't dialled 999.

On the other hand, Alan was technically my boss and he'd have been livid if I'd sent the police round just because he'd been having a fight with his girlfriend. I knew how things could get out of hand. When Liz and I were in full flight, so was the crockery. Then I thought of the blood on the door-step. I inspected the brown mark on my finger and smeared it off on my soaked jeans.

The rain had stopped by the time I pulled up outside our five-bedroom house in Roehampton. I parked on the gravel driveway beside my wife's Fiat Punto. Liz had left the coach

5

lights on by the front door of our detached Tudor-style home, illuminating the black wooden beams and white plaster panels of the building's fascia. I set my mobile phone to recharge and dissolved a Paracetamol tablet in a glass of water. I took it upstairs to bed, treading gently on my sprained ankle. I hoped that Liz was already asleep but the lights were on in our bedroom. She was reading in bed with her spectacles perched on the end of her nose, the pillows banked up against the button-backed headboard. Liz's elfin face glistened with the Clinique cold cream she applied at night in an attempt to turn the clock back on nine years of married life. She looked up and scowled at me.

'So did you kill anyone on the way home?' she asked.

'I told you I was all right to drive,' I said. My hand trembled as I raised the glass of Paracetamol to my mouth.

'Which is why you're slurring your words and drinking that muck.'

Liz had recently discovered homeopathy and now had little time for the fruits of Western medicine.

'I've got a headache, that's all,' I said.

'*Quelle surprise*, Steve,' she said, turning a page of her book, *Women Who Love Too Much*, a book that she'd bought for its title alone. I climbed into bed and tugged gently at the duvet to unfurl some *Lebensraum* from Liz's side of the bed.

'Alan was still up when I got back there,' I said.

'I bet he was pleased to see you again.'

'I didn't see him. I knocked on the door but there was no reply.'

'Then how do you know he was still up?' she asked. Tiny points of light gleamed on her creamy face.

'There was music playing. All the lights were on and Claire was there. Her Mini was parked outside.'

'So you had another chance to ogle her tits? That must have been nice.'

'Oh, come off it. I just wanted a cup of coffee for the drive,' I protested. All the same I wondered if it was partly true that the sight of Claire's car had prompted me to knock on Alan's front door. Liz's long dark hair lay splayed on the pillow beside me, as twisted and tangled as human motive.

'Look, I heard something going on inside his house. Violence, people fighting,' I said.

'What do you mean, violence?'

'Someone getting hit, falling over and moaning. I shouted but no one came to the door. Then I called Alan's number. Someone picked up the phone and I heard a struggle in the background.'

Liz raised her eyebrows. Her spectacles slid down the greased slope of her nose to stop at its *retroussé* tip.

'A struggle? So naturally you called the police,' she said.

'No, but I thought about it.'

'Oh, but you should have, Steve! They might have given you a Community Action Trust award. If they didn't arrest you as a Peeping Tom.'

'I thought he might have been having a row with Claire,' I said. 'And, anyway, I saw his car drive off when I got back from the phone box.'

'Then what on earth are you worried about?' she sighed.

'It could have been a burglar at the wheel. Alan might be lying in his house bleeding to death.' I pictured him on the carpet, a claw-hammer lying by his head in a pool of blood.

'Sure, sure. I'm bored of this bullshit. I'm going to sleep,' said Liz. She switched off the light and we lay silently in the dark.

'I'm not making this up,' I said.

Liz put the light back on. 'Right then,' she said. 'What's Alan's number? I'm going to call him.'

I told her the number and she dialled it on the bedside phone.

'It's engaged. Maybe it's off the hook. And it was definitely Claire's car you saw?'

'I'm sure it was. The blue Mini we saw in the drive outside her house.'

'How d'you know it was hers?' she asked, trying the number again.

'Parked right outside Alan's front door? Same colour and year? There aren't that many around.'

Liz dialled the operator and asked to have Alan's line checked. It took a few minutes to discover that his phone was out of order. Liz began to lose interest.

'I find it hard to imagine Alan beating Claire up,' she said. Her eyes widened as if she relished the idea.

Liz turned off the light. Her application of face cream meant that she didn't want to make love and she soon fell asleep. I tossed and turned, feeling bad that I hadn't called the police.

Like Liz, I found it hard to picture Alan in a scene of domestic violence. He was too controlled. In the three months since he'd joined our company he'd hardly even raised his voice. Alan was a couple of years older than me but he looked younger. He had the kind of self-confidence you can't buy from a therapist or a dealer. I wondered if he'd got it from public school. Over the last couple of months I'd been hoping some of this confidence might rub off on me.

I couldn't sleep. After half an hour I left my dormant wife and went downstairs to dial Alan's number. The engaged tone beeped in my ear like a heart monitor and I asked the operator

8

to check the line. I was put on hold and stared at our wedding photograph on the desk. Two young Kodachrome strangers smiled at me through the glass.

I'd been an art student at Chelsea when I'd met Liz at Taboo, a discotheque in Leicester Square. Nineteen years old with silver hair, Liz had been going through what parents like to call a phase - awaydaying into London from the stockbroker belt, smoking spliff in the train toilet and struggling with her eyeliner pencil against the bends in the track. Then Liz moved into a flat on Beaufort Street with two girlfriends and I courted her assiduously, beating off two rivals. One of them was a glum guitarist with a Second Division New Romantic band - not that there were any First Division New Romantic bands. Liz and I fell in love that summer and around the same time she began to get work as a model. When I asked her to marry me the following year on a whim I'd envisaged a quick trip to the registry office, but Liz's mother had insisted on a proper wedding. We were married in Liz's parents' local church in Hampshire. Between us, Liz and I received seven matt black Filofaxes as wedding presents.

But that all seemed like a thousand years ago as the operator informed me that Alan's phone was still out of order. I went back to bed and replayed the evening in my mind, trawling my memory for a clue.

.

3

Love Is . . .

ALAN HAD ASKED LIZ AND ME OUT TO DINNER so we had arranged to meet for a drink at his place before going on to a restaurant. I'd been glad that Liz was going to be there because it meant I wouldn't have to discuss the company's problems all night with Alan. I was in a good mood for once and I didn't want to lose it.

For the past week Alan had been trying to get me to support him in his plan to fire Tony Mold, my partner in the fashion business that we'd started together in the mid-eighties. Tony and I had been friends since art school. I wanted no part of his sacking, especially since he had just kicked his way out of the closet after ten years of marriage and now faced an enormous alimony bill. However, as soon as I was inside the mews house near Gloucester Road Alan raised the subject of Tony again.

'Steve, I've got to level with you on this. We can't afford to keep paying out three executive salaries. There's no way Sally'll buy it.'

'Hey, give it a rest,' I said. 'Let's have a drink.'

Alan shrugged and fixed me a vodka and tonic. Sally Moore was our backer and we'd hired Alan as managing director at her suggestion. She had called a board meeting for the following day to discuss further investment in our company.

'It's just that we don't need Tony's design skills right now,' Alan continued. 'It's the import lines that we're making money on, the business you built up yourself. If we can pull through the next year or so, Tony can come back.'

'Look, please, give it a break. Liz'll be here any minute and I don't want to talk about this in front of her. Tony's an old friend.'

'Well, whatever you say, boss. But we do have to talk it over.'

'Boss' was a nickname. As managing director, Alan had the power to make the major business decisions, leaving Tony and me free to concentrate on design and marketing.

Alan went upstairs to get changed. I looked around his sitting-room, a showroom of bachelor living with modern furniture and black hi-fi and video equipment. His CDs were arranged in alphabetical order from Aerosmith to Frank Zappa. Alan had bought the house two years before and it still looked immaculate. The magazines and books on the coffee-table were piled in a neat ziggurat, square to the edge of the table.

Alan had spent some time in Public Relations before he'd hit the jackpot importing a designer beer, selling the company for a large profit. Then he made some astute moves in the property market and began hiring himself out as a company doctor. I was replenishing my drink in the kitchen area when he bounced down the stairs in an untucked denim Stüssy shirt, black jeans and biker boots, looking crisp and hygienic. I've

11

got the standard-issue no-frills suburban body, a '64 model with roomy well-upholstered stomach. I felt like a fat slob beside Alan. I asked him if I could have a wash and he told me to go upstairs, second on the left.

His white sparkling bathroom was squeezed between a bedroom and a small study. I spent a while in there hoping that Liz would arrive so that Alan couldn't harangue me about Tony. I opened the medicine cabinet and found nail-scissors, cotton-buds and razor-blades laid out on a cloth like the instruments in an operating theatre. There was quite a collection of male fragrances and some shampoo from a trichological clinic that I'd visited at the first signs of hair-loss two years earlier. I couldn't see why Alan went there since he still had an abundant crop of red hair that he wore long. When I'd finished with the soap it was black, and I felt obliged to rinse it under the tap before returning it to the dish. Then I heard a knock at the front door and went back downstairs.

Alan was double-kissing Liz who was wearing a new floral-print dress that hugged her breasts and flared out at the hips. She was laughing at some joke of Alan's and broke off to peck me on the lips without much enthusiasm.

'Oh, Alan, you said that you were going to get a nice bright rug and jolly the place up! This room's so cold!' Liz illustrated her point with a little shiver. 'It's crying out for some colour. Some flowers at least.'

'I know, I know. I'm sorry but I just haven't had the time,' Alan said.

'Then you should get someone in to do it for you. A decorator.'

'I like it as it is,' I said. 'Organized, no frills.'

'Organized? It's antiseptic! And what would you know about "organized" anyway?' she said to me.

'No, Liz is right,' Alan said. 'This place is too eighties. It needs a more organic feel.'

'A nice painting over the fireplace or something. And that print's got to go. It's ghastly!' said Liz, indicating a reproduction of an op art painting by Vasarèly, a distorted grid in blue and grey that appeared to pulse and press out through the frame.

'Don't you like it? I've had it since I was at university,' said Alan.

'Well, you can afford something better now, can't you?' Liz said.

I studied the picture until my eyes began to ache. We had another drink and then Alan drove us to an expensive Italian slow-food restaurant on the Fulham Road called La Paesana. I'd never heard of it but Liz said she had lunched there with a friend. I wondered if Alan would be putting the bill on his company credit card. The restaurant opened onto a covered garden at the back where waiters in dark-blue T-shirts ministered to an upmarket clientele. Tanned middle-aged men in open-neck shirts sat with their wives or girl-friends. There were no kids or black people to be seen. The manager flashed his capped teeth from beneath a talking-point moustache, greeted Alan by name and showed us to a table at the back of the garden next to a couple of striped shirts with their Diana-style womenfolk. Alan asked the manager for a bottle of Chardonnay while Liz scoped out the other punters.

'Have you noticed how all the women are blonde?' she asked us.

I peered over the top of the A3 menu. Besides Liz I could see only two other brunettes.

'I bet half of them are dye-jobs,' I said.

13

Alan turned round to give the room a sweep. 'More than half, I'd guess,' he said.

'It's like they come complete with the hair, gold jewellery and the clear-varnished fingernails,' said Liz. 'And they can only wear navy and beige. Yuk! I reckon they grow them to full-size in vats of nutrient underneath Harrods.'

Liz saw herself as cooler and more Bohemian than the blondes, but despite her teenybopper rebellion and subsequent modelling career, she'd been to the same schools as these women and now she probably used the same hairdresser. I'd heard this described as the Narcissism of Minor Difference at a seminar on fashion retailing.

'They're just your Basic Pleasure Model Sloanes, like in *Blade Runner*,' Alan said.

'Steve and I saw *Blade Runner* on one of our first dates. God, it was embarrassing!' Liz cried. 'Twenty minutes into the film Steve put an arm round me and I thought, oh God, here we go, but he just started rubbing my elbow. And he kept rubbing it for the rest of the film! I thought he was some kind of freak. He told me later that he'd thought it was my tit.'

Alan laughed and I smiled weakly. Liz had told this story many times to many people.

'Apparently some people have a fetish for elbows,' Alan said. 'Seriously. I think it's the wrinkly bit of skin at the tip that turns them on.'

Liz pulled a face and Alan treated us to a well-polished anecdote of his own about the perils of cinema-dating.

'I was about eighteen and I took a girl to see a film,' he said. 'I'd just had my appendix out and they'd shaved all my pubic hair off before the operation. But I hadn't told my date about it and when she put her hand down my pants she whipped it back out and said, "I didn't think you were as young as that!" Can you imagine? It was a real toe-curler.'

Alan was so smooth that it was hard to imagine him being embarrassed. There was something of the replicant about Alan - the effortless gestures, the complex sums he did in his head and the way his face looked like it had been cast in plastic from a mould labelled 'conventional good looks'. He used an electric razor twice a day to heighten this effect, patrolling the frontier between himself and the rest of the world.

'What happened afterwards? Between you and the girl?' Liz asked him.

'We went out together for a few months.'

'That sounds like a long relationship by your standards,' said Liz, her face reddening at the realization that she might have pushed it too far. When Liz had first met Alan she'd spent half an hour char-grilling him about his failure to achieve a committed relationship.

'Have a care, Liz,' I said.

'No, no. It's a fair comment,' Alan said. 'But I do think I'm ready for a serious relationship now.'

'What, a full twelve-round title bout?' I asked, refilling my wine glass.

'Why not? If I met the right person.'

'Are you doing anything tomorrow night?' Liz asked him.

'I'm having dinner with my aunt,' he said.

'Well, why don't you come over for a drink afterwards?' Liz asked.

'Aren't we seeing Mary tomorrow night?' I said.

Liz kicked me under the table. Mary Marighela was Liz's best friend, a Model-turned-Divorcee with a seven-year-old son. I could see what Liz was planning. She'd been setting Mary up with men for the past two years without success.

'Come over if you can, Alan. It'd be fun. What do you say?' Alan raised his palms in surrender and said he might be able to make it since his aunt was elderly and lived in Barnes, not far from us.

We ordered food and the conversation zipped along, punctuated by brays of laughter from the surrounding tables. Liz was more animated than she had been for weeks, regurgitating insights that she'd gleaned from television as she picked at a plate of pasta. Alan sliced through his calves' liver and I worked on my veal and the Chardonnay.

We'd reached dessert and Liz's warmed-over analysis of Quentin Tarantino's *oeuvre* when a blonde girl came into the restaurant with two callow youths. The three of them went to the bar and ordered long drinks. The girl was beautiful and I was happily surprised when she weaved her way through the restaurant to our table. She tapped Alan on the shoulder with a giggle and bent down to kiss him.

'Hi, Alan. How are you?' She seemed excited and a little insecure. Alan swivelled round with delight.

'Claire! What are you doing here?'

Alan introduced us as Liz assessed Claire with quick eyes. The girl was old enough to know she was beautiful but too young to know quite how to handle it. Slender and feminine, she smiled at Liz and me from behind a curtain of ash-blonde hair.

'Why don't you sit down and have a drink?' Alan asked her.

'I'd love to, just for a minute. We're waiting for a table,' she said.

'Who are you with?' asked Alan.

16

'Just some friends from college. Rupert and Tarquin,' said Claire.

Alan turned round as she pointed them out. The boys looked over from the bar, sullen and self-conscious. One of them was wearing a leather jacket that looked like one of our designs but was made of better leather, a three hundred quid item.

Claire sat down and swept her blonde mane back over her shoulders. I poured her a glass of wine and guessed she was about twenty-two, a sophisticated twenty-two in her Agnès B jacket. She took a sip of wine through her full lips and reached for a Camel Light. Her shoulders were lopsided from an adolescent shyness but you could tell that she'd be a real handful in a few years. I wished I'd changed my shirt before coming out and hoped that Claire wouldn't notice my stale armpits as I sparked her cigarette. I saw Liz give me a disapproving look.

'How's the revision going?' Alan asked Claire.

'Oh, not too bad, thanks. I've only got one more paper to go, thank God.' Her eyes were set wide but there was a cleverness there. The frown mark between them registered the strain of her exams.

'Claire's taking her finals,' Alan explained, covering her hand with his own on the tablecloth. She put her other hand on his. I felt a snip of what I recognized as jealousy. I wanted to put my own hand on top of the pile and start a childish game.

'What subject are you doing?' asked Liz, whose own further education had been limited to a Foundation course in Southampton.

'Philosophy,' Claire said.

'God, you must be clever!' Liz said. The line was soaked

17

in acid to my ears. Poor Liz, double-whammied by youth and now brains.

'You must be joking,' Claire replied. 'I'll be lucky to get a 2.2.'

'Oh, don't be silly!' Alan said, giving her hand a squeeze. A look passed between them and Claire's shoulders dropped. When she took off her jacket I saw a bruise above the scoop-neck of her white T-shirt. She hadn't got it playing lacrosse.

'You poor thing. Finals must be hell,' Liz said, smiling as she roasted Claire on a subterranean spit in her imagination. 'I've got a friend who still has nightmares about the finals she took ten years ago. Honestly. She dreams she's going back for her final term and she hasn't done any work so she has to run around borrowing essays from her friends. Then she has to try and learn them by heart.'

'Maybe I should borrow some essays myself,' Claire said.

'What are you going to do when you get your degree?' I asked her, hearing myself come over like a boring old jerk.

'Oh, I'll get a job, I guess. Maybe travel a bit first. I haven't really decided what I want to do.'

Claire didn't seem too concerned about it. I wondered if she'd just drift along without purpose until someone married her. It looked like a possibility because there was a fecklessness about her, as if she'd seen things she shouldn't have at her age and knew what adult life could hold in store for people. I would have bet money that she came from a broken home. Like everyone else.

'That's a good idea, Claire. Travel while you can,' said Liz.

'Did you travel a lot when you were modelling?' Alan asked Liz.

'God, I went all over the place! But I wouldn't call it

18

travelling exactly, it was just work. I saw a lot of airports and hotel rooms. No, I haven't travelled much at all.'

Liz had never hit the big time as a model but nevertheless she'd made enough money in five years to put a deposit on our house in Roehampton.

'Oh, come on,' I said. 'We went to India together and we spent a month in Peru, went to Machu Picchu.'

'Yes, and when we climbed to the top we found a stark naked American tripping with his underpants on his head,' said Liz. 'Have you ever thought about modelling, Claire?'

'No way! I'm much too heavy,' Claire said. She'd obviously been brainwashed by the body-fascists because I could have circled her waist with my hands.

'Nonsense,' said Liz. 'You'd do well. There's always a demand for the fresh, wholesome look.' There was an edge to the compliment that Claire picked up on. Fresh and Wholesome wasn't a million miles from Young and Unsophisticated.

'Are you still modelling?' Claire asked.

'Oh, not for years. I didn't have the bone structure to keep going. No, I design handbags now. With a friend.' Liz had developed a few designs with Mary Marighela but the handbag world was proving tough to enclasp.

'I'd love to go to South America. Alan's been there,' Claire said dreamily, as if Alan's one-time presence on the sub-continent was in itself reason enough to make the trip.

'I went when I left school,' Alan said. 'I was there for six months. It was a pretty dangerous place at times.'

'Really? Even then?' said Liz.

'It wasn't that long ago!' Alan protested, trying to contract the ten years that separated him from Claire.

Alan had had it easy. When I'd left school I'd worked in a strawberry jam factory for eight months and the sight of a strawberry still made me heave. The boy in the leather jacket sloped over from the bar area. Claire introduced him as Tarquin. He treated us to a diffident scowl and told her that he and his friend Rupert were tired of waiting for a table. They wanted to go to Pizza Express. Claire listened to him as though she wouldn't have cared if he'd decided to hang himself from a street lamp.

'I'm not really hungry. I might just go home, you know?' Claire said, tapping cigarette ash and taking an unhurried drag. Tarquin shrugged, acutely self-conscious, convinced that everyone in the room was staring at him.

'Okay, whatever. See you tomorrow,' he sniffed, a public schoolboy trying to improvise some cool. I watched him slouch off between the tables to tell Rupert what sad cases Claire's friends were. I hoped fervently that none of my tax contribution had gone towards the cost of his jacket.

'Is he your boyfriend? He's really good-looking. Sort of Johnny Depp,' said Liz.

'Oh, God, no! He's just someone I know. He gave me a lift back from college,' Claire said, keen to distance herself from Tarquin's retreating figure.

'He's got a car? I thought you said he was a student,' Alan said.

'Well, I've got a car, haven't I?' said Claire.

'The Mini? You said it was your mother's,' he said.

'It was, but she gave it to me for my birthday.' A waiter arrived and we ordered coffee. Liz frowned when I asked for a Grappa to go with my double espresso.

'I want to hear all about your adventures in South America,' Liz said.

'No, you don't. It's ancient history,' Alan said.

'Oh, please, Alan. You've got some incredible stories,'

Claire said. Alan turned to Liz and embarked on a tale about a Colombian hippy that he and his schoolfriend had met on a bus ride from Bogotá.

Liz sat forward with her chin on her hand like a kid watching cartoons, but I felt that Claire had heard this story before and was just miming rapt attention. Then Alan began to describe the wondrous effects of Colombian weed and she started to work at her split ends. One day she'd learn a sad truth: Love is . . . listening to your partner's favourite story for the thousandth time and still mustering a convincing smile at the denouement.

The waiter arrived with the coffees and my Grappa. Alan's tale climaxed with Alan and his friend being ripped-off at gunpoint by their new friend, Carlos.

'And you were only a teenager at the time, right? What a nightmare,' said Liz.

'Oh, it was all our own fault. We should have known better. It was just that Carlos was so plausible. You know, the strange thing is that I think I saw him a couple of years ago walking down Carnaby Street wearing a poncho.'

'Carlos? You never told me that!' said Claire. 'What did you do?'

'Well, I couldn't be certain that it was him, of course. And anyway, what if it was? In his place I'd probably have done the same thing. He only ripped off a couple of gringo tourists.'

'Oh, you don't mean that!' cried Liz.

Alan shrugged and asked for the bill which he insisted on paying. I was happily surprised that he used his personal gold American Express card. When we stood up I helped Claire put on her jacket. She smelt like a new-born baby. The manager came over and shook Alan warmly by the hand. Then he moved on to Claire.

'*Ciao,* Claire,' he said, embracing her. She didn't appear to enjoy the experience.

'Shall I give you a lift home?' Alan asked Claire as we walked out into fresh air and the first drops of rain.

'Sure, that'd be great,' she said. If she was disappointed to be spending the night alone she did a good job covering it up. Alan drove us all to Kensington with Liz and Claire in the back. We pulled into the short semi-circular drive of a large detached house set back from the road. A little blue Mini and a Mercedes 190 were parked side-by-side.

Lights were on downstairs and Claire got out of the car. She turned to wave before she disappeared through the front door and we rolled off across the gravel.

'She's a bright girl,' I said to Alan. 'How did you meet her?'

'Through her brother. Yes, she is bright,' he said distractedly.

'She's a little young for you though, isn't she?' Liz sniped from the back seat.

'Oh, it's nothing like that,' Alan said with a laugh and turned the music up. We arrived back at the mews and parked beside my Shōgun. When he asked us in for a nightcap I agreed before Liz could say no. Alan fixed Liz a Diet Coke and when he poured my brandy she shot me a frost-look behind his back.

Eventually I took pity on Liz and bolted the brandy. We thanked Alan for dinner and said goodnight. Liz said she'd drive so I climbed into her car, assuming that she'd drive me back in the morning to pick up the Shōgun on my way into work.

'That was fun, wasn't it?' I said, buckling myself into the Punto. Liz didn't say anything till we'd pulled out of the mews and I knew I was in trouble by the set of her jaw.

'Christ, you're so insensitive!' she hissed as we turned onto the road. 'Couldn't you see that he only asked us in to be polite? You're such an oaf when you drink like this.'

'Hang on a second! I thought we were all having a good time!' I said. 'I didn't have any more than anybody else.'

'Oh, please! And the way you kept leering at that stuck-up little bimbo! When she took her jacket off I thought you'd burst a blood-vessel.'

'That's ridiculous,' I said. 'And I didn't think she was stuck-up.'

'Because you had your double vision trained on her tits. Do you think I didn't notice?'

'Give it a break,' I said, sinking deeper into the contour of the seat to watch the rain pebble-dash the side window. We drove in silence for a while. I put Liz's bad spirits down to the fact that she was alone with me again.

'Anyway, Alan seems to like her,' I said.

'Claire? He was just being nice,' said Liz. 'I'm not saying he wasn't flattered, but didn't you see how she irritated him? I suppose you didn't, not with your Chardonnay goggles in place.'

'Well, she's scuppered your plans for Alan and Mary, that's for sure. They're obviously having an affair,' I said.

'Alan and Claire? Don't be daft,' she scoffed. 'She's much too young for him. He's thirty-three for God's sake,' said Liz, running an amber light on Cromwell Road.

'Can you give me a lift to get my car in the morning?' I asked.

'No way, Steve. I'm working on the handbags with Mary.'

'Oh, shit. Turn round then. I'd better get it now,' I said.

'No chance. You've drunk far too much to drive.'

'But it's on a double yellow line. I'll get a bloody clamp!'

'You should have thought of that beforehand.'

We had a row about my drinking. Liz refused to drive me back to the Shōgun. In the end she dropped me at Hammersmith roundabout and I caught a cab back to Alan's place to collect the car.

Much later that night I tossed and turned beside my sleeping wife, tormented by a number of violent and increasingly bloody scenarios involving Claire and Alan. In the end I crept downstairs to call Alan once more. This time his phone rang twice and Alan picked it up.

'Hello . . . Hello. Who is this?' he said.

Alan sounded wide awake and very close. It freaked me to hear his voice and I didn't know what to say. I hung up. It was almost four o'clock.

4

Solpadeine

Each effervescent tablet contains
Paracetamol Ph. Eur. 500mg.
Codeine Phosphate Ph. Eur. 8mg.
Caffeine Ph. Eur. 30 mg.
in a special effervescent base
containing sorbitol.
Store below 25°C.

SOLPADEINE © Sterling Health

CHEEP! CHEEP! CHEEP! CHEEP! The digital alarm
clock woke me at 7.00 a.m. the next morning proclaiming its
low retail value in a high-pitched warble. Liz groaned beside
me. When I climbed out of bed, my head swam to catch up
with my body as if I'd taken a sleeping pill the night before.
My ankle wasted no time reminding me that I'd twisted it on
the cobbles of Alan's mews. I limped to the bathroom to
descale my teeth with an abrasive smoker's toothpaste. On the
shelf lay my Gillette Sensor with its sprung blades and white
strip of lubricant, the Lubrastrip.

My concern about Alan and Claire had dwindled a little with the dawn and, given the drinks I'd consumed and the fact that I'd hardly slept, I felt surprisingly good. But I didn't notice the arrival of a mole-hill pimple that had popped up on my cheek overnight. My razor's twin blades decapitated it to release quick scarlet blood into the shaving foam. I pressed a finger to the damage, groped in the cupboard for a Styptic pencil and stabbed the spot with the anhydrous stick. Electrifying pain staunched the flow. I hobbled down to the kitchen to munch through a mound of fibrous breakfast cereal and read Liz's *Daily Mail,* itself a powerful laxative.

I looked out into the garden through the diamond grid of the leaded window and saw our empty swimming-pool. The pump had broken a couple of weeks earlier and needed to be replaced. Beyond the pool the sun rose over the golf course that abutted our property, a great gold golf ball that appeared to be teed on a cedar tree at the horizon waiting for God's eight-iron to thwack down and zap it westwards.

On the radio a disc jockey ferried his audience towards the sunshine cereal bowl of the Top 40 breakfast format. He flirted with Debbie in the Flying Eye, pausing to transmit birthday greetings to someone's unloved relative in Putney. I made a cup of tea for Liz and took it upstairs. Since she was still asleep I left it on the bedside table to skin over as a token of my kindness.

I pulled out of our driveway and skirted the golf-course for a quarter of a mile to the main road. The traffic was light on the way into town and I tooled along in the Shōgun, head and shoulders above most of the other drivers. I parked in Soho near Tony's flat on Shaftesbury Avenue, intending to tell him of Alan's plan to sack him at the board meeting. I leaned on the buzzer until Tony let me in, night-soiled and shrivelled in a faded aubergine robe.

'What are you doing here, Steve? I'm still asleep! God, what time is it?' he moaned.

'Eight-fifteen. We've got to talk, Tone.' The bags beneath his eyes had transformed themselves into brown Louis Vuitton travelling-trunks.

'Not yet, I can't face it. Give me five minutes,' he begged. 'Go and get us some milk or something, will you? I'll put the kettle on.'

I bought a Tetra-pakked pint and some dried-up croissants from a delicatessen. When I got back Tony was already dressed and lay sprawled across the sagged orange couch in his little sitting-room. He slit open a puffed eye to indicate a coffee-pot gurgling on the counter of the kitchenette. I supersaturated some coffee with sugar and took it to the sink to add a piddle of cold London tap water so that I could drink it without scorching my tongue.

'Have a good time last night then?' Tony asked. He was still bitter that Alan hadn't asked him along.

'Fair to crap. You didn't miss much. What did you get up to?'

I didn't really need to ask. The previous night was written on his face in red Gothic script.

'I had a few after work and gave the car a little knock, nothing serious. I left it at the office,' he said, supping a fizzing beaker of Solpadeine, the champagne of over-the-counter analgesia. Tony looked ill.

Outside in the street the traffic-lights conducted worn brake-shoes and blown silencers in a carbon-monoxide concerto. I went over to shut the window. If Tony had opened it for fresh air he was further gone than I'd thought. I saw him reach for the phone.

'Who are you calling?' I asked.

'Someone I met last night.'

'Leave it out. You've got enough trouble.'

We'd been here before. Since his divorce Tony had been seeing the world through flesh-coloured spectacles.

'I've got to catch him before he goes to work. He was gorgeous,' he said.

'Is that right? I'm surprised you can remember what he looked like.'

I chugged the coffee down and headed for the lavatory. The bathroom was a scene from *Stalker* with blotches of brown damp revealed by the glare of a frosted glass window that gave onto a mews. A waiter from Gerrard Street had been killed out there, hacked to death with a melon knife. They'd sat on him while someone chopped off his arms and legs, leaving the torso to wiggle to death. The previous tenant had seen it all from this very window early one Sunday morning and moved out the same day, which explained why Tony had got a cheap sub-let on his three rooms. It was the first place he could call his own since his divorce. Laura's lawyer had taken him to the cleaners and had him professionally sand-blasted. It was another incentive for me to try to patch things up with Liz in Marriage Guidance.

Tony was still hanging on the telephone, trying not to move his head around too much, with a telephone book propped on the coffee-table before him. Suddenly he sprang to life or something like it.

'Hello, could I please speak to Jim, please? Thank you.'

Tony spoke in his phone voice, contracting his plaited scouse vowels in a pinched and misjudged stab at received pronunciation as he tried to 'reach out and touch' the 'Jim'.

Tony liked them young. I wondered if the Jim still lived with his parents. I caught Tone's bloodshot eye and tapped my sports watch. He nodded and smoothed his dry thinning hair back towards the new pony-tail that he'd grown to compensate for the recent deforestation of his frontal lobes. As yet the pony-tail barely brushed his top vertebra, a flat black comma typed on his shirt-collar.

With eyes and nose two sizes too big for his five-and-a-half-foot frame, Tony had always been obsessed with his appearance. This morning a plaid shirt was buttoned at his neck to drape like a teepee from his scrawny shoulders, giving him the look of a withered raver. It was Tony's current incarnation, the latest of a stream of fashion avatars I'd witnessed since the time we'd opened a stall in Kensington Market together in the mid-eighties. At that point Tony had been into a transitional Neo-Punk look, time-travelling on the 31 bus from Chelsea to Kensington High Street.

Kensington Market was a fire-trap warren of tiny retail units, a tacky fashion kasbah comprising a hundred clothes' stalls on three floors of a building next to Barker's Department Store. Many of our fellow stallholders looked as if they'd walked straight off one of the government's heroin-screws-you-up posters. We rented our first stall with a loan from Tony's dad, called it Oktober and began to sell the pinstripe Zoot suits that I had made up in the East End to Tony's design. Although Tony and I were still technically art students, from that time on we spent most of our time hanging out at the market thinking about business. It was the high-water mark of the Thatcher revolution and, except for Red Wedge, everyone was at it.

Oktober was only six feet deep by ten feet wide, a beacon of style between a patchouli-dripping head-shop run by a Dane and Naveen's leather-jacket emporium. Naveen's jackets retained the pungent reek of the tanning process and our own stall served as a battleground in the aroma war that Naveen and Thor had been conducting since the seventies. If ever Naveen achieved olfactory supremacy with a particularly pungent consignment of leather flares or waistcoats, the Dane would torch up a bundle of joss-sticks in retaliation, setting punters and stallholders alike stumbling out into the street.

Fortunately our clothes sold through well enough to allow us to move to a bigger stall across the road in Hyper Hyper, a smart new fashion market. It was Tony's idea to call the new outlet Rotogravure because it suggested machinery and gravitas, two concepts that were big at the time. A graphic designer from *The Face* bought a polo-neck on the day we opened. He was so robotic and humourless that I knew we'd got the name right.

Tony and I had expanded the company throughout the eighties, ripping-off the top designers and importing container loads of worn jeans from the States as a lucrative sideline. We made a great deal of money, re-investing much of it in the business. Then the recession struck. Five years later we were barely hanging on with a string of shops in London and a wholesale operation selling work-wear and rave-garb under the name of Puffa Group.

The company was facing bankruptcy but Tony seemed oblivious, perched on the edge of his sofa waiting for the 'Jim' to come to the phone.

'Hello, ah . . . Yes. I'm a friend of Jim's. Is he there by any chance? I see. You don't know a Jim Forbes then? I see . . . Tosser,' he hissed as the line clicked dead.

'Wrong number?' I asked.

'I can't find the bit of paper he wrote it on so I'm trying a few names from the phone book. Lucky he's not called Smith.'

'Or Macaulay Culkin. Don't be a prat, Tone. Come on, we've got things to discuss.'

'Just one more go,' he said, even as his fingers stabbed the next set of digits into the phone. It wasn't libido so much as a bad case of raw emotional need that Tony had suffered since the divorce, the pent-up yearning of years spent scuffing his shoes against the closet door.

I went over to the window and looked out into the street. A crocodile of Scandinavian schoolchildren was winding along the other side of Shaftesbury Avenue blocking the pavement in front of the Chemist's, the kids' sportswear bright through the summer dust. Tony's window rattled as a juggernaut boomed by. I saw a long-haired teenager cross the street behind it and enter the Chemist's wearing one of our leather jackets, a £160 item from last year's range. It had worn in nicely. Tony tried another number.

'Give it a rest, Tone. What's the use? It's pathetic,' I said. 'We've got things to talk about.' I thought of Alan and my nerves cranked up a few notches.

'I want to catch him before he goes to work. He gave me his number and that means he likes me, right?'

'Forget it. He probably just made it up to get you off his back. Why don't you shave? We could get in before Alan for once. To let him know you're taking this seriously.'

'Alan? Who gives a fuck about Alan? It's Sally we've got to worry about.'

'Yeah,' I said. 'But she listens to what he says.'

'Come off it, Steve. You know what the toe-rag thinks of me. If he wants to give me the push, so be it. I couldn't care less. Are you telling me it'll make any difference if I try to schmooze him now? Are you serious? What d'you think I've been doing for the last couple of months?'

'You dragged him off on a couple of bar-crawls and he hardly drinks.'

'That's his problem. What time do we see Sally?'

'Four, remember? We see her at four,' I said. My patience was wearing thinner than a Giacometti with anorexia.

'And what's the time now?' he asked.

'Eight-forty.'

'Are you on a meter?'

'No,' I said.

'Then you've probably already been clamped,' he sniggered.

'Oh, Jesus, no.' My mind reeled as I visualized a ghastly yellow shackle on the Shōgun. I'd parked it on a double yellow line.

'Let's go then,' I said, jittery from the coffee.

'You go. I'm going to shave and have a shower like you said. Freshen up a bit.'

'Suit yourself,' I said. At that moment I didn't care if Alan sacked Tony at the board meeting.

I limped downstairs and out into the concentration of the street. Moving down Shaftesbury Avenue and side-stepping pedestrians, I tripped over a teenager asleep in his sleeping-bag. His legs stuck out from the doorway of a tax-free cloth shop and I fell over them, landing heavily.

'Sorry, mate,' I said. His head popped out of the pupa.

'Spare some change?' he wheezed, coughing up a tuber-cular oyster.

'Haven't got any,' I lied, faking a pocket search while I got my breath back.

His head retracted into its chrysalis and he sealed himself up again, a street-larva refusing metamorphosis from the pavement stage. I peg-legged it up Wardour Street filling my lungs with the morning of a million cars. The Shōgun was manacle-free. I'd been spared. I took the inevitable parking ticket from the wiper and gleefully ripped it to confetti.

It was a beautiful summer day as I lane-swapped up Tottenham Court Road, the sky a wedge of blue perspective fanning out from the north. My mind was speeding from Tony's coffee but I felt good, on top of things, capable of ice-sculpting a crystal chandelier in my imagination. I took my mobile from the pocket of my old Chevignon blouson and dialled Liz in Roehampton to hear the flat southern drone of my own recorded voice through the Cellnet. I sounded peculiar, uptight and depressed.

'There's no one here right now, so please leave us a message or call back later . . . Beep.'

'Hi, it's me,' I said. 'Just to say I hope you have a good day. I'll call again from the office. Love you, mean it. Bye.'

My chirpy tone rang a little hollow. At the side of the road a middle-aged Rasta stood by a green Ford Orion being grilled by a policeman. There was something about the cop that caught my eye. I slowed down to get a better look at him. He seemed familiar and I realized that it was because he was a dead-ringer for me. With a beer-gut hanging over his belt he could have been my twin. I braked at a red light on Euston Road and stared up at the enormity of the Euston Tower looming above the intersection.

That's when it happened. I was staring mindlessly at the steel-and-glass skin of the building when the structure's graph-paper panes appeared to soften and expand as though conforming to some internal pressure. To my amazement the mid-section of the building bubbled out like a piece of op art. I sat forward in horror and checked the Shōgun's windshield for some warp in the glass that could explain this effect but found no flaw. When my eyes refocused on the building it had returned to its former stability.

Behind me someone beeped their horn. I jerked back to reality. The lights had changed and I took off across Euston Road, turned left into Drummond Street and slid into my reserved parking space in a vacant lot that was being fingered by the long shadow cast by the Euston Tower. Badly freaked by the hallucination, I breathed deeply to pull myself together. I cut the engine and tried to convince myself that the hallucination had just been a symptom of stress, a psychic speed-bump telling me to slow down. Inside I was deeply alarmed. It was terrifying to think that my mind could play a trick like that. I wondered if it had something to do with the bad trip I'd had in 1984. Was it possible to have a flashback after so many years?

I pulled myself out of the car and saw the big scrunch across the front of Tony's Porsche in the bay next to mine. This was the 'little knock' he'd had the night before. A mangled headlight flopped loose from its socket like the eye of a brutalized boxer and half the cherished number plate PUF 4 A had broken off. Alan Denton's bay was empty. I was glad that I'd have a little time to pull myself together before I had to face him. I rode the lift to Puffa Group's headquarters on the third floor of a large Victorian warehouse, two thousand square feet of cheap storage space which we had partitioned into offices.

Gigantic colour prints of last year's range hung against the whitewashed brickwork of the reception area and the odd pane of frosted glass chequered the metal-framed windows that ran along one wall. Beneath a big cut-out of Puffa's logo, a skate-boarding Michelin man with dreadlocks, Gudrun sat at her desk being receptive. She was talking on her new phone, a mic and earphone combination that left her hands free to type. It was so inconspicuous that it seemed as if she'd gone mad, babbling to herself beneath her hayrick hairdo. I sat on the edge of the desk listening to her side of a call.

'Alan's not in yet, I'm afraid. Shall I ask him to call you? No problem, I'll pass on the message . . . Yesyes . . . Bigkiss . . . Byeee.' She looked up at me through a pair of mascara raccoon-rings. 'Hi, Steve. Nice evening? Goodgood?'

'Not too bad. What's up?'

Gudrun pulled a sad face and told me that a consignment of the Paraguayan Ranchwear we imported was being held at Heathrow in a bonded warehouse. I would have to go down and sign for it in person. The Ranchwear was one of our most popular wholesale lines and the consignment was already three weeks late. I drove out to the warehouse to find that Customs and Excise had opened up all of the crates. It took me the whole day to sort out the mess.

I didn't get away until seven o'clock. Then I was locked in sheer weight of traffic on the M4 for an hour on my way home. Grid-locked behind a BP tanker, I watched carcinogenic emissions sprout like grey broccoli from its exhaust pipe with metronomic regularity. The tanker's tick-over was only just out of sync with the indicator light of a Ford Mondeo flashing in the middle lane. The effect was so hypnotic that I fell into a daze until the tanker moved forward a few yards to prevent the Mondeo cutting in front of it.

5

The Blind Date

When I arrived home I found Liz in the kitchen cooking dinner with her friend Mary. The two women had become particularly close following Mary's divorce from Lenny, her rock-guitarist husband. My wife's tendency to compete with other women meant that she had few female friends but Mary was an exception. As a former model herself, Mary had shared some of Liz's disappointments, not least in the marriage department. Mary had recently bought a house across the golf course for herself and her son Jonah with part of her divorce settlement.

Alan had called to say that he'd be coming over later, and Mary was feeling nervous about meeting him. She reminded us that she hadn't had sex for over a year and she was worried that it showed. It struck me as ludicrous that such a confident and self-assured woman should get so worked up about meeting a total stranger. Mary asked Liz if her make-up was okay.

'I don't know why you use any with your peaches-and-cream complexion,' said Liz.

'The cream curdled a long time ago,' Mary said.

She applied some powder from a little compact and rearranged her hair with the heel of her hand. The thick blonde cash-crop had been her unique selling point as a model, featuring in several shampoo commercials before her marriage to Lenny.

Mary sat down and I refilled her wine glass on the pine table-top.

'I'd rather have a joint. I feel like a bloody teenage wall-flower,' Mary said.

'Drugs aren't the answer if you're feeling nervous,' I said.

'No, Steve, I know drugs aren't the answer,' she replied. 'Drugs are the question. And the answer is yes.'

'It's in the blue jar,' Liz said. 'But don't smoke it too near Steve. You know how he gets passive paranoia.'

It wasn't far from the truth. For the past year one Bisto-whiff of marijuana had given me the same hollow, dead feeling that I'd experienced on acid. I'd discussed this feeling in Marriage Guidance, sensing that it was in some way connected to the welling sadness I'd felt as a kid when my dad left home.

Mary rolled a hash joint with a Marlboro Light and Liz took a token hit off it. Mary smoked the rest of the joint, taking deep doper drags, holding them in to allow her lungs to wrest every last druggy molecule from the smoke. When she could hold it in no more, her lungs collapsed like the ceiling in a gold-mine to release a cloud of smoke from her mouth.

We ate the roast chicken. When we had finished the meal Mary went to the bathroom. I asked Liz how Alan had sounded on the phone.

'He sounded fine. So much for your little story,' she said.

'Something was going on over there last night,' I said.

'He was probably just re-arranging the furniture. And I don't want you saying anything about it when he gets here either. This is Mary's night. And don't drink too much.'

I'd only had a couple of glasses of red wine with dinner. When Mary came back I fixed us both another. Mary's anxiety was getting to me and I needed some alcohol to take the edge off before Alan's arrival.

Mary rolled another joint which put a dreamy smile on her face but when the doorbell rang the current electrified her. She was up smoothing her clothes and striking a languid pose by the sink before I'd even left my seat.

I opened the front door to find Alan smiling on the threshold with a bottle of champagne in each hand. I checked him over for cuts and bruises but there were none to be seen. He was dressed in a crew-neck pullover, jeans and Docksiders. I took the proffered booze and told him he shouldn't have bothered.

'Look, you deserve it after all that trouble at the airport. Gudrun told me about what happened,' he said.

'It wasn't that bad. Come on through. We're still in the kitchen.' When he'd kissed Liz I introduced him to Mary who gave him a stoned smile.

'Look what Alan's brought,' I said holding out the bottles. Liz and Mary gasped in wonder.

'Wow! Rock-and-roll mouthwash! Wicked!' cried Mary with inappropriate stoned exuberance. Alan seemed happy but I felt that he'd overdone the generosity. One bottle would have been enough.

'Why don't we all go next door and sit soft?' Liz suggested, and we filed into the sitting-room. I opened the

Bollinger and poured four units into flutes while Mary put a Frankie Knuckles track on the CD. Alan checked her out as she bent down over the console.

'What a lovely room. This isn't a house, it's a home!' said Alan. 'I wish you could give me a hand with my place, Liz. Where did you find this lovely rug?'

'The Conran Shop,' said Liz.

'You mean the Con-Man Shop,' I said. Given Puffa's recent troubles I was worried about the amount of money Liz and I were spending. Brown envelopes on the doormat had begun to give me bill-terror, a feeling I remembered from my student days.

'Oh, stop moaning, Steve. It wasn't that expensive. It's from Turkey,' said Liz.

'Aren't the colours great? The pattern's really intricate,' said Mary, transfixed by the blue and red whorls.

Alan went over to the French windows and expressed an interest in the garden. I led him outside for a quick tour before the light went. The garden ran forty feet back to a fence which bordered the golf course. Liz and Mary stayed inside and it made me uneasy to be alone with Alan. I could hardly contain my curiosity about what had been going on at his house the night before but Alan made no mention of it. Instead he peppered me with questions about the various shrubs for which I had no answers. We skirted the drained swimming-pool.

'I feel like we could be in the country. Do you play golf, Steve?'

'I took it up when we moved here but I'm still lousy. Mary's good though. She lives just over there. Behind those trees.'

'On her own?'

'With Jonah,' I said. 'Her son.'

Alan leaned on the fence and looked across the golf course towards the setting sun. Half of it had disappeared beneath the ornamental lake to leave a bright orange Kilroy. The sun's reflection drooped across the water to form a pendulous nose and the dying rays caught Alan's hair, turning it cooker-ring red in the dusk. When Alan mentioned Tony and the board meeting, I suggested that we discuss it at the office the following morning. He agreed reluctantly.

'Is anyone else coming over tonight?' Alan asked. When I told him it was just the four of us he looked a little disappointed.

We went back inside and joined Liz and Mary in the sitting-room. I sat beside Mary on the zebra-striped seventies sofa. Alan took my director's chair on the other side of the coffee-table. I refilled the flutes.

'Steve tells me you play golf,' Alan said to Mary. She squirmed at the prospect of having to hold a straight conversation together.

'I used to. I was taught as a kid. My parents played all the time,' she said. 'But I'm more into Jeet Kune Do now.'

'What on earth's Jeet Kune Do?' asked Alan.

'It's a martial art developed by Bruce Lee. It translates as The Way-of-Intercepting-Fist,' Mary said, sparking up a Marlboro Light.

'The Way-of-Intercepting-Fist? Where did he invent that? In a San Francisco bath-house?' Alan laughed at his joke but Mary was unamused. Her brother was gay and Bruce Lee, the Little Dragon, was her number one hero. She had a full-size poster of him in her hallway.

'Actually he developed it in Hong Kong. It's a free-form fighting technique,' she snapped, ready to blind her blind date. Liz asked Alan if he liked cooking.

'Not really. I just go to Marks and Spencer's,' said Alan. 'I live on the stuff. Just bang it in the microwave and, hey presto, it's ready.'

'You use a microwave? You want to be careful, they're dangerous,' said Mary. 'I wouldn't have one in the house.'

'Oh, that's nonsense! They're perfectly safe. It's just that people are snobbish about fast food,' said Alan.

'That's like saying people are snobbish about Lysteria. Or cancer,' Mary said.

Despite the fact that she smoked joints all day and drank like a fish, Mary was obsessed with healthy eating. On one occasion I'd even seen her use Evian water to steam some fish.

Alan popped the cork on the second bottle of champagne which ricocheted off the ceiling before coming to rest on the rug by my trainers.

'When I was in California I read about a short-order chef who worked with a microwave and died from it,' Mary said. 'They did a post-mortem and found that his liver and kidneys had been completely cooked through. Apparently the door hadn't been closing properly and his insides had been roasted.'

'That's horrible!' cried Liz.

Mary fell into an overlong marijuana laugh and gangwayed out of the door towards the bathroom. The champagne and the spliff were enduring a sticky date of their own in her central nervous system.

The pearl light-bulb in the desk lamp glowed strangely. It seemed dimmer than usual but somehow deeper and clearer. It began to pulse slowly and when I concentrated I could make out a blue-tinged halo that circled it like the rings of Saturn. I imagined that this light-bulb was connected to all the other light-bulbs in the world, that they enclosed the globe in a luminous hairnet that was only visible at night. I wondered if I was getting a contact high off Mary.

'So, Steve tells me you have a son,' Alan said when she returned. Liz shot me a reproachful look for letting the cat out of the bag so soon.

'Yes, I do,' said Mary. 'He's staying with my ex in California at the moment. I'm really missing him. Jonah's only seven.'

'Is your ex-husband American?' Alan asked.

Mary glued three cigarette papers together and emptied the tobacco from a Marlboro Light on top of them. 'No. Lenny's English but he lives in Los Angeles. He's a session guitarist.'

'What kind of things does he do?' Alan asked.

'He's working with one of Simple Minds' producers on a solo project at the moment,' said Mary, unwilling to be drawn on the subject.

She singed the corner of the Lebanese resin with her Zippo, sucked at a wisp of smoke and sprinkled crumbs of dope over the tobacco.

'I used to want to be in a band,' said Alan.

'Who didn't?' Mary said. 'But it's not all it's cracked up to be.'

In Lenny's case 'crack' had proved to be the operative word. He'd ended up at the Betty Ford Clinic but now he was two years clean. I went to make coffee and camomile tea. When I returned to the sitting-room with the tray, Liz was reminiscing about her modelling days.

'Do you remember that swimwear shoot we were on in Miami, Mary? For that German company? What a nightmare!' Liz groaned and turned to Alan. 'The client was so obsessed with Mary that we used to have to lock our door at night. He'd get hopelessly drunk at dinner, profess eternal love to her and

42

then sulk all day with a hangover. He gave everyone a really bad time. The stylist spent the whole two weeks in tears.'

Liz often made out that she'd only missed supermodel status by a whisker, but in fact she'd never been close. With two *Elle* covers to her credit, she had been marginally more successful than Mary but for most of the time they'd both made their money in the grim but highly lucrative world of the fashion catalogue.

Mary passed Liz the joint. When she'd taken two hits she stood up and danced over to offer it to Alan. He smiled and shook his head. Liz re-activated Frankie Knuckles with the remote control.

'Come on everybody, let's dance!' said Liz, pulling Alan out of his chair.

Alan began to make a few jerky moves, completely out of time with the music. Mary danced on her own with her eyes closed. I did my usual low-energy shuffle and Liz came over to put her arms round me. As we swayed to the music, Liz pushed Alan gently towards Mary.

Alan jigged about in front of her with his lower lip pinched between his teeth, really feeling the music. Mary kept to her flowing-hippy dance-style and started to get the giggles at Alan's dreadful dancing. He tried to laugh along with her but then he got irritated and sat down on the sofa to slurp coffee. I joined him and we watched Liz and Mary dance together till the track came to an end.

Alan said he had to go home and rose abruptly. He thanked Liz and then he turned to Mary.

'It was great to meet you. Perhaps we could go out dancing one night. I'd really enjoy it. You're a great mover.' I couldn't tell if he was being ironic but Mary certainly took it that way.

'Sure,' she said, and shook his hand coldly.

I walked Alan over to his car and the women went back inside. He thanked me and reminded me that we'd have to discuss Tony's position in the morning. I waved him off and returned to the sitting-room. Mary was smoking another joint and bitching about Alan. She was lying on the sofa. Liz was flat on her back on the rug.

'Christ, he was awful! He was so far up his own bum, one day he'll just be a pair of Docksiders floating around in mid-air,' Mary said. They both broke into extended druggy laughter.

'He's not that bad,' Liz protested, massaging her ribs.

'Not that bad? He's a vain little smoothie, except when he dances and then he's worse than Bono.'

'He's just straighter than most men you know, that's all. And better-looking,' Liz said.

'There was something really creepy about him. You wait and see. He'll marry a submissive little fluff-head and have loads of affairs. I can't believe you thought he'd be right for me.'

I hung around until I began to feel nauseous from the pot smoke, stacked the dishwasher and went to bed. Before I turned off the bedside light I inspected the bulb. It was perfectly normal. I drifted off to sleep lulled by the low thud of reggae music from downstairs.

6

Fear & Clothing

*W*HEN I LEFT FOR WORK THE NEXT MORNING Mary's ageing Range Rover was still parked in the drive. I assumed she'd stayed over, too wasted to drive home. As I drove along the side of the golf-course the trees and rocks looked as if they were made of fibreglass. When I put on a tape by The Aphex Twin each note was charged with its own special significance. It was almost too much for me. I felt oddly apprehensive, as if I was on the brink of some important and not wholly welcome discovery. When I reached Puffa I found Gudrun behind her desk drinking a take-away cappuccino.

'Hi, Steve. All okay at Heathrow then? Goodgood?'

'No problem. Is anyone else in?'

'Not yet. Lawrence called from Covent Garden. He asked if you could go down to King's Road. Jill's having trouble with the till. I haven't heard from Dean.'

'I doubt you will.'

Dean shifted our wholesale range on commission and

with the way things stood there was no guarantee he'd ever get paid. I asked if there'd been any messages. Gudrun told me that Julia from Sally's office had called to confirm the meeting for four o'clock.

Julia was Sally's assistant, an old-school yuppy who had arranged the investment package and had stayed in our hair ever since. She wore her own hair in a shiny black bob, an insect headpiece. You felt that if you flipped back her fringe the words 'I WANT' would be tattooed on her forehead in Chanel's typeface. Her boss Sally Moore had her own wholesale business, In Deep Fashion, and her money had allowed us to expand Puffa.

That was when we'd developed our 'cash-flow problem'. The shop-rents, the business rate and the recession were strangling us. Sally had been helpful when Tony and I had been to see her about it in her Covent Garden office a few months before, oozing concern and encouragement across the grey slate plane of her desk which was bare but for a flat telephone and a Bonsai tree. Sally had encouraged us to build up the wholesale side and run the shops with as little loss as possible until the leases expired over the next couple of years.

The frayed carpet-tiles of Puffa's corridor felt like a gang-plank on a ghost ship. I saw fading Post-it notes stuck to dead PC screens like patches of decay, desks littered with ring-bound files and Styrofoam coffee-cups. In one half-empty cup the rotten milk had formed an archipelago of bacteria.

Alan had fired eight of our employees when our creditors had started baying for blood. With no help forthcoming from the bank, he'd asked In Deep to invest more money to finance the restructuring plan he'd devised. This would give Sally a controlling interest but Tony and I would still hold forty per cent of Puffa between us. Tony had been on an alcoholic bender ever since Sally had called a board meeting, convinced that Alan had persuaded her to fire him.

I shut myself into my glassed-in cubicle feeling numb and listless, unable to muster the energy to phone our King's Road shop. Alan had fired the shop manager a month back to 'safeguard the jobs of the rest of the workforce' and promptly hired a young student called Jill to take his place for half the money. Jill had already had problems with stock-taking and the anti-theft tags. Now her miserable finger had evidently fallen on the till. But Jill's problems were nothing compared to the trouble I faced on the Bigger Screen, my own private 70mm Disaster Movie. For devotees of distress there's little to beat the possibility of imminent bankruptcy washed down with a bucket of marital strife.

Gudrun put through a call from my wife.

'Liz on line one, Steve.'

'Hi, how's it going?' I said as the line clicked in.

'Fine. You were up early. Do you think Alan had an awful time last night?' she asked.

'He'll live, he's a big boy.'

'Look, I just wanted to remind you we've got Marriage Guidance at five-thirty.'

My jaw dropped.

'Really? God, I clean forgot. And we've got the board meeting with Sally Moore at four. I thought I told you?'

I twirled about in my executive swivel chair looking for a way out. Liz groaned at the other end of the line.

'You never tell me anything. It's not good enough, Steve. If you're so scared to face things then there's really no point going on. I know it's painful, but it's our last chance to change things. You have to be committed. No one said this would be easy, you know.'

47

I winced at her use of 'committed', the C-word.

'I can't mess Sally Moore around,' I said.

'Heaven forbid. Well, I'm not going to call Joanna. You do it and see if you can make another appointment. Call me later and tell me what she says. If you can find the time, that is.'

'I'm really sorry, Liz . . .'

She hung up on me.

I flicked through my copy of *We're All Special People* by Dr Joe Sorrell, a Californian psychologist. Joanna, our Marriage Guidance counsellor, had given me the book, suggesting that I attend a seminar of Sorrell Interactive Therapy at the SIT Institute outside Swindon. The two-day intensive residential course had promised to 'strip away the old patterns of fear and guilt' according to the tenets of Joe Sorrell. Joanna felt that Joe's 'program' would help me to release the 'suppressed anger' that was 'poisoning my relationships' and put me 'in touch with my feelings'. She'd ganged up with Liz until I'd agreed to spend Easter weekend in 'intensive residence'. Although I'd driven to Swindon with reluctance, my filthy mood had soon fallen away like so much disagreeable sportswear, and I had been able to 'drink deeply of the experience'.

I remembered feeling apprehensive as I crossed a nail-clippered lawn towards the large white neo-classical building that housed the Institute. There was a polished brass mandala on the front-door that resembled the logo of the Queen's Award for Industry. The door was opened by a young man with a pony-tail who showed me to a comfortable room and left me with a schedule which I skimmed in vain for a list of amenities - pool, Jacuzzi and other things Californian.

When I went downstairs to meet my group of fellow students a bald counsellor named Jerry introduced the nine of us by first name only and sat us in a circle. One by one we were asked to describe what had brought us to SIT. A thin vapid woman to my right was so petrified that she could barely speak. She eventually managed to whisper that she suffered from M.E. When it was my turn I resisted the urge to inform the group that my problem was O.T.H.E.R. P.E.O.P.L.E. Nevertheless we all opened up and from then on the weekend was filled with one-to-one interactions, lectures, Mirror-work and group sessions, performing psychological striptease and revealing - trembling, naked - our 'New Me's.

I put Joe Sorrell's book down and sat up in my swivel chair to practise the Positive Thought techniques I'd learnt at the seminar, repeating projections from the Self-Image Repertoire - SIR, for short - that I'd developed in the group sessions. 'I am a young god,' I told myself. 'A bright red lion on a flag at Agincourt snapping in the breeze . . .'

'What are you doing, Steve?'

I opened my eyes and saw Alan Denton peering round my door, his face as sharp as a cartoon, bright and curious.

'Nothing. Come in,' I said. 'How's it going?'

'Not too bad, boss. Thanks for last night.' He went to sit in the other executive swivel, moving in his studied 'laid-back' way. I asked him what he'd made of Mary.

'Oh, she was all right,' he said. 'But if they ever filmed her life story they'd call it *Gone with the Flow*. How's it hanging yourself?' he asked. The vernacular pinched painfully in his tight-laced Lobb of an accent.

'By a rope.'

'Try not to worry too much about the meeting. I've gone over the three-year forecast budget and the numbers aren't looking all that bad. Sally'll probably go for it,' he said, putting his feet up on the desk and leaning back in the swivel like a head boy in the common room. Beneath the long hair, baseball cap and Hysteric Glamour tour jacket lay an unreconstructed public schoolboy of thirty-three.

'Tony in yet?' he asked.

'Not yet, no.'

'Have you said anything to him about what we talked about?'

'About you wanting him out? No, nothing.' I shook my head vigorously.

'Good. Well, we have to discuss it, Steve.'

'Whatever you want to do about Tony, I told you there's no way I want any part of it.'

'Okay, okay . . . By the way, did I tell you Sally's got her own personal astrologer now? Julia told me. She consults her about everything. Just like Yoko Ono.'

'Or Hitler.'

Alan laughed and noticed a speck of crud on the leg of his jeans. He scratched it off with a fingernail, preserving the force-field of personal hygiene that surrounded him like a Ready-Brek kid. I once met Princess Di at one of Mary's charity galas and she had the same squeaky-clean aura. The sun flared above the Euston Tower and Alan gleamed as though he'd been dipped in vinyl, as plastic-smooth as an Action Man. He leaned forward and laid his hands on my desk.

'Steve, I can't get away from one thing. Overhead! Overhead! Overhead! There's no way Puffa can justify three executive salaries right now. Between you, me and Tony it's a hundred and fifty thousand a year right there, excluding the cars and everything. And have you seen Tony's expenses? I don't think Sally'll overlook them and I don't think she should.'

'Are you saying we should all take a cut?' I asked. All three of us were on the same salary.

'Not exactly. Listen, I appreciate your loyalty to Tony but I think he could use some time to sort himself out. He needs treatment for his drinking problem. Did you see his car out there? He could have killed someone.'

'He wasn't pissed when it happened,' I said.

'If he wasn't actually drunk then you can be sure he had a hangover.'

'Alan, please get one thing straight. Tony and I have run this business together for ten years. No way will I help you shaft him, so don't insult me by suggesting it.'

'But you must agree he's not pulling his weight.'

'The reason he's drinking all the time's that he thinks you're trying to give him the push and he's terrified. Why don't you take a cut, Alan? You know, last one in?'

'If that's how you feel, fine. I'm simply trying to turn this company around and I really don't need this,' Alan said. He got up out of his seat and I panicked. I knew in my heart that without his help we'd never make it through the board meeting.

'I'm sorry. Please sit down. I'm just stressed out,' I said.

'Okay. I know this isn't easy,' he said. 'But, remember, if Tony left the company for a year or so he'd still have his twenty per cent of the equity, and it would give him time to deal with his problems.'

'I think it'd just give him a lot more trouble. He's just come through a divorce. Can you imagine what that must be like?'

'I can't, but I don't think it can help his self-esteem to draw a salary as a passenger,' he said pompously. I could see him at thirty-six running a privatized utility company.

'Hang on a minute. If we're talking about Tony's self-esteem, what do you think it does when you order him around like an office-boy?' I said.

Alan took a deep breath.

'I agree I have a communication problem with Tony but I really wish you could leave emotions out of it and consider this rationally. What about your own future? Liz's? Why do you think Sally's called this board meeting? She wants to see a restructuring and if we don't sort things out between us she'll do it for us. Please, Steve, I know this is a hard call but let's not allow it to jeopardize our friendship. You know as well as I do that I'm only trying to do what's best for the company.'

I was getting sick of it.

'Was everything all right after we left your place the other night?' I asked.

It pulled him up short. 'Yes. Why? Shouldn't it have been?'

He looked straight at me across the desk, motionless as he tried to read me.

'It's just that I rang you at about twelve-thirty when I got home and it sounded like there was a fight going on or something. A struggle. Someone cried out. A woman.'

He didn't bat an eyelid.

'Why didn't you mention this earlier?' he asked.

'I don't know. I thought it might have been a wrong number.'

'It must have been. I was fast asleep by twelve-thirty,' he said, inspecting his fingernails for microbes. I knew he was lying and it gave me a feeling that I had something on him, that the balance of power had shifted in my favour. I wanted to hear Claire's side of the story.

'The phone rang at about three-thirty, but the caller hung up. That wasn't you, was it?' Alan asked.

'At three-thirty? No, it wasn't me,' I said. 'Obviously another wrong number. Maybe you should have your line checked?'

Alan sat forward, working out how to play it.

'Look, Steve, you're bloody good at your job,' he said. 'With your marketing skills and a free rein for me on the business side, we'd turn Puffa round inside a year. Tony's a great designer but how much of our stuff do we design in-house right now? Not a lot and it doesn't sell through. The figures speak for themselves. Puffa's got a great future in wholesale, the network you've developed. I just want you to think about it, that's all . . . Look, why don't you go down to Chelsea and help Jill out? Gudrun tells me she's having trouble with the till.'

'Yeah. I was planning to do that anyway,' I said.

'Great. I'll look after this end. By the way, what did you want to talk to me about when you rang the other night?'

The question caught me off-guard.

'Oh. It was just what you'd said about Tony. It was on my mind, that's all. I couldn't sleep,' I said.

It didn't sound convincing. Alan shrugged, stood up and shook my hand. It was a strangely formal gesture from someone wearing a Hysteric Glamour tour jacket. His hand felt cool and prosthetic.

I tried to fix up some 'Guidance' for the following Wednesday but Joanna's phone was engaged. I stared at the back of the Euston Tower across Drummond Street, a monochrome Mondrian executed by a robot. I was glad it didn't start squirming about the way it had done the day before.

I left the office and it felt good to be heading south in the Shōgun, floating above the traffic in the soft, womb-like Japanese interior. The car was one of the few places I felt safe, like the bath. I turned on the radio and the infantile babble of Capital's DJ supplied the aural dimension to this sense of regression. The DJ was certainly in touch with his Inner Child. I imagined him in a sound-proof eyrie, broadcasting in a romper suit beneath a Mothercare mobile. All that was missing was a dummy in his mouth.

I zig-zagged south-west to Lancaster Gate and drove through Hyde Park. The leaves on the trees shone in the sunshine, sparkling with exhaust deposits. Through the Shō-gun's smeared windscreen I watched a jogger aerobicize on filthy air as he crossed the Serpentine Bridge. He was wearing a headband with Head written on it.

I found a meter near enough to the Puffa shop at World's End and fed it some coins. Emerging from the tree-lined side-street I turned right and walked up the King's Road over the same paving stones I'd trod fifteen years before, raking my studded jacket along the sides of the smart cars, fuming with solvents on school Saturdays.

This end of the King's Road had smartened up a lot in fifteen years, smartened up and promptly died. There were hardly any punters around and a hundred traders desperate for custom. To Let signs dotted the buildings and red Sale posters suffocated in silence behind dreary display windows. I walked into the Puffa shop and Jill was nowhere to be seen. Massive Attack were playing on the shop's cassette. I called out her name and Jill scuttled out from the stockroom.

She was a brown girl in her early twenties, fresh down from Manchester with her hair in grungy locks, looking fashionably exhausted. I gave her a lesson on the till and she told me about her obsessive boyfriend and the trouble he was causing with her flatmates in Hackney. For a while her patter helped to take my mind off Tony and the board meeting. I looked out at the world past ranks of Puffa jackets and T-shirts that weren't selling. A local schizophrenic wandered past the window in his dressing-gown.

A couple of white middle-class teenagers came into the shop wearing pale yellow Timberlands, plaid shirts and regulation woolly Smurf-caps. They gawped around with dead fish-eyes and all the charisma of a pair of Health Trust managers.

'Can I help at all?' I asked with what was meant to pass for enthusiasm. I wanted to show Jill how to close a sale.

The boys looked bored.

'Just looking,' grunted the taller one. They inspected one of our best-selling T-shirts, a blow-up of Elvis's last prescription from Dr Nick. They read the mind-boggling list of pharmaceuticals as if it was a spreadsheet, hung it back crooked on the rail and left without another word.

Jill and her emotional woes began to enervate me. I decided to stroll down the road to the Picasso Café for a coffee and a sandwich. The usual group of grey-haired swingers were sitting at their pavement table clocking the young girls as they walked past in the sunshine. Among them was Ken, a fifty-year-old regular with tight blue jeans and teased white hair who ran the cowboy-boot shop across the road. His business had been steady for twenty years because, as he put it, dwarves always need heels. I sat and bullshitted with him until it was time to head back to the office.

I got there just before three. Gudrun was busy working on her nails, long Fu Manchu curlers that clacked on her keyboard and broke all the time. She told me that Tony and

Alan had gone out for lunch around twelve-thirty. Tony hadn't come back yet and apparently Alan was worried sick. When he saw me he bowled out of his office.

'Tony's not at home and his mobile's switched off. Gudrun's trying his numbers. We've got to leave here in twenty minutes.'

'It'll be okay. He knows about the meeting. He hasn't called in at all?' I asked.

'Not a squeak. I had lunch with him and he said he had to go to the bank. Do you know where he could be?'

I had the feeling that wherever he was, there'd be a sign saying 'Licensed to sell beer, wine and spirits' above the door.

'He'll be here. He knows it's important. You didn't say anything to him over lunch? About sacking him?'

'No. We talked about the restructuring plan, that's all.'

'Well, if he doesn't show up then we'll just have to go without him, you and me.'

'We can't do that,' Alan said, going white at the prospect.

I thought I knew why he was so worried. If Tony wasn't at the board meeting, they couldn't sack him. Ten minutes later Tony reeled in with glazed eyes. He sat down with a thump on the sofa in reception and I felt like hitting him.

'You fucking prat,' I said. 'You're pissed. I knew it!'

'I'm sorry, Steve,' he slobbered. 'Get me some coffee, would you?'

I called out to Alan and poured a thick cup of stewed filter for Tony. Alan and I watched him burn his lips on the coffee.

'I'll be right as rain in just a minute. Just a bit tired,' Tony said.

'Great,' said Alan. He banged his forehead with his palm.

'Where've you been? I wanted to go through things again before we leave.'

'S'all right. We've been through it enough, haven't we?' said Tony, glaring at Alan with drunk hostility.

Alan went to change into the suit he kept zipped up in a plastic body-bag on the back of his door. I poured coffee down Tony's gullet until we had to leave. I drove us all to Covent Garden in the Shōgun with Tony propped in the front seat chewing spearmint gum. I parked on a meter round the corner from In Deep's offices. We were on Westminster Council turf and it was four quid for two hours, a real bargain. I pumped the coins into the slit and followed Tony's frisky pony-tail as he trotted unsteadily down the pavement.

We rode the lift to In Deep's fifth-floor offices. Tony looked sick in the neon light as we lurched a hundred feet into the air. I put a hand on his shoulder.

'Don't worry, it's going to be a piece of piss,' I said, trying to rally my own spirits as much as Tony's. I wondered what I'd do if Alan and Sally tried to dump him. I hoped that I'd have the strength to fight them.

The three of us filed out of the lift into In Deep's vast reception area which overlooked the Piazza. We trekked across a veld of carpet to the dark-wood desk that was womaned by a skinny secretary in a T-shirt with 'Babe' printed across it.

'Good afternoon,' said Alan in his garden-party accent. 'Alan Denton from Puffa Group. We've a meeting scheduled with Sally Moore.'

'Ah, yes,' she trilled. 'Please take a seat. I'll tell them you're here.' She directed us to some enormous leather chairs

57

and sofas that were bunched around a low smoked-glass coffee-table like hippos at a mud-hole.

We parked ourselves on the deep-grey furniture. Tony's feet barely brushed the floor. It felt like a trip to the head teacher's office. Alan flicked through a business magazine, cool as a freeze-chilled cucumber. Julia swanned up in a power suit and led us into Sally's office. Julia's hair was so black you could imagine Stan Lee inking in a blue highlight. Behind the surface affability we were all tense. Tony's face had started to pour with sweat. I caught his eye and gave him the thumbs-up sign. He tried to smile back but he was sick with fear. I asked myself again what I'd do if they tried to sack him. Tony and I should have worked out a strategy.

The Covent Garden Piazza lay beneath a plate-glass window that ran the length of Sally's office. I watched the teeming shoppers down below as Sally glided her tanned gym-body round the desk to welcome us one by one with an Ultra-brite smile. She looked good for fifty. Her skin was tight on her face and her white hair was scraped back off a no-make-up look to brush against the beige linen shoulders of her Japanese jacket. She sat us at the conference table in high-backed chairs, an elegant monkey to Julia's white-faced vole. Except for the deep tan everything about Sally was drained of vulgar colour as befitted someone who had made a fortune from stone-washed denim.

'Hi, Steve. You look great, really good. Here, take a seat,' she said. There were some glasses on the table and a bottle of mineral water that had come all the way from Helsinki. I tasted some and discovered that it hadn't travelled well. Julia opened a file, pen poised to take minutes. After some banter that reeked faintly of goodwill, Sally got down to business.

'So basically I've been over the figures with Julia. I agreed some weeks ago that In Deep would buy a further share of the company if you could come up with a viable strategy between you.'

She scanned us expectantly with her pale eyes and smiled, her teeth flashing on like an arc-light. I looked across to Alan but he didn't move a muscle. Sally took a breath and pressed on.

'Alan told me today that this hadn't been possible, despite all your hard work.'

'But what about the restructuring?' I asked Alan. He just shrugged and I turned to Sally.

'Have you seen the plan?' I asked her.

'Yes, I read Alan's proposals. I agree with all his suggestions but I don't think they go far enough. There are certain conditions you would have to meet if we're to invest more money. Firstly, cutting your losses and closing the shops. Secondly, the relocation of Puffa's offices. The lease on Drummond Street expires in September and I'd want to move you over here.'

'What, into this building?' I asked. I began to feel distinctly uneasy.

'Why not? There's enough space and there'd be a big saving,' she said.

'It sounds like a take-over, that's all. With you owning sixty per cent.'

'I see it as synergy.'

'More like colonization,' I said. I immediately regretted it.

'Steve, if you can raise the money elsewhere, fine. Otherwise hear me out,' she said with a whip in her voice.

'I'm sorry. Please go on.'

'Very well. Then we come to the sad fact that Puffa cannot at this time justify three executive salaries,' she said.

I looked at Tony and knew it was coming. These were the exact words Alan had used. Tony was staring at his reflection in the table-top and Sally turned to me.

'I'm sorry, Steve, but if In Deep is going to make a further investment we're going to have to let you go,' she said.

'Me?' I stammered. I couldn't believe it.

I tried to speak but nothing came out.

'You can't do that to him!' Tony said to Alan. 'You didn't say anything about that!'

'Don't worry, Tony,' I said, scrabbling around for some composure. 'Sit tight. They can't do a thing without our agreement. We've still got control of the company.'

'But I don't have a vote any more!' cried Tony.

'What do you mean, you don't have a vote?' I asked.

'Alan's bought my shares,' Tony said.

I couldn't believe it.

'Let's all try to calm down,' Alan said, trying for a 'more-in-sorrow-than-in-anger' tone. 'I feel awful about this but you should know that I already hold Tony's shares. He made them over to me earlier today. There was no other way to save the company. Please make sure you get that down, Julia.'

Julia nodded and scribbled away in shorthand. Tony hunched over, racked by the remains of his conscience while Alan leaned back to watch me. I caught him wiping a grin off his face. Alan had planned the whole thing.

'You fucking bastard!' I yelled at him. 'How could you?'

Sally laid a hand on my arm but I didn't take my eyes off Alan. He held my gaze for a moment and then shuffled some papers around.

'Please, Steve,' Sally said. 'It's a business decision, it's nothing personal. You'll still retain twenty per cent of the equity.'

'You bastard!' I shouted at Alan. 'You've stitched me up, you little shit!'

He raised his palms and shook his head. I felt like smashing him in the face. He was behind it, scheming and manoeuvring, manipulating Tony and me like a pair of puppets. I could see it now. He'd even got me out of the office for the day so he could twist Tony's arm. Tony couldn't look me in the face.

'I'm sorry, Steve, but I had to think about Laura and the kids,' he whined.

'But you've just divorced her, you toss-pot! How long do you think you'll last with me gone anyway? He just needs your vote to give him control and then he'll cut you out too. Don't you see that, you drunken fuck?'

'Steve, whatever you may think I want you to know that I feel very sad about this,' Alan said.

'You what? You feel *sad*? Come off it, Alan! It's your wet-dream come true!'

'If you look at it objectively . . .' he started.

'You're an idiot, Tone,' I said. 'What'd he give you for the shares? Fifty grand?'

'That's a private matter,' said Alan. 'If you could calm down you'd see that Puffa's profitability depends on Tony's design expertise. It's for the best. Think of your own investment in the company.'

'Yeah, yeah. Which is tied up for at least two years. What am I meant to live on, for fuck's sake?'

Sally turned to face me, the way the manuals say you should when you fire someone.

'I can't believe you'll find it hard to get another position. Just for the time being, until we pull through this difficult period,' she said.

There was a flask of liquid oxygen behind her ribs where her heart should have been.

'What, in Burger King? Bollocks to that!' I yelled.

'Listen, Steve,' said Alan. 'I suggest you think this over very carefully and weigh up your options. There really is no alternative. It's this or the company faces receivership.'

'You're right, I haven't any options. You've made sure of that! Fuck you, Alan!'

I circled the table fast and hit him hard in the middle of his face. Alan went over backwards in his chair as I felt an astonishing pain in my knuckles. Blood poured from Alan's nose as if I'd turned on a red tap in his head.

He got up and came at me. He was quick and he grabbed my throat with both hands, tucking his chin into his chest as I tried to uppercut him in the face. I struggled to break his hold and kick his legs away.

His hands were choking me. Blood welled in my head. I couldn't breathe. I got a handful of his hair, pulled his head back and clubbed his face with my fist. He wailed in pain and I reeled back, dragging air into my lungs. Fresh blood gushed from Alan's pulped nose to ruin Sally's carpet. He was pouring red pints. The sight transfixed us all for a moment. Alan was making little croaking noises like a frog. His eyes were on me, primitive and hateful.

Tony grabbed my arm. I brushed him away as Alan lunged at me, catching me in the ribs with his elbow as I stepped to the side. I managed to kick him in the back of the knee as he went past. He fell heavily against the edge of the conference table before sliding to the ground. I kicked him hard, burying a Hi-top in his gut. I went for his face as he curled up in a ball to protect himself.

The women were screaming. Tony and Julia pulled me

off him. Alan knelt on the carpet and pinched the bridge of his nose to staunch the flow of blood, glaring up at me like a psychotic animal. Sally screamed at me to get out.

'All right, all right! I'm going!' I shouted.

On my way to the door I grabbed the baby bonsai tree from Sally's desk and slung it at Alan. He got a hand up just in time to stop the porcelain base hitting the side of his face. I walked out in disgust.

I went to get a drink in a pub just off the Piazza, the Prince of Wales. It was full of office workers preparing for the trip home in the tube trains. I pushed my way to the bar and the barmaid measured out my Scotch, her profile haloed by the blue ring of an Insect-O-Cutor.

My heart was running at two hundred beats-per-minute. I felt sick. My right hand began to swell up around the knuckles. I downed the Scotch and felt it burn my stomach. I wanted to cut Alan's throat and stick his head on a stake. An office worker brushed against me. I felt weak and vulnerable, a fly with its wings pulled off.

I sat there drinking until I'd calmed down sufficiently to call Louis, my lawyer. A suit was spluttering drunk love-talk into the pub's pay phone so I went back to the car and used the mobile.

Louis assured me that he'd look into my contract and advised me to collect all my papers from the office in case we wound up in court. I headed home and the rush-hour traffic crawled towards the sun as it expired in disgust over west London.

7

Mirror-work

THE SUN WAS FALLING BEHIND OUR HOUSE. Pulling into the driveway, I speculated as to how long we could afford to live in it without my salary. The big mortgage would keep ticking twenty-four hours a day. Alan's words 'Overhead overhead overhead' ran around my brain.

It was hard to believe I'd really been sacked and this sense of unreality hinged on the inexplicability of Alan's change of mind. It made no sense for him to sack me. I felt that if I could only talk it over rationally with Julia and Sally, I could persuade them to reinstate me. As I trudged across the gravel it all began to feel like a sick joke.

I de-activated the burglar alarm and found a note from Liz saying that she'd gone to yoga class at the health centre with Mary and would be back at ten. Light-headed with hunger, I prepared some spaghetti bolognese. Cooking helped to take my mind off Alan's betrayal. As the spaghetti boiled and the bolognese mix bubbled beside it, I searched the cluttered sideboard for the pepper mill and located it by the bread bin.

It felt different - heftier and better made. The bulbous head rotated on a series of precision-engineered clicks like the dial on a combination safe, effortlessly crop-dusting the sauce in two dark diagonal swathes. It was a delight to operate and the operation reminded me of the time I had twisted the head off my sister's doll. It was a surprise that the mill suddenly worked so well. I felt a surge of delight and wanted to buy more of these pepper mills and give them to all my remaining friends.

A £3.99 item from a Habitat bargain bin, Liz and I had bought the pepper mill for our first flat in Finsbury Park. Of course the mill had soon revealed the poverty of its Czech manufacture. The poorly lathed pine squeaked alarmingly in operation like a note tortured by Stockhausen to a universal goose-pimple frequency. The top-screw was forever twisting off loose alloy threads to roll beneath the cooker.

I dished up the spaghetti and it was so delicious that I wondered if some external force was improving not just my sensory perceptions but the contours and flavours of my im-mediate world. I looked at the pepper mill standing before me on the table. The once-white pine was camouflaged by a thousand fingerprints, tiny whorls etched in oil and red wine.

Observing the pepper mill closely, it surprised me to discover that this smudged veneer proved to partially obscure not cheap Czech pine but a wood I had never come across before, something like a compacted bird's-eye maple with the intricate fractal curlicues of walnut. I peered more intently, concentrating until I detected a shimmer like the beginnings of Brownian motion in the grain. It looked as though the wood itself was boiling. However, as soon as my eye focused directly on the areas of turbulence they fell static again. Sensing a connection to my hallucination in front of the Euston Tower, I told myself it was just a symptom of shock and fatigue. I sucked up the last thread of spaghetti anteater-style and was putting away the pans when I discovered a second identical pepper mill in the cupboard. It rattled, nearly empty, and when I assayed an experimental twist there was the familiar unedifying squeak of the clapped-out mechanism. This was the original for which Liz must have found a replacement.

I went into the sitting-room and watched the news. A baby had been abducted from a supermarket in Leeds and when the mother appealed for its return, her despair shot through me. Swamped by waves of sorrow and loss, my mind began to torture itself over the mess I'd made of my own life.

I heard a car fizzle to a stop on the gravel outside. My wife came into the sitting-room in her yoga gear: an aerobic leotard and new trainers topped off with a T-shirt bearing a Yin and Yang symbol for the right spiritual touch, just long enough to cover her bottom.

'Did you call Joanna to fix up another appointment?' Liz asked.

If she'd gone to yoga class to release some tension it hadn't worked too well. She scoffed when I told her I hadn't had a chance to make the call. Then she asked me about the board meeting.

'You'd better sit down,' I said. She lowered herself warily onto the director's chair and I gave it to her straight. Liz didn't believe me at first. I told her exactly what had happened. She sat there opening and closing her mouth like a goldfish as the truth sank in.

'How could they do that, Steve? It's your company. You and Tony own most of the shares!'

'But I told you Tony sold Alan his shares and that gave Sally and Alan control. Alan conned me, made me think he wanted to get rid of Tony so I wouldn't suspect him. Then he scared Tony into selling him his shares.'

'God, I can't imagine Alan doing that! It must have been Sally Moore. Do you think you'll be able to get another job?' she asked.

'It's going to be tough. I may have run a business for ten years but it's not as though I've got any proper qualifications.'

'What about redundancy? They'll have to give you something, won't they?'

I could see the fear behind her eyes: penury, repossession, the DSS, b. & b.s in Paddington. We'd been living high on the hog for quite a few years and there were going to have to be some painful adjustments. Liz enjoyed spending money.

'I've already been on to Louis about it,' I said.

Liz took a deep breath and steeled herself to sound positive. 'Well, it'll be all right. We'll muddle through until you get another job, won't we? You've got bags of talent,' she said, trying to get some feeling into it.

In Marriage Guidance they call that a 'stroke', an unsolicited compliment that the recipient should treasure and hopefully repay at some later point, though not too soon lest it appear a purely mechanical exchange. For the next half-hour we went over what had happened, going round in circles and getting nowhere.

'How was yoga?' I asked, aware that whatever small measure of relaxation she'd obtained from her class had long been nullified by my news.

'Oh, it was all right. Mary came with me and we mainly did the breathing stuff.'

'How's Guru Gerry?' I asked.

'Knackered. He's got a new girlfriend.'

Liz turned away from me and fixed her hair in the mirror. Guru Gerry was her yoga instructor, a neo-hippy jerk Liz had slept with a few times the year before. This had emerged in Marriage Guidance and it still hurt. Liz went upstairs to have a shower.

Slumped on the sofa and bathed by the television's Deadly Orgone Radiation, I picked over the carcass of my marriage. Seven-year itch had developed into nine-year eczema. Counselling, retailing at ninety pounds an hour, had staved off talk of the 'D-word' for the time being, but the lineaments of our desire were still a pair of death masks at absolute zero, the relationship reduced to a tired ritual which was becoming ever more circumscribed. Liz's ropey tubes and my limbo-dancer of a sperm-count had led us down a dusty track to a cobwebbed Petri dish. We'd tried every available fertility treatment but Liz still hadn't conceived. Only habit and fear held us together now. I wondered how long we'd last without money.

These thoughts, the very thoughts that had led me to SIT, now assailed me on the sofa. 'Sit up,' I told myself. 'Detach. These are negative programmes you can change.' I winched myself up, doused the electronic baby-sitter and climbed the stairs for some Mirror-work.

As I passed the bathroom I could hear Liz taking her shower. I undressed, sat cross-legged in front of the full-length mirror in the bedrooom and addressed the white Buddha before me. My eyes travelled over my reflection, from the tinged flesh around my armpit, across my chest to the marzipan folds of my stomach area and beyond.

'You are the godhead, the thousand-petalled lotus blossom,' I incanted. 'You are perfect and yet you improve, an alpha male, poised, resplendent . . .'

After ten minutes I stood up and saw my old green Pringle crew-neck on the back of the chair. It felt extremely soft, almost cashmere, and very different from the swarf-like Shetland-meets-the-wash-cycle texture that I remembered. I sniffed at the sleeve for some trace of a new breakthrough fabric conditioner but smelt only new wool. This puzzled me but I told myself to accept pleasure. After all, I deserved it.

Liz came into the bedroom with a towel wrapped around her head. She shook off her robe and I kissed the back of her neck. She turned round to embrace me, hot from the shower with steam rising off her body. Her eyes were big and wet, the whites as bright and box-fresh as her new trainers. The crêpe flesh around them seemed smoothed-out and the dark dope-smoker rings had gone. Her distended pores had contracted too and her slack cheek now cleaved tight to the bone.

It wasn't just the flattering glow from the bedside lamp because I saw my own hand on her shoulder and the blue veins wriggled beneath my raddled skin like the roots of a Syc-amore. Hardening like the very trunk of the said tree, I was amazed how much I wanted my wife. Once I'd got over the surprise and let go I was in heaven. I realized that I wouldn't even have to pretend I was with somebody else, projecting home movies on the button-back headboard in order to achieve an orgasm.

However, I needed a pee before we made love so I broke away and padded off to the bathroom. The light was on and the room smelt delicious, the air still steamy and thick with scent. Liz's yoga clothes were strewn across the floor, bless her untidy little heart, and there was water all over the carpet.

I was pissing a perfect parabola when I saw that the array of cosmetics surrounding Liz's sink had multiplied as if the potions and unguents had germinated in the fetid atmosphere. There were two big glass bottles of scent with their tops off, the same stuff I'd blowtorched my Barclaycard for in New York. I replaced the stoppers before heading back to the bedroom.

When I entered the corridor something caught my eye in the upper panel of the bedroom door. An area the size of a dinner plate was pulsing, a bubbling disc upon which minuscule currents eddied, Voyager's footage of the windswept surface of a frozen planet. I examined the paintwork closely. The movement in the gloss surface slowed into a milky moiré which began to shimmer like the surface of a pond on a breezy day.

Puzzled, I pushed the bedroom door open and there was someone fucking my wife on the side of the bed, his flanks a blur of flesh in motion, his legs braced against the chest of drawers.

'Liz!' I yelled.

'Steve!' she squawked as the attacker pounded into her.

I yanked him off her by the hair - he wasn't as well-built as me - and threw him against the wardrobe. I hit him and kicked him on the ground in a red rage until I heard Liz screaming at me to stop. I turned and held her. She was in shock, trying to speak through her sobs.

'Hey, it's all right now, it's over,' I said.

My mind raced as I looked at the naked rapist curled up on the floor in a ball, groaning. There were red marks coming up on his back where I'd kicked him. I hoped he was a haemophiliac. I wanted to call the police but Liz held me tight.

'Steve,' she groaned. 'Oh, Steve!'

'I'm here, don't worry.' I stroked her hair and kissed her.

'What have you done?' she cried.

Her face was white and she was trembling. She sobbed and threw herself on the bed. I rolled him over and reeled back in horror.

The room span.

He had my face! He had my bloody face. I couldn't believe it. I looked at Liz, cowering in fright with her mouth agape. The man was breathing.

'Look!' I ordered her, pointing to her assailant on the carpet. 'What's happening? What is this?'

Liz was still sobbing into the pillow and my heart ran a tin cup along my ribcage.

I forced myself to look at him again. He had my head, my bulbous nose and the same cleft in his recessive chin but his geometry was clearer, not so customized, almost good-looking. He had much more hair, glossier with less grey, and carried much less fat than me, and though I hate to say it, a lot more penis. (Maybe he was still detumescing.) Liz sat up while I stared at the supine interloper.

'Who is he?' I asked her, even though I knew the answer.

But I had seen him before, every day of my life, reflected in shop windows or while I Lubrastripped my jowls in the mirror.

Liz was shaking and I saw the pain of our married life soldered onto her face. She fled downstairs, keen to leave the scene of her unwitting adultery.

I tried to regain some equilibrium with a SIT technique. I shut myself in the spare bedroom but the world followed me like a gas, pressing in around the door-frame, squirting up through a cigarette-hole in the rug. Like a flasher it couldn't help but obtrude. I went back into the bedroom.

On the carpet the replicant stirred. He had a suntan. The white buttocks were marked with eight tiny red crescents, four on each cheek like a cluster of UFOs. I thought they might have been tattoos but they weren't. They were indented scallops freshly impressed by Liz's fingernails, the very index of her passion. I touched his shoulder. It was warm and solid, real flesh and blood.

I stumbled down to the sitting-room and tried to think it through. After a few minutes I heard him coming downstairs. The clone found me, smiling sheepishly as if to say that it wasn't his fault if the Cosmic Cardsharp had cast him as a joker in the pack, a mere wannabe. The beating I'd given him seemed to have had little effect. He didn't appear particularly shaken by what had happened, just excited and confused. The sight of him horrified me but I tried to act calm.

'This is amazing! I always wanted a brother,' Steve Jr said. 'Not to be the only son. It's incredible! I feel like I'm dreaming. You know, I think I know what might be happening. I read about this in a book, *Beyond the Mirror Stage*. It's an analysis of the doppelgänger phenomenon, the search for the invisible twin. Specular reduplication, the demystification of narcissism. I guess it suggests we could've fantasized each other, or rather that one or both of us represent the other's psychotic delusion – that is, if I've grasped Politzer's thesis correctly.'

'Come off it,' I said with a laugh. 'I've never heard such a load of bollocks! I'm completely sane. So what does that make you? A nutter!'

I observed our guest, my better half. Not only was he considerably slimmer than me but he comported himself with a poise and grace rarely evinced by the inhabitants of south-west London. He perched himself on the huge zebra-striped sofa like a speck of crud on a bar-code. I took my director's chair by the desk and tried to mask the hostility I still felt towards him. I had to try and find out what was going on. I wanted to interrogate him.

'Are you feeling all right?' I asked.

'Yes, thanks. I'm fine now. I'm really sorry about what happened upstairs,' he said.

'Forget it. I'd like to ask you some questions, if that's all right?'

He nodded enthusiastically.

'Tell me what you've been doing today,' I asked.

'I went in to work and had a meeting with Sally Moore at lunch-time.'

'Before the board meeting?' I asked him.

'That's right. It went very well. I managed to persuade her to increase her investment in Puffa without sacking Tony Mold.'

'And how do you feel about Alan Denton?'

'Alan who?'

'You haven't appointed Alan Denton as managing director of Puffa, then?'

'God, no. Tony and I run the company between us.'

'And nothing strange happened the night before last?' I asked him.

'The night before last? I had a wet dream, that's all.'

Myself, I hadn't enjoyed an unassisted orgasm in over ten years. Maybe it was a dietary thing. I'd ask him about it later. Meanwhile I probed deeper.

'Do you remember the name of the headmistress at your nursery school?'

'Yes, I think so. The school was called St James's, and the headmistress was . . . er, no, it's on the tip of my tongue but I can't quite remember. I'm sorry.'

I could. Her name was Miss Sheppard and she'd made my little life a misery. I still had a holographic voodoo doll of her preserved in my head, plus the steel pins to go with it. Steve Jr couldn't even remember her name. I felt encouraged.

'What O level grades did you get? Which subjects?' I asked him.

He reeled them off by rote, and then the retakes. Fair enough. You don't forget humiliations like that in a hurry.

'So, as far as you're concerned, you've just been living your normal life until one day, zap, you meet your double while you're in bed with his wife. Right. How's your marriage going by the way?' I asked him.

'Same as for you, I guess. It's a good marriage. We've been lucky, Steve. It's a rare thing these days.'

I'd told the same lie a thousand times myself.

'Are you still working with Tony Mold?' I asked him.

'Oh, yes. Very much so. We've been in business for ten years. He's a good friend as well as my partner.'

'And you never had a thing with Tony's wife?'

'You mean Laura?' he said, fidgeting on the zebra. 'Of course not. They're happily married.'

Another discrepancy. Two in fact. Firstly, I'd had a desultory affair with Laura when my own marriage hit the permafrost. Secondly, Tony had divorced her in a blood-soaked legal bout a year after she gave birth to the triplets.

And now for the *coup de grâce*: a secret I had repressed for twenty-five years and only just released during a gruelling one-to-one interaction at SIT, the ultimate therapy-credential, the Big Bang that retroactively excused all my own infractions. The acid test.

'Did you ever get interfered with by Uncle Sid?' I asked him.

'God, no! That's ridiculous! No, never. Why, did you?'

'Yes, I did. When I was about four. It was after my bath and I was drying myself by the gas fire.'

I didn't go on. I didn't need to. It was conclusive proof that I was the real Steve and I was exultant. It would be tough on Steve Jr but that was life. I'd help him find a job and maybe rent him a small flat until he got on his feet. We'd keep in touch, of course, for our birthdays and so forth.

Meanwhile Steve Jr sat skewered by the black stripes of the sofa, horrified as his identity collapsed around him in a flutter of cheap cardboard. It's a hard blow to have it confirmed that you are a dyed-in-the-wool phoney. I saw a tear well up in his eye and burst over the levee of his lower lid. I went over and hugged him, the poor sod. I felt bad for him.

'I'm so sorry, I'm so sorry,' he sobbed. 'It must have been awful for you. It's so unfair, I feel you've had to bear all this pain for me through the years. What can I say, Steve, except, "Thank you"?'

His words hit me like a truck.

In a flash I realized that I'd drawn a short straw a long time ago. I began to cry myself, a Mississippi of tears for the abused kid inside me, the inner child as they say at SIT. I didn't care which one of us was real anymore. It didn't matter if Steve Jr was a happier, luckier me from a parallel universe or a sloppily programmed robot. In the dreadful light of memory he held me like a brother.

Steve Jr went into the kitchen and I lay stricken on the sofa.

8

Steve Jr

I WOKE SLUMPED FORWARD ON THE KITCHEN TABLE, my left cheek impressed with the mirror-image of the table's grooved pine surface. The door to the sitting-room was ajar and I tip-toed across the hall to peek through the crack. My sad bald double had been asleep in there the last time I'd looked, his bloated stomach inflating on the sofa with each snore.

He was gone.

In the grey glow of dawn I saw a fresh crop of butts in the ashtray by the sofa. The tobacco-reek lingered on the still air. Before leaving the room I opened the window, glad that I had never smoked myself.

I searched the house and found Liz fast asleep in the spare room wearing all her clothes. There was no sign of my unfortunate clone. I assumed he'd just disappeared back into the ether. I put on my Timberlands and slipped out through the back door to take my usual early morning walk.

At the bottom of the garden I climbed over the fence onto the golf-course, relieved that I hadn't had to see my negative double again. It was depressing that someone who resembled me so closely had made such a cock-up of their life, wasting so many opportunities for happiness. If the coin had flipped the other way it could so easily have been me.

My muscles loosened up as I strolled the great green Wilton of the fourteenth fairway, lit by a cold strip-light of dawn at the horizon. I skirted a bunker and reached the green as the sun rose above a hillock. I felt its rays on my face. As I retraced my steps on the way home, I observed the gradual disappearance of my outward footprints as the dew evaporated in the heat of the sun.

When I got back to the house there was still no sign of the other Steve. Liz was sleeping and I kissed her lightly on the forehead. My heart brimmed over with love for her as I drove into town. The sun was already warming the air and if the breeze cleared the smog it would be another beautiful day.

I parked in my space on Drummond Street, climbed the stairs to Puffa and found that I couldn't open the door with my key. It just wouldn't turn and I saw that the barrel of the lock had been changed. The new metal gleamed brightly. I guessed that we'd been burgled again. I dialled Tony at home on the mobile but the liquid crystals displayed the fact that my phone was 'Out of Service'. It was the second little ruck in the starched white collar of Friday morning.

I took away a cappuccino and sat on the steps outside Puffa massaging my right hand while I waited for someone to arrive and open the office. At nine-thirty a shiny blue BMW pulled into the street. The driver parked and primed his car alarm before heading across the road towards me. He had a black eye and a bandaged wrist. He didn't see me until he'd almost tripped over me.

'Good morning,' I said with a smile. He was wearing a loud striped shirt and black Levi's. I had no idea who he was.

'Steve! What the fuck are you doing here?' the man asked. I wondered how he knew my name.

'I can't get into my office. The lock's been changed,' I explained.

I stood up and he backed off, running a shaky hand through his long red hair.

'Just get away from here! Just get lost, all right?' he cried.

'Hey, calm down,' I said. 'What's wrong?'

I went to put a consoling arm on his shoulder but he shoved me away.

'Are you kidding? You fractured my bloody wrist! And my nose might have to be re-set!'

I had no idea what he was talking about and I told him so. He stepped back.

'If you don't leave right now I'm going to call the police,' he said.

'Come on, let's go inside and talk it over,' I suggested. It crossed my mind that he could have been smoking crack.

'You're not allowed in the office!' he yelled. 'I had the lock changed!'

'What do you mean, you had the lock changed?' I asked, utterly bewildered.

'To keep you out! In case you decide to steal stuff, smash the place up. After yesterday's performance.'

The man glared at me with paranoid anger, kicking at a hardened blob of chewing-gum on the pavement with his cowboy boot.

'Why do you think I'd want to smash the place up?' I asked gently.

'Are you telling me you can't remember? Sally fired you. Gave you the chop, boss. The old heave-ho,' he said with a little grin.

It was the grin that triggered my memory, the same grin he'd worn as his plan had unfolded at the board meeting. My head exploded. I ran at Alan through a red mist, hit him in the gut and got an arm round his neck. He tried to break my grip. When he pried at my swollen fingers I howled in agony and released him.

'You fucking piece of shit!' he yelled.

He rushed me, pushing me to the ground. He tried to stamp down on me but I rolled on the pavement and grabbed hold of his leg. He hopped around and fell over, taking the weight on his bandaged wrist. His face went grey.

I got to my feet and kicked him in the chest. I tripped over his legs and fell beside him. We scrambled to our feet simultaneously. He stood hunched forward, clutching his solar plexus and gasping for air. I was bigger and heavier but Alan was much fitter than me, a gym-freak. Despite his wrist we were about evenly matched and I wanted an unfair advantage.

I saw an empty beer-bottle by the steps and picked it up by the neck. I broke off its base against the wall and waved it at him. Alan's lower lip trembled as his eyes fixed on the shards of green glass glittering in the sunlight.

I went for his throat. He jumped back from the bottle but I caught him across the cheek. A lip of pale marbled fat opened up. The blood flowed from it like a red sideburn. I slashed at him again but he weaved out of the way and grabbed my forearm.

We wrestled each other for the bottle. I dropped it to lock an arm around his neck. Blood pumped out of his cheek to daub my sleeve scarlet. I tried to wrestle him to the ground but he tripped me over and I fell, cracking my head on the pavement.

9

Oblivion by Calvin Klein

I CAME ROUND AND *ALAN WAS ON TOP OF ME*. His face had changed shape, swollen and crazed, warped with aggression. His hands gripped my windpipe, cutting off my air-supply. The psychedelic design of his shirt started boiling in front of me, blurring and swirling like an over-dressed kaleidoscope. I smelt his fragrance and that's the last thing I remembered. *Oblivion* by Calvin Klein.

I circled the lagoon beneath a lead sky. The air was thick and hard to breathe. The island had a sad tropical feel: the water of the lagoon looked viscous and unhealthy. Grey paralysed palm trees loomed above me in the stillness as I trudged along the sand. There was something black and massive along the shore. A pall of greasy smoke coiled above it in the dead air. It was a beached whale and a man was cutting at its side. Wearing a laboratory-coat splattered with blood, Alan Denton was carving chunks of blubber from the dead mammal with a curved blade and reducing them in an oil-drum over a pit of burning driftwood. The blubber hissed and Alan grunted with his exertions. I shrank away to notice a lilac fish darting about in a rock-pool at the edge of the water. As I watched it, I came to realize that the fish's apparently random movements were in fact highly significant, that it was tracing the movements of the Invisible Hand that controls all our lives.

I woke in a bed with too many blankets piled on top of me. Through a chink in the tapestry curtains I could see that it was another sunny day outside. It was so hot and close in the room that a candle on the bedside table had drooped over in the heat, prostrating itself before some white roses in a crystal vase from which the water had evaporated to leave a brackish deposit. The walls were hung with seventeenth-century por-traits. A red museum-rope ran along the left side of the room between two doors. The general public would be filing through these doors in a couple of hours but I was in no hurry to get up. Then one of the long-stemmed roses leant down and whispered to me.

'Wake up! Replenish my supply! I'm thirsty, Steve, and I must drink!'

Then I was in the delightful position of knowing I was asleep.

I woke up in limbo, underwater, but it was just the inside of my head, my own private darkness. I opened my eyes and saw only dim shapes. Everything felt rough and papery, the sheets, my face, the pillows, as though my skin and the bed linen had been mulched and recycled together. On the bed-side table some lilies were dying. When I looked out of the window I saw that it was twilight. Across the street an office worker was being economically active in his strip-lit cubicle.

My own room was no bigger. I made out the essentials: table, built-in cupboard, chair, wall-mounted TV. Through the open door I caught two or three frames of a middle-aged woman in an orange robe shuffling past along a corridor. I pressed a red button that glowed above my bed. Someone came and turned on the light. My eyes adjusted and I saw a short middle-aged nurse with steel-rimmed spectacles.

'Hello, Mr Cork, I'm Nurse Barnes. How are you feeling?' she asked.

'Not good,' I mumbled, sloppy-tongued. 'I'd love a cup of tea.' I had a bad taste in my mouth. My brain felt like a pale-grey blob of chewed gum squidged into my skull-cavity.

She went to get my tea and I examined the room in greater detail. The decorator had enjoyed a Pampas mood during Lady Thatcher's third term and there was a screen-print of an empty deck-chair by a pool for the Mediterranean touch. Nurse Barnes came back with a plastic cup of tea. I took it from her with both hands.

'Thanks,' I said. 'Where am I?'

'The Webster Clinic on the Marylebone Road. You came in on Friday.'

'Friday? What day is it today then?' My tongue couldn't form the words properly.

'It's Monday. You've been here for three days.'

I'd lost the whole weekend. 'What am I in for? I mean, what's wrong with me?'

'You had a minor breakdown, Mr Cork, but you're much better now. We've given you some medication. Doctor Mahmood will be along just as soon as he finishes with another patient. He'll explain everything to you. Just relax and drink your tea. If you need anything just press the buzzer.'

Nurse Barnes left and scenes came back to me in a slideshow of jumbled memories: the board meeting, my fight with Alan, the blonde girl in a restaurant and something terrible in the bedroom with Liz that had finally flipped me out. I remembered seeing Liz's fully clothed body on the bed in the spare room. Had I hit her? Christ, had I killed her? I spilt some dishwater tea at the thought but because of the medication my anxiety was muffled like a row in the house next door.

A thin silver-haired man of sixty-five came through the door. I thought he'd got the wrong room until he introduced himself as Dr Mahmood. He had a sing-song voice and moved towards me in such a stiff jerky way that I found myself looking for the strings.

'How are you feeling, Mr Cork?' he asked.

'Not great,' I said.

He looked less like a doctor than the kind of international businessman who reads the *Wall Street Journal* in first-class aeroplane seats. In place of a white coat he wore a tailor-made three-piece suit with a gold watch-chain spanning a small pot belly. His sallow cheeks were brogued by old acne scars.

'I'm really worried about my wife. Have you spoken to her?'

'Oh, yes, yes. I met her when you were admitted on Friday and we had a chance to talk a little. A charming woman. She's coping very well.' He smiled to demonstrate his confident bedside manner and revealed a row of small yellow sweetcorn teeth.

'Is she really all right? I thought maybe I'd hurt her.'

'Oh, no, she's perfectly well. She said that you became very confused on Thursday night. You were very agitated when you came in on Friday and we gave you something to help you relax,' he said, his brown eyes twinkling beneath thick grey eyebrows. The diamond pin in his red silk tie made me wonder how much this consultation was costing me.

'You had a breakdown. Do you remember much about it?'

I told him what I remembered about the board meeting and about the way I'd been eclipsed by my double. Our identities were still overlapping each other in my mind like a Venn diagram. Replaying the night's events for him, I tried to pinpoint exactly when I'd lost the plot but it was still unclear. I did know that Steve Jr had departed whence he came, that nobody had been able to work a lunch-time miracle on Sally Moore. I'd lost my job, my marriage was probably beyond repair, I was broke and was possibly facing criminal proceedings for assault. And now I was a patient in a mental hospital.

'This is very encouraging. You're gaining some valuable insights,' said Dr Mahmood, beaming with unaccountable good cheer, like a head teacher who had discovered the pleasures of soft drugs on retirement. 'Try not to alarm yourself, Mr Cork. One out of four adults require psychiatric treatment during their lives. It's not as uncommon as you might suppose and the vast majority of our patients make a full recovery.'

'How long will I have to stay here?' I asked. I felt as if I was floating on a spongy cloud and that he'd never let me off it.

'Well, it's a little early to say. It really depends on your progress. I intend to reduce the medication gradually and see how well you get on over the next week or so. How do you feel about that?'

'All right, I suppose. What medication am I on?'

'Oh, nothing serious. Just a tranquillizer and something to help you sleep.'

'Tell me, do you know if I'm covered by medical insurance?' I had the feeling I was bleeding money by the bucket.

'I wouldn't know, I'm afraid. That's not really my department,' said Dr Mahmood, far above such matters. 'By the way, do you have family in America? I knew a Jeffrey Cork when I was at Harvard, a Boston man. He was a cousin of the Kennedys.'

'I do have a cousin called Jeff, but he's a butcher in Wolverhampton.'

Dr Mahmood made a little horseshoe smile and stood up, flapping his arms to shoo away the black crows of insanity. He told me that Liz was coming to see me the following morning. When he turned to leave I noticed a tiny dandruff galaxy spread across the dark blue shoulders of his suit.

On Tuesday morning I lay in bed and waited for Liz to show up. I felt apprehensive about our meeting. Although I was still confused about the events that had led to my admission, I remembered Claire and wondered how she fitted into the picture. I was still trying to piece it together when Liz arrived in her mackintosh. She hesitated, unsure in the doorway. Stress had drawn and pinched her face into little points like a Euan Uglow portrait. I managed a smile and she rushed over to hug me, the raindrops on her shoulder wetting my cheek with a spatter of ersatz tears.

'God, I'm so glad you're better. I've been so worried,' she said, burying herself in my neck.

'I'm sorry, Liz,' I mumbled. 'I'm sorry about all this.'

'You've been ill. It's not your fault. How are you feeling?' she asked, looking into me for an answer. I could see my own fear reflected in her eyes.

'Much better. I still feel dopey from the drugs but things are getting a bit clearer. I can't believe I've lost three whole days.'

Liz stood up, took a hanger from the wardrobe and hung her mackintosh on the back of the door.

'I talked to Doctor Mahmood and he's very pleased with your progress,' she said, perching herself on the edge of the bed and taking my hand with an earnest smile. 'We're going to pull through this, I promise.'

The line sounded rehearsed. It was a Movie-moment and I couldn't quite buy it, convinced that Liz was playing a role. I knew my next line, 'Darling, I love you.' I'd heard it a thousand times on television but I couldn't bring myself to use it. Our problems hadn't just vanished in a puff of smoke. Like my memory, they were reconstituting themselves by the minute.

'Tell me, I didn't hit you on Thursday night, did I?' I asked.

'God, no,' said Liz, shocked at the idea. 'You broke the mirror in the bedroom, that's all. We were in bed and you went crazy,' she said. 'You saw your reflection and you thought it was real and you smashed the mirror. Then you started talking to yourself. I didn't know what to do. I called the doctor but he couldn't come until the morning. You calmed down eventually and when I woke up on Friday you'd gone. Alan Denton rang me from the office. Apparently you attacked him on the street and he knocked you out. When you came round he realized you were hallucinating and brought you here.'

'Oh, yeah, I'd forgotten about the fight.' I'd been trying to puzzle out why I had a lump on the back of my head. 'Bloody Alan,' I said. 'I could kill the bastard.'

'Oh, don't say that! Alan's been so kind! He came here with you in the ambulance. They were going to section you.'

'Section me?' I said. 'What does that mean?' I imagined my skull split in half like a walnut and stuck in a display case.

'Committed. Under the Mental Health Act. Yes, Steve, you were almost committed for once,' she joked, relishing the C-word. It was a relief to see the old sardonic Liz poking through. 'It's lucky you didn't make a fuss about coming here. Do you remember cutting Alan's face with a broken bottle? Apparently you almost strangled him to death.'

'Maybe so but he sacked me, Liz! From my own company!'

'Alan's been really worried about you. The board meeting was just a business thing. Sally was behind it. Alan feels awful about what's happened and he wants to come and see you in a couple of days. And he told me that he's not pressing charges for assault.'

'I don't see how he can complain in the circumstances. This is the fucker who's screwed up my life and you're making him out to be the Good Samaritan!'

'For God's sake, Steve! Do you think this has been easy for me?'

She looked into my eyes and I saw my reflection in her pupil, my head ugly and blob-like. Beyond it there was nothing but the sucking nihil void of our mutual isolation. A tear rolled down Liz's cheek. I should have been disgusted with myself for making her cry but I didn't really care. I just watched the teardrop progress down the powdered slope of her cheek, wondering if it had enough mass to make it to her jaw-line.

Liz snuffled at a peach-coloured tissue from a floral-patterned box on the bedside table. Neither of us had the energy to fight.

I was worried about the state of our war chest and asked

Liz about medical insurance. She threw out the dead flowers and said that Alan had told her that Puffa Group's BUPA insurance would cover the Webster's bill. Then she fixed her make-up and kissed me goodbye. I felt very tired.

'I'm with you in this. You know I love you,' she said from the doorway.

'I love you too,' I replied wearily, and she was gone.

We'd got the whole scene in one take.

BUPA cared . . . The following afternoon Dr Mahmood came to my room, crossing and re-crossing his legs while we twisted my mind around like a Rubik's cortex. Pressed for details of the run-up to my breakdown, I described the way the Euston Tower had bubbled out and what had happened when I'd gone back to Alan's house the previous night.

'Are you quite sure you really heard a fight taking place in the house?' asked Dr Mahmood. 'You didn't actually see anything and you say there was a thunderstorm at the time.'

'I'm sure I heard a fight. It was nothing like the hallucination with the building,' I said.

It was an effort to concentrate on anything for long. Dr Mahmood drew the session to a close after half an hour. I mulled over my troubles and realized that there was no particular moment when things had gone bad for me, no one wrong fork that I'd taken on life's decision tree. Instead there had just been a whole procession of minor miscalculations that stretched back to infancy. In this sense my breakdown had been no catastrophic reversal but the inevitable culmination of my life.

The tranquillizer muddied my thoughts. The demarcation between sleep and wakefulness was still blurred. Day and night were spliced together in a random barcode sequence. If I slept for more than an hour I woke feeling like an astronaut emerging from a light-year of oblivion. Double glazing insulated the ward from the traffic of the Marylebone Road, leaving only the drone of the Webster's air-conditioning. It sounded like the distant hum of a great engine, as though the ward was itself a spaceship passing through the universe in search of its senses.

The next morning my head felt a little clearer and I went to explore the ward, which took up the whole of the Webster's third floor. Thirty or so private rooms fanned off a corridor that circled the building, enclosing the kitchen, consulting rooms and the nurses' station that constituted the hub of the ward. The windows of these inner rooms gave onto a central well that was veined with drainpipes: a grey shaft of grime, pigeon shit and little light.

On my journey I encountered one of my fellow patients and realized why Dr Mahmood held comparatively high hopes for my recovery. I was relieving myself in a gents' toilet on the other side of the building when I heard a keening sound coming from one of the cubicles, a sound beyond tears, a muezzin call from Jonestown.

I called out to see if the occupant was all right. Since there was no answer I knocked on the locked door. The ululating whine got louder as I climbed onto the seat of the adjacent lavatory to peek over the partition. There was an old man in there standing to attention, stark naked with his clothes folded on the toilet seat with origami precision, making this dreadful sound with tears squeezing out of his eyes. I called to him and tried to tap his shoulder but my arm didn't reach. I went to the nurses' station and told them what I'd seen.

Liz came to see me that evening, bringing Mary along

for moral support. I was glad to see Mary because things were usually easier between Liz and me when she was around. Liz brought me some grapes and Mary gave me a translucent pebble, explaining that it was a healing crystal. She had her hair in pigtails which made her look even spacier than usual. Liz was in a much lighter mood and I wondered what had brought about the change.

'How are you feeling today?' Liz asked me with a bright expectant smile.

'Not too bad, thanks,' I said, trying to match her daytime television tone. My breakdown had reduced us to soap-actors, unable to face what had happened to me and to our marriage.

'I talked to Doctor Mahmood earlier,' she said. 'He's really pleased you're doing so well. He says he's already started taking you off the tranquillizers.'

'Yeah. I begin group therapy tomorrow,' I said.

'But what I want to know is if they're giving you any good drugs? Prozac or anything?' Mary asked, picking a grape from the bunch.

'Sure, Mary, I'm on a sort of supercharged Ecstasy. What do you think? No, it's just tranquillizers and the odd puff of skunk-weed when I can score it off Nurse Barnes.'

I glanced at Liz and caught a fleeting look of cosmic disappointment on her face. It was the look of a woman who'd had it all at nineteen, a successful model pursued by rock stars, but who'd somehow ended up in a childless marriage with an overweight, imminently bankrupt lunatic.

Liz switched on a smile and told me that Gudrun sent her love. 'She wanted to come and see you too but the doctor said just family and close friends for the moment.'

'You haven't told Mum about this, have you? It's all she needs right now.'

Liz shook her head. My mother's boyfriend had recently walked out on her, and the dry-cleaner's she managed in Croydon was facing bankruptcy. We weren't a close family. I'd been out of touch with my dad since my teens and my sister lived with her quantity surveyor husband and their two toddlers in a north London semi with kiddy-art magnetized to the fridge door. They were the very picture of functional family bliss but Liz and I didn't see them very often. Liz didn't like to spend time around happy couples with small children.

Liz and Mary got up to leave and my wife kissed me goodbye.

'I'll come and see you tomorrow evening. Alan might come with me. Unless you're still blaming him for everything.'

'No, no, of course not,' I said. I was keen to avoid a row.

When they had left I lay in the dark and subjected myself to some introspection, a session with my Inner Torquemada that failed to extract a worthwhile confession.

10

F.O.R.E.S.T.

Freedom Organization For The Right To Enjoy Smoking Tobacco
2 Grosvenor Gardens, London SW1W OBD
0171–823 6550

*A*T TEN O'CLOCK THE NEXT DAY, Dr Mahmood came to see me with a preppy young woman wearing a grey pleated skirt and a navy cardigan. He introduced her as Dr Katherine Parker.

'Pleased to meet you, Steve,' she said with a firm hand-shake. 'Call me Kate. I'll be looking after you on a daily basis from now on.'

She bristled with enthusiasm and her informal manner stood at odds with her clothes. Quite attractive with a snub nose, wide mouth and shoulder-length blonde hair, she had bright lively eyes that turned down at the corners. They observed me with what I was supposed to take for keen professional interest. I found the force of this scrutiny mildly unsettling. Dr Mahmood sat himself in the armchair and I noticed that he'd trimmed the wiry hair in his nostrils since our last encounter. Dr Parker took the straight-backed chair by the wardrobe. When she crossed her calves with a swish of nylon, Dr Mahmood shot a surreptitious glance at them and cleared his throat.

'I'll be popping in for a chat every few days, but I'm happy to hand over to Katherine now that you're ready for group. How are you looking forward to meeting your fellow patients?' he asked.

'I'm not holding my breath,' I said.

'You're doing very well, Steve. And the group is vital to your recovery. Now that we've reduced your medication, it's very important for us to be able to monitor your progress with your fellow patients,' he said.

'How do you mean?' I asked.

'Well, from what you've told me, it's not so very different from SIT. Your interaction with the others will allow us to assess your progress. It's the best gauge we have.'

I'd mentioned my visit to SIT during one of our little chats. I'd told him all about it except for the part about Uncle Sid.

'So what pills am I on now? Tranquillizers?' I asked.

'Perhaps Doctor Parker would explain? She'll be looking after your medication from now on.'

Kate shifted in her seat. Her smile was coolly flirtatious and she held my eyes while she spoke.

'Doctor Mahmood started you off on Haloperidol which is a tranquillizer, what we call a high-potency neuroleptic. You needed it to bring you down off the high you were on but we've been gradually reducing the dosage as you've responded so well. And we've started you on lithium carbonate.'

'Jesus, I've heard of it. It's heavy stuff, isn't it?'

I'd read about lithium in the papers. From what I remembered, once you were on it, you were on it for life.

'It's just a mood-stabilizer. You can live a perfectly normal life on lithium,' she said. 'It's not really a tranquillizer at all in the pharmacological sense. It's the salt of the element lithium and it occurs quite naturally in nature. It'll help us to make sure that you don't get too high again by keeping your mood from fluctuating. There was a paper recently about a small town in Texas that has an abnormally low incidence of mental disturbance. The population is also pretty much crime-free. A research chemist analysed the town's water-supply and discovered an unusually high lithium content in the water.'

'Really?' I said. I looked to Dr Mahmood for corroboration.

'Oh, yes, it's quite true,' he said. 'I read the paper myself. We've been prescribing lithium for years but we're finding out more about it all the time. You're actually very lucky that this treatment is available to treat your condition.'

'Which is what exactly?' I asked, feeling anything but privileged.

Kate took the ball. 'It would be rash to make a cast-iron diagnosis at this stage but Doctor Mahmood and I are pretty confident that you are suffering from bi-polar affective disorder. In other words, manic depression.'

Her words hit me a soft blow in the chest. I felt tagged and skewered like a butterfly on a pin.

'Hang on a second. What does that mean exactly?' I asked, dry-mouthed. 'Everyone gets depressed, don't they?'

'Yes, they do. And most people experience moments of

euphoria,' she said. 'It's all a question of degree. But I'd suggest that during the manic phase of the attack you became convinced that a lot of things were happening which didn't really happen at all.'

'So I went mad?'

The doctors exchanged a glance.

'That isn't a word we feel comfortable with and I'm not sure how helpful it is any more,' said Dr Mahmood. 'Sanity, insanity. These are elastic terms, an out-dated polarity. I'd prefer to say that you suffered from certain delusions because your mind was being overloaded. By the way, has anyone in your family ever had an experience like this?'

'No, not that I'm aware of,' I said, racking my brains. My mother had streaked naked across a municipal car park in the early seventies, but then so had half the population.

'I don't mean to pry,' said Dr Mahmood. 'It's just that there's often a genetic component associated with this condition and it might help to confirm our diagnosis.'

'Well, I'm afraid I can't help you there. How long will I have to take this lithium drug?' I asked Kate.

'I'm afraid it's much too early to say,' she said.

'A week? A month?' I asked.

Kate shrugged. 'Perhaps indefinitely. As a prophylactic measure,' she said.

'I wouldn't worry about it unduly,' said Dr Mahmood. 'After all, diabetics have to take insulin every day of their lives. It's really quite a small price to pay for one's health. Look, it's almost time for Group so if you're ready . . .'

I didn't have the bottle to probe any further down this ghastly track. Imagining my future as a nutter hooked on riverbed scum from Texas, I swung my legs off the bed, bid farewell to Dr Mahmood and followed Kate's blonde mane as it swung down the corridor distributing whiffs of Chanel No. 5. I wondered if Dr Mahmood had told Liz the good news about lithium and manic depression. I remembered the element lithium from long-ago chemistry lessons, up in the top left-hand corner of the Periodic Table. Was it radioactive? My guts twisted at the idea.

I'd been dreading the group, anticipating a menagerie of bandaged wrists and Napoleonic delusions. In fact the quality of psychosis was strained through the tight sphincter of English formality. It was like teatime in a seaside boarding house with neither tea nor table, just a load of ashtrays. Kate Parker ushered me towards a loose circle of grey plastic stacker-chairs. Three of these chairs were already occupied. The patients broke off their analysis of the Webster's cuisine and Kate introduced me to them by first names.

Carol was a plump sun-tanned woman of fifty-five in a pricey brown velvet-style track suit, trainers and gold jewellery. Then there was Bernard, the old man I'd found howling in the lavatory. Dressed in a graph-paper-pattern shirt and maroon tie he seemed withdrawn, ill-at-ease with the whole dreadful business of Personal Discovery. A wan young man called Joshua held up a hand in greeting and then a florid bovine slob of forty entered the room to be introduced as Angus.

'How d'you do,' Angus said, strangling the vowels with a Hooray accent.

He sat down and I watched his lips move silently as he struggled to read the logo on my Champion sweatshirt. There was some dried egg on the lapel of his brass-buttoned blazer. A girl called Maria arrived late and apologized in a quiet Australian accent. She was tall and broad shouldered but so thin that her body appeared to exist in only two dimensions, a razor blade sketched by Gustav Klimt. Kate opened the proceedings.

'Now that you've met everyone, would you like to say something about yourself, Steve?'

'Er, where should I start?'

'Well, you could tell us about how you're feeling now,' she suggested.

Reminded of my first day at SIT, I delivered a flat five-minute account of my hallucinations and admittance to the Webster. Once I got started it all plopped out easily enough. No one even raised an eyebrow. Carol stared blankly at me throughout, faking concentration and waiting for my lips to stop moving. Joshua absorbed himself in a brutal manicure while Maria just seemed lost inside herself. I noticed a smudge of melanin of her left cheek, a patch of brown skin the size of my thumbnail just visible through its face-powder camouflage.

'Thank you, Steve,' said Kate when I'd finished. 'Perhaps someone else would like to share their feelings with the group?'

Carol took the floor with a show of reluctance. Bernard sighed audibly and passed around a packet of Silk Cut to delay her soliloquy. Everybody smoked except Kate, and Bernard torched up our cigarettes with pyromaniac glee. His hand trembled and I wondered if it was a side-effect of the tran-quillizers. Dr Mahmood had warned me that there was a chance that the Haloperidol might cause these tremors, and said that he had prescribed me another pill to counter this effect. I was glad to see that my own hand was steady as I reached for Bernard's cigarette. I'd have preferred a Marlboro because I could actually taste a cigarette now that I was on a lower dosage of Haloperidol. The drug had slowed and buffered everything. Smoking had been reduced to a formal nullity, a mime of the stress and involvement I hadn't been able to feel.

The room soon resembled a F.O.R.E.S.T. convention and I watched my smoke as it coiled up to intermingle above our heads with the other plumes to form a smoke-signal, a votive offering to BUPA. In this swirling nicotine fog I made out the profile of Alan Denton, emerging like a Rorschach blot from the corridors of my mind where my Inner Child stalked him with a Bowie knife. The cigarette burnt down to scorch my fingers and I snapped back into the group. The tube of ash lay in my lap like a fossilized worm as I tuned in to the sound of Carol's voice, dolorous and posh.

'. . . and so when I finally got the part, it was terrifying. I mean I hadn't worked for years. Well, I'd worked of course, bloody hard as a wife and mother as a matter of fact, but nothing just for *me,* you see. And I just cracked, fell completely to pieces. Lionel was very understanding at first, research being part of the job. I'm not into the Method or anything, but if I was going to play a bag-lady on television, I had to know how it felt. And I kept spending more and more time down by the railway line with the others. I didn't want to go home, wouldn't change my clothes for weeks. And I was drinking, of course.'

It transpired that Bernard had been a civil servant with special responsibility for the town-twinning programme. He'd come home one night to find his wife's headless body sitting in her armchair with his shotgun propped between her knees. Bernard had retreated into a catatonic state following her suicide and Kate was still trying to get him to explore his feelings.

Joshua had a problem with water. He felt compelled to

drink so much that it washed all the minerals and vitamins through his body and made him ill. The nurses monitored his intake. He wasn't even allowed flowers in his room because given half a chance, he'd drain the water from the vase.

Maria was an anorexic who'd been shedding body bulk like a Saturn V rocket prior to her admittance. She'd tried to kill herself with an overdose of Paracetamol the year before, a simple gobbling process that she'd muffed on account of her difficulties with ingestion. I watched a fly buzz around in a holding pattern and tried to join its imaginary dots until Kate called things to a halt. In one way or another, society's pliers had done their work on all of us. There was one good thing about mental illness. It was no snob.

Liz phoned to say she couldn't make it that evening because she had a headache. I wondered if she was telling the truth or if she had something better to do. A nurse woke me and ushered Tony Mold into my room. He had frightful glittering eyes. Purple blood-vessels covered his face like a cocked-up Maori tattoo.

'How you doing, Steve? Are you okay?' he wheezed. 'Hey, can you hear me in there? It's me, Tone.'

He swayed slightly, peering at me through a drink-fog while I rubbed my eyes. I guessed he'd started drinking at lunch-time and hadn't stopped since.

'Yeah, I can hear you. Sit down,' I said. 'I'm surprised they let you even get in the lift. I'm told there's an alcohol and drug abuse unit on the ground floor.'

Tony laughed and then his smile dropped in a drunken mood-change.

'Shit, I feel bad about selling Alan the shares, Steve. I mean, if I could put the clock back . . .'

'Look, Tone, Alan fucked us both over. He played us off against each other. You're not to blame.'

'That's crap,' he said.

'Listen, I thought he was going to try and give you the push and I didn't even tell you about it, did I?'

'I still shouldn't have sold him the shares,' he said, making a mess of the sibilants.

'Spare the whining, Tone. We were outplayed, that's all,' I said. 'When did Alan first tell you he wanted your shares?'

'Not till the day of the board meeting, just before lunch. As soon as I agreed he got straight onto the lawyers and they sorted it out in an hour. They had the papers biked round to the office. Alan didn't say anything about getting rid of you. That didn't even enter my mind. I thought you two were thick as thieves, you know. I was certain it was me that he wanted out. And I needed the money badly.'

'You know something, Tone? When I get out of here I'm going to kill him.'

'Are you serious?' He shifted uneasily, reminded that he was on a mental ward.

'It's just my little joke,' I said.

'I heard you had another go at Alan on Friday. He looks like a fucking safety-belt ad.'

'Good. By the way, don't tell him we talked about any of this, all right?'

'I don't tell him anything,' Tony said. 'Have they given you any idea when you can go home?'

'They've put me on this lithium stuff and they've got to make sure the dosage is right before I go anywhere.'

'Lithium? I've heard of that. Axl Rose is on it, Steve. You should think about a career in the rock world, make a late bid for pop stardom!' Tony laughed and relaxed a bit without staying for longer than ten minutes.

When he'd left I pondered what he'd told me. As I'd suspected, Alan had changed his tactics at the last minute. The longer I thought about this volte-face, the more convinced I became that it was connected to what I'd overheard when I'd been back to the mews. I needed to find out what had been going on in Alan's house that night, and that meant that I would have to talk to Claire.

Kate stopped the Haloperidol when my lithium level was where she wanted it to be. She'd explained that lithium wasn't like other drugs. You had to let it build up in your system and then top it up twice a day to maintain the level. I didn't like the way it felt like a clamp at the back of my neck and levelled my emotions into a gentle rolling plain. Although it was a lot better than having them tarmacked and steam-rollered by Haloperidol, the lithium was still a barrier, a psychic condom rolled down over my mind. Kate said she'd discussed it with Dr Mahmood. They wanted to keep me on it for a couple of months and then reassess the situation.

'It may well be that you can stop taking it after a while,' Kate said one afternoon in my room. 'Since you haven't had a previous attack, it's possible that this was just a one-off episode brought on by the pressures we've been talking about.'

I put Kate around thirty and guessed that her life had not been a bed of roses. There was too much pain around her eyes. Her hands fought a bloody civil war, picking each other's fingernails to bits.

'Tell me, Kate, when do you think I can go home?'

'Another week, something like that? When we're sure we've got the level right. I talked to Liz yesterday and we had a chat about it. How are things between the two of you?'

'Like I said, we've been together for a long time and I guess we've just grown apart. I told you we'd been going to Marriage Guidance before all this started.'

Kate just sat there waiting for me to continue, beaming empathy at me.

'I don't know, maybe it would have been different if we'd been able to have kids,' I said.

'How long have you been trying for?' she asked.

I told Kate about the ovarian pantomime Liz and I had been living through for the last three years. The doctors had originally focused on a problem with Liz's tubes but they'd soon invited me down to the fertility clinic to check my sperm count. I had to face the possibility that the Cork line might have finally run out of gas in a genetic cul-de-sac. Jacking off into a laboratory beaker for the express purpose of having your sperm measured under a microscope comes low on the squash-ladder of sexual experiences.

The results from the test hadn't been encouraging but the situation wasn't hopeless. It had come as a shock to realize that my sperm count was so low, but apparently there were just enough earnest little tadpoles wriggling around in my goop to give Liz and me a percentage chance of conception. This had heralded a time of charts, hormones and thermometers for Liz, ice-cubes for me. Before each programmed coitus I had to lay my bollocks in a bowl of crushed ice to lower the sperm temperature. It was a nice touch.

The doctor at the clinic had spelt it out. 'Unlike the female eggs, the testes hang outside the body to keep them cool. We increase their chances of fertilizing an egg if we ensure they don't overheat,' he'd said. 'Oh, and one more thing. Tight jeans are out from now on, Mr Cork.'

I'd replied that they'd been out since the seventies.

Liz and I had fucked like clockwork robots for two years with no result. It had been enough to derange anybody. Retailing at two grand a pop with no money-back guarantee, our two failed IVF attempts hadn't helped either. It would have been far cheaper to buy some Romanian surplus but Liz had been desperate for her own child.

'So we've more or less given up trying to conceive after all that,' I told Kate. 'Liz has finally started thinking about adoption.'

'And how do you feel about it?' Kate asked.

'Well, I was really up for it until last year, but now I'm not so certain. I think Liz sees it as a chance for a new beginning but I'm not sure if we should even stay together. Things aren't good between us. I don't think we should be adopting a baby to sort out our marriage. And that's what it feels like.'

'Liz thinks you can make it work, but that it depends on you making a commitment. What do you think?' Kate asked.

'I think she's just kidding herself that everything's suddenly going to change. I keep having to hold back so we don't have a row.'

'What do you think you might row about?'

'Anything. She's been making out that the bastard who double-crossed me is some kind of angel.'

'You mean the man who made you redundant?'

'Alan, yeah. I don't know, I just can't see how anything's going to be better with Liz because I've lost my job and we haven't got as much money.'

'But you still want to go home when you leave here?' she asked.

'Sure. The sooner the better,' I said.

I was glad that Kate accepted that things were difficult with Liz and didn't push me to get enthusiastic about adopting a baby. It was easy to talk things over with her. Unlike Dr Mahmood, Kate seemed to inhabit the real world and I felt that she understood how bad things can get between men and women. The sun re-emerged from behind a cloud to throw a bar of light onto the carpet by my bed. When Kate stood up to leave, she set a thousand golden motes swirling in the sun-beam.

At noon the next day Liz showed up unexpectedly and told me I had a surprise visitor. She made it sound as if she had Mickey Mouse in tow.

'I don't know if you're ready,' Liz said. 'But he'd like to see you. I talked to Doctor Parker earlier and she said it would be all right if you feel up to it.'

'Who is it?' I asked.

'Alan,' she said.

The name chilled my blood.

'Look, if you don't feel ready to see him, that's fine. He'll understand. He knows you've been ill and he just wants to wish you well. I told him it's ridiculous but he still feels he should have stood up for you when Sally gave you the sack. He cares about you.'

'Where is he?' I asked, my heart thumping. I felt scared and angry in equal measure and wondered if I could handle meeting him.

'Down the corridor. The last thing he wants to do is to upset you, but I think it might help you to see him.'

'Sure, I'll see him,' I said. 'It'll give me a chance to apologize for beating him up.'

Liz went to fetch Alan and I steeled myself to give a good performance, hoping that the lithium would be enough to take the edge off my nerves. Alan came into the room, re-moved his Arnet sunglasses and walked straight over to shake my hand with a sympathetic smile in place. He was sporting a gauze bandage over the cut on his cheek, a plastic splint on his wrist and a pink sponge neck-brace.

'Good to see you, Steve.' He shot a nervous look at Liz.

'Thanks for coming, Alan. It means a lot. Why don't you sit down, have an orange juice? It's all I can offer.'

'I'm okay, thanks,' he said, taking the chair.

Liz sat on the bed and held my hand.

'The doctors say Steve can come home in a few days,' she said to Alan. 'He's doing really well.' She made it sound as if she was talking about a child with learning difficulties.

'That's great,' said Alan. 'God, it must have been hell for you, Steve. I couldn't believe it when the doctors explained what had happened.' I scanned his face in vain for a glimmer of mendacity.

'Look, I'm really sorry for all the trouble I've caused, attacking you and everything,' I said. 'I didn't know what I was doing.'

'Please. Of course. No harm done. They did a great job sewing up my cheek and this is coming off in a couple of days,' he said, adjusting his neck-brace. He smiled and sat back in the chair.

'No, I do feel bad about it. Especially since Liz told me how you got me here and how much support you've been giving her,' I said.

'You were wonderful, Alan,' said Liz with a smile. She looked radiant, years younger, and I put it down to the relief she must have felt at my recovery.

'It was the least I could do. I'm just glad you're on the mend,' he said to me. 'Look, I know how you must feel but I want you to know that there was nothing personal in what happened at the board meeting. It was a business decision and

I had to go along with it. I had no choice. I wish it hadn't turned out the way it did.'

I drank some water before I replied. 'Thanks for saying that, Alan. It means a lot. We were always friends, ever since you joined us.' I smiled at him with chummy sentiment, even though I wanted to rip his eyes out.

'I'd like to think we still are,' he said.

'Of course. That goes without saying.' It was hard to get the hang of all the bullshit. I'd been out of practice. 'So who was behind it then?' I asked.

'Behind what?'

'My getting the shove. You buying Tony out.'

'Does that really matter now?' Liz intervened.

'It's no big deal,' I reassured her. 'I'm just curious, that's all.'

'Well, it was Sally's idea that I should buy Tony's shares,' said Alan. 'To tie me to the company. And I had to go along with Sally.'

Liz gave me an I-told-you-so smile and said she was going to get a cup of coffee. Her subterfuge was transparent. Kate had just walked past in the corridor and I knew Liz wanted to grill her about my progress.

'It must have been terrifying losing your mind like that. I can't begin to imagine it,' said Alan when Liz left the room. 'Liz told me you attacked your reflection in the mirror.'

'So I gather,' I said, my paranoia cranking up now that I was alone with him.

'Do you remember why? I mean, what was going through your mind exactly?'

'I thought I saw my double and it flipped me out.'

'What was your double doing?' he asked, sitting forward. I shrank back instinctively into the pillows.

'Raping Liz,' I said.

'That's incredible,' he said. His curiosity was prurient and I could feel him getting off on it like a tourist in Bedlam. 'But it was really you, wasn't it? Reflected in the mirror, with Liz?'

'Yeah, it was me . . . Look, about the board meeting,' I said. 'Didn't Sally sound you out about their scheme? Ask your advice or anything?'

Alan sighed but I wanted to press him while Liz was out of the room.

'I told you, Steve. The first I heard about it was when Julia phoned me on the Thursday and suggested that I make an offer for Tony's shares.'

'But you knew something was going on before that?' I asked. Alan smiled wearily.

'Listen, I thought they were going to let Tony go. I'd talked to them about that, his drinking and so on. They did ask me about your mental state but I didn't tell them anything.'

'My mental state? What do you mean?' My voice came out high and strained.

'Well, you have to admit you'd been behaving rather oddly before the board meeting. Imagining things. Talking to yourself, that kind of thing.'

'You mean in my office that time? I was meditating for God's sake! Thousands of people do it.'

'Well, what about that phone call you said you made to my house? You said you heard a fight or something.'

Alan's eyes were on me. This was it. I acted dumb and he waited on my reply.

'Oh, that. I'd forgotten all about it. It was just a wrong number, wasn't it?' I said.

'Or maybe you just imagined the whole thing, like the man in your bedroom.'

'Maybe. Incidentally, how did Claire's exam go?' I asked.

'Claire?'

'The girl we met in the restaurant. You know, your friend.'

'Oh, Claire. I don't know. I haven't seen her.'

When he moved in his chair I flinched, convinced that he was about to attack me. I looked round for something to defend myself with and saw a pair of nail scissors on the bedside table. I reached for them but my hand was shaking so badly that I only succeeded in knocking them to the floor.

Alan stood up. I braced myself for violence but he just picked up the scissors and handed them to me.

'Are you all right?' he asked.

'I'm fine, thanks,' I stammered. 'It's the pills, they make me clumsy.' He loomed over the bed. 'Look, I'm sure you're right about that call I made being a wrong number. It was dark and raining and I probably just hit the wrong buttons in the phone box.'

'The phone box?' said Alan, backing towards his chair. 'The other day you said you called me from home.'

'Oh, yeah. I did. I'm talking crap. Forget it. Like I said, it's just the pills.'

He gave me an odd look. Liz came back just in time to stop me putting my foot right down my throat. Alan said that he had to go and we exchanged warm goodbyes for Liz's benefit.

'I'm so glad you've sorted things out with Alan,' Liz said when he'd gone.

'Me too,' I said with a forced smile.

I was horrified to have let slip that I'd made that call from a pay phone. It didn't prove that I'd been back to the mews that night, but I remembered telling Alan that I'd made the call from home. At the very least he would wonder why I'd lied to him.

11

The Ovarian Pantomime

TEN DAYS LATER KATE ALLOWED ME TO GO HOME. I was sitting with my Adidas sports bag in reception waiting for Liz to collect me when a skinny bloke in a frayed anorak walked in off the street. He asked the receptionist if he could sell her a copy of the *Big Issue.*

'It's a charity paper for the homeless,' he explained, revealing some bombed-out teeth. She shooed him away. Bigger issues were at stake here and BUPA's care was selective. Five minutes later a grey-haired gent arrived and walked over to wait by the lift. He looked me over in my jeans and trainers as though I was counterfeit currency. When Liz arrived I was glad to leave the place.

'I don't want to go back there. Ever,' I said, as Liz swept us up onto the hot grey haze of the Westway. It felt strange to be back in the real world. I peered at it through the windscreen with the fresh wide eyes of the convalescent.

'Of course you won't. Just for counselling,' she said. We were both feeling nervous.

'I mean if I go whacko again. That place is such a rip-off and we're virtually broke.'

'We'll manage,' Liz said with grim determination. As she steered the Punto through Kensington, I wondered if I'd be able to find Claire's house again.

We arrived back in Roehampton and the broad thirties boulevards felt as insubstantial as a film set. I'd always appreciated the kitsch charm of our house but now it struck me as a schizoid mock-Tudor nightmare. I was almost disappointed that Steve Jr hadn't moved back in while I'd been away. When I phoned Louis he told me that under the terms of my contract Puffa only owed me three months' wages in severance pay. This nickel-alloy handshake would barely cover Louis' fee. Then Liz informed me that the leasing company had repossessed the Shōgun. Alan must have enjoyed asking Gudrun to make that particular call.

I settled down a little after lunch and we made love. I'd been feeling hornier since I came off the Haloperidol but upstairs in the pale afternoon light it didn't feel quite right with Liz. Nevertheless we undressed and slipped under the cool duvet.

Liz shivered in my arms, running her hands around on my back. When we kissed her saliva was cold and tasted of fluoride. I wondered how she'd managed to clean her teeth without my noticing. It made me think she was apprehensive about making love. My erection lost some heftiness but I was confident that it would return during the extended foreplay that Joanna had prescribed for us in Marriage Guidance. The stakes were high. We hadn't made love since I'd flipped out and today was meant to signal a new chapter in both our lives.

I brushed a strand of loose hair from Liz's lips as her nails raked my chest-pelt.

We rolled around and I hardened up as her hands began some exploratory forays down to my abdomen, brushing the tip of my cock as if by accident. I moved down and kissed her nipples, switching from one to the other, circling them with my tongue like a manic potter. Liz clutched the roll of fat at the back of my neck. She moaned and pushed my head down to her vulva. I grabbed a pillow to put under her arse en route. Her fluffy pubic hair tickled my nose and I smelt wet leaves.

Liz rubbed a smooth Philli-shaved calf against my cock and I slipped a finger inside her, pressing up directly below her clitoris which I flicked with my tongue. She shuddered and yanked my hair hard as I slid another finger into her rectum, pulling it up below the one in her vagina the way she liked me to.

'Stick it in,' she whispered. I moved up the bed and pushed inside her. Liz squeaked like wet rubber. She grabbed my love-handles and ground her hips up against me, her eyes black saucers staring into mine as she hooked a yoga-leg onto my shoulder. We went through a medley of our favourite positions. When Liz saw that I was about to shoot my blob of Lo-Cal genetics she turned onto her stomach, lifting her arse to get a hand to her clitoris and chase me to an orgasm. She made it just in time.

We lay panting with the sweat cooling on our bodies.

Things were better between us after that but it didn't last long. When Liz went shopping the following morning I phoned Russell our accountant, and he gave a depressing appraisal of our financial position. I needed to get a job quickly but I knew it wouldn't be easy because I'd only ever worked for myself. Then Liz came home and raised the subject of adoption. It was the last thing I wanted to discuss.

'You know the situation,' she said. 'The older we get the less likely it is that they'll let us adopt. Thirty-four's the limit. I know it's not a good time but we have to think about it.'

'I can't face it just now. I've just been talking to Russell about money,' I said. 'Christ, I could kill Alan!'

'I thought you were over all that,' she sighed.

'Russell said that the surrender value on the policies is poxy, and you know we've got negative equity in this place,' I said.

'That's another thing to consider. We've got to be able to provide a secure future for a baby. To even stand a chance. And I'm not sure how the agency'll take the news of your illness.'

'Oh, yeah? Great. Suddenly I'm Anthony bloody Perkins!'

'That's not what I said.'

'Come off it. You think I'm a psycho, don't you? Why don't you just come out and say it?'

'Oh, for God's sake! Get a grip and stop feeling so sorry for yourself!' Liz snapped. She turned away and started to fill the fridge with groceries.

'I found that book you've got. What is it? *Living with Schizophrenia*? I'm not bloody schizophrenic!'

Her face drained of colour.

'Where did you find that? In my bag? That's low, Steve.'

'Oh, I don't know. In a close, open relationship like ours . . . Anyway, you go through my things the whole time. You read my diary, remember?'

She left the room to perfect her sulk on the moral highground. In accordance with Joanna's suggestion for such moments, we gave each other our space for the rest of the day and managed to negotiate a civil path through dinner. However, when we tried to make it up in bed, physical love just pulled us further apart. My fat thighs were slapping against Liz's firmed yoga-buttocks when I turned my head to watch our reflections copulate in the mirrored doors of the wardrobe.

I remembered seeing my double with Liz the night I went mad. I gasped in horror and Liz misread it as enthusiasm, moaning in response to my call. I looked down at her profile half-buried in a pillow but the memory of my hallucination had invaded my mind and I lost the rhythm.

'God, don't stop!' cried Liz, pushing back hard against me.

I tried to keep it going but in my head I was smashing the mirror with my hand, smashing my reflection and Liz was screaming. I began to lose my erection. Liz sensed this and attempted to regenerate my soft-on by rubbing my perineum. When this strategy failed she tried to rush her climax with her fingers. This time she missed the bus and sighed.

'What's the matter?' Liz asked, with as much sweetness as she could manage in the circumstances.

'I'm sorry. I just couldn't, you know?'

'Hey, it's all right,' she said, rolling over with a sigh as my mange-tout fell out of her with a sad plipping sound. I buried my face in her breasts.

'It all came back to me. The row we had,' I said.

'It's okay. It was great.' She stroked what remained of my hair and my ego.

'Yeah, it was great,' I said, echoing her empty phrase.

We made it in the end for the purpose of mutual reassurance but there was too much expectation and too little spontaneity between us. I had to trundle out a few fantasies, air-brushed replicants, to give me a hand. I didn't feel too good about it but what can you do? There was even a term for it in Marriage Guidance. 'By-passing,' Joanna called it. Liz wasn't really there any more than I was. We performed the sex act without much relish on either part. Her actressy moans and faked-up lather were the very antithesis of abandon and impinged on my own attempts to achieve orgasm with a composite dream-girl on the Caribbean beach in my brain.

The warm, soft sand showed coral pink against the micropores of her imaginary shoulder. On the rise before the long descent, Liz squawked the encouragement of her own faux-coming and almost broke the spell. I fantasized Claire's young body squirming beneath me like a caramel seal-pup and managed to rumble up a doleful blob of DNA with my face pressed into the pillow beside Liz's head.

Liz had faked her orgasm and I wondered if she'd been trying to get there with her own home-movies. *Keanu in Kenya* or *Cruise in Cuba*, or maybe just Guru Gerry on a gym-mat? We were propelled back into the world of patterned duvet-covers, fitted sheets and my own stray hairs on the pillow. I asked Liz if she was ovulating and she said she wasn't. We chatted to fill the void between us until she turned over to go to sleep.

The following afternoon I was due for my first out-patient group session with Kate at the Webster and felt glad for the chance to get out of Roehampton. I had an idea how I might find Claire without having to search all over Kensington for her house. To this end I'd phoned Tony at home that morning, arranging to meet him before Group at a café near Puffa. I went over to the double garage beneath the laburnum tree and operated the remote-control device on my key-ring. When the garage door whirred up it revealed only empty space. I'd forgotten that Alan had repossessed the Shōgun.

Liz had gone shopping in the Punto. I thought about ordering a cab but, mindful of economy, my eye fell on my mountain bike at the back of the garage. I'd bought it the previous Christmas and it was still wrapped in its cardboard packaging, testimony to another blown New Year's resolution. The delivery note hung from the handle-bars, curled and yellowing. I unpacked the bike and pedalled off towards the city but it was hard work and the gears proved tricky. I left my toy padlocked to the railing by East Putney Underground Station.

I hadn't used public transport for a long time and the station was dirtier and more oppressive than I remembered. I bought a ticket and joined the crowd of people milling about on the platform. I felt anxious and paranoid among so many strangers. People pressed in on my space. Two twelve-year-old boys began to punch and kick a third by a broken vending machine. The train took ten minutes to arrive.

I took a seat and a red-haired kid with a personal stereo sat down opposite me. He reminded me a little of Alan Denton. Tinny Techno leaked from his earplugs and his freckled face looked as if someone had flicked shit at it. I changed trains at Victoria and got off at Warren Street to emerge into a warm drizzle. As I walked to the café the raindrops grew as big as grapes, their surface tension stretching credulity until they splatted as dark blotches on the pavement. I reached the café just as the rain started to power-shower.

Tony showed up ten minutes later wearing a new green Adidas track suit, breathing hard and soaked with a mixture of rain and his own evil sweat. His face pulsed like a Belisha beacon at every heart-beat and cardiac arrest seemed imminent. Bent over with his hands on his knees, Tony gulped air and explained that he'd been jogging.

'What happened out there, Tone? You look a bit peaky,' I said.

'I'm getting into shape, that's all. Sorry I'm late, but it

took longer than I thought. It's all a bit of a shock to the system. After all, the closest I usually come to a cardio-vascular workout is masturbation.'

When his breathing levelled he broke the filter off a Camel Light and sparked it with his lighter.

'How far did you run?' I asked.

'Just half a mile or so. You have to take it easy to begin with, build up gradually. You feel a right idiot running on the spot at the traffic lights but you have to. Otherwise you don't aerobicize. And I'm off the sauce too. Two days already. I feel great, really pin-sharp. Look, Steve, tell me what this is about because I've got to get going. Things to do, people to see.'

He looked out anxiously into the street. Rods of rain had jailed a group of pedestrians beneath a shop-awning on the other side of the road and slowed the traffic to a crawl.

'I know you're a busy man, Tone. I just want you to photocopy Alan's address book for me.'

'His address book? You're joking! What do you want it for?'

'I want to find a girl called Claire, a girlfriend of Alan's. I think she had something to do with Alan sacking me. Louis thinks I might have a case for wrongful dismissal,' I lied.

'Yeah? I can't see how . . .'

I cut him off. 'It's not your problem. All you've got to do is copy his address book,' I said.

'I can't, Steve. If I got caught . . .'

'Why should you get caught? Just wait till Alan's out of the office and bung it on the photocopier. He'll never know.'

'I'm not sure. I reckon it could be illegal. Alan's already trying to push me to resign so I don't get redundancy. The atmosphere's got really bad.'

'Alan came to see me in hospital. Told me it was Sally's idea that he should buy your shares,' I said.

'That's bullshit,' he snorted.

'That's what I thought. Look, just get me a photocopy, Tone. If he takes his address book home there's always the back-up, the one Gudrun uses.'

'Yeah, well, I'll see what I can do,' he said, bending down to retie the laces on his Nikes. I knew he would put it off for as long as he could.

'Just do it. As they say. But if you can't then lend me your keys to the office. I'll do it myself.'

It took me five minutes to persuade him to lend me his keys on the understanding that I'd give them back to him the next day. Tony could be a tricky sod.

'Hey,' he said, poncing one of my Marlboros. 'Have you heard that song by Nirvana called "Lithium"? You should really think about pop stardom, Steve. You've got the credentials now and it's never too late. That bloke in the Pet Shop Boys was older than you when he started.'

Tony bought a can of isotonic sports drink and drained it off in one go.

'It's meant to replace your body fluids,' he explained with a belch. 'Which is why it tastes like urine.'

I caught a bus down the Marylebone Road to the hospital. The Webster's receptionist directed me to Room 3 on the first floor for Dr Parker's outpatient group. Kate was surrounded by some neophytes in a big white room with the usual plastic stacker-chairs, the grey machinery of psychotherapy. Maria walked in and I was glad to see a familiar face. She was dressed completely in black and reminded me of a girl in the Woodstock film, the one who wouldn't take her clothes off by the lake.

'Hi, Maria. They let you out then?' I asked.

'Yes, I went home two days ago. I'm just coming in for Group now,' she said, her mouth widening to reveal a zip of grey teeth that underlined her thin nose.

Kate kicked off by asking us all to introduce ourselves with a brief personal history. It was like a card game in which an anorexic was beaten by a bulimic, an alcoholic trumped by a crack addict. A junkie thought she'd won the hand with a sickening description of her last overdose, only to have it snatched away by Maria's lurid account of full-on bulimia. Maria described the way her knuckles had been rubbed raw by her front teeth as she shoved her fingers down her throat, how her teeth had themselves been rotted by the gallons of acidic stomach-juice that she'd spewed across them over the years. As she spoke I noticed the corner of a family bag of M&Ms poking out of her handbag.

Encouraged to make a contribution by Kate I began to describe my money worries, only to be interrupted by a recovering cocaine addict called Edward who told us about the huge trust fund he'd blown on the drug, redistributing wealth in a trickle-down effect via his clapped-out septum into the sink estates of north-west London.

The group stripped down and reassembled each other's psyches for an hour and a half. When it was over Kate asked me to come for a blood test to check my lithium level. I said goodbye to Maria and took the lift with Dr Parker to her tiny consulting room on the third floor.

Kate found my file and leaned against the edge of her desk to make a couple of notes. She smoothed her cardigan and I found myself admiring the curve of her breast as she asked me to roll back my sleeve. I'd had blood tests taken before and hadn't enjoyed the experience. It was usually left to the nurses and I hoped Kate had taken the time to develop a reasonable technique. She was a bundle of nervous energy, darting around the little office for a syringe like a kid who had been given too much sugar.

'How are you finding the lithium?' she asked.

'No problem. I'm not feeling so tired any more. It fits me like a glove.'

'That's great,' she said, removing the orange jacket from the needle.

'Feeling nervous?' she asked.

'Just a bit.' She came round the desk with the assembled hypodermic held aloft like the truth serum in a sixties spy film.

Kate wrapped a Velcro tourniquet round my arm. I made a fist and saw her degree framed on the wall. She'd taken medicine in 1988. I felt the needle prick through my skin.

'Hold still now. This won't take a second. You've got good veins,' she said.

'Really? That's good to know.' I felt hysteria mount as I visualized my blood squirting up into the barrel. Kate was wearing a different scent that day, maybe Eau de Métal. I didn't look down at my arm.

Kate pulled the needle out. It stung and she pressed a disinfectant pad into the crook of my arm with a bitten fingernail. Her face was inches away from mine. She stuck a plaster over the hole and called for a nurse to take my sample to the Pathology lab.

'That wasn't too bad,' I said. 'Eight out of ten.'

'Thanks,' she said, relaxing a little. The intimacy and tension had tested us both. 'I'll have the results when you come in next week.'

I left her and took the lift down to reception. The rain was so heavy that I asked the receptionist to call for a taxi. I was still waiting for it to arrive when Kate walked out of the lift fifteen minutes later. She was surprised that I was still there and I explained that I had ordered a cab.

'This is the rush hour, Steve. It'll take ages. Why don't I give you a lift? You can pick one up in the street,' she said. It made sense and I asked the receptionist to cancel the taxi.

'Which way are you going?' I asked.

'Kensington. Where are you headed?'

'Home, but Kensington's fine. I can catch a tube from there.'

We scurried across the road to the hospital car park. Kate unlocked an old red Audi and we climbed inside, thrown back into physical proximity. The rain drummed on the roof as Kate reversed out of the slot. It felt strange to be with her outside the Webster.

'How are you and Liz coping?' she asked.

'I don't know. We had a row this afternoon.'

'What about?'

'Adopting a baby,' I said. 'Liz thinks my breakdown might screw things up with the agency.'

'It must be hard for her, wanting a child so much,' said Kate.

'Yeah, it is. Plus me going nuts.' Seeing it through Kate's eyes, I empathized with Liz. I could really see what she'd been through.

Kate nosed the Audi into the traffic which was oozing at glacier-pace along the Marylebone Road. Through the rain-beaded window I saw the tensed profiles of other motorists hunkered over steering-wheels, their cars tin cans of compressed human rage and impatience. There was a dark blue BMW up ahead. My stomach iced as I thought I recognized the back of Alan Denton's head.

'Are you okay?' Kate asked.

'Yeah. I thought I saw someone I know from work. Alan, the guy who fired me. I told you about him.'

'And is it him?' she asked.

'It's some other jerk.'

'Do you still feel hostile towards him?'

'No, he doesn't mean much to me. It was just a business thing.'

'Alan's surname isn't Denton, is it?' asked Kate.

I tensed, on red alert. 'Why? Do you know him?' An alarm bell went off in my head. My world had no depth, and the two-dimensional scenery was being wheeled away by a demonic stage-crew.

'I thought I saw him at the hospital the other week. I do know him, or rather I used to. Tall, good-looking, red hair? I think he lives somewhere around South Kensington.'

'That's him. He came to see me with Liz,' I said. 'How come you know him?'

'I haven't seen him for years,' said Kate. 'We were at university together and he used to go out with a friend of mine.'

'Really? What was he like?'

'Pretty self-assured. I only knew him for a couple of terms. He broke Janet's heart. She found out he was sleeping with two other women.' Kate braked to allow a British Telecom van to cut in front of us.

'As a matter of fact he was charged with rape in his final year,' she said.

My cortex lit up like a Christmas tree. 'What happened?' I stared straight ahead through the windscreen to stop myself from grabbing her lapel.

'It was after he and Janet split up. He was quite lucky to

get off apparently. Janet said it was touch-and-go - that the case could have gone either way.'

'But what exactly did he do?' I asked, sparking up a cigarette without bothering to obtain clearance. My mind was spinning on fast cycle. Kate buzzed her window down an inch. The traffic started to move.

'He met this girl at a party and he walked her home,' Kate said, concentrating on the road as the traffic picked up what passed for speed. 'They were both a little tipsy and when he asked if he could stay the night she made a bed up for him on the floor of her room. And they went to sleep. Then she woke up and he was in bed with her raping her.'

'You're kidding!'

'Come on, Steve. It goes on all the time. Date-rape.'

'And what happened then?' I asked.

'She said he turned into a completely different person, that he held her down with a hand on her throat so she could hardly breathe. She thought he was going to kill her. When he was finished he got dressed as though nothing had happened and went back to his college. The girl was in a terrible state. In the morning she told the other students in the house that he'd raped her. One of them called the police and Alan was arrested.'

'And so? How did he get off?'

Kate switched lanes for a ten-foot advantage. 'He had his own version of events. He said she made up a bed for him on the floor but when he told her it was uncomfortable she said he could get into bed with her. They wound up having consensual sex. It got a bit rough because she enjoyed it that way.'

'Rough? How do you mean rough?' I asked, recalling the bruise on Claire's neck in the Italian restaurant.

'I don't know exactly, but I remember Janet saying that Alan liked to pin her arms when they made love, pull her hair, that kind of thing. He said in court that he and the girl started play-fighting and she liked it, that she asked him to scratch and slap her. His barrister suggested that she'd felt ashamed about what they'd done so she told her friends that she'd been raped. The girl was Catholic. Alan's barrister made a lot of that.'

'So it was just her word against his?'

'Exactly. And this was the eighties. One of the other students saw him leave the house but no one heard anything. But the fact that Alan was seen leaving counted in his favour because his barrister argued that it forced the girl to explain to her friends what he'd been doing in her room.'

'So you think he did it?'

'Who can tell? From what Janet said he'd probably be convicted if the case was tried now. Attitudes to rape have changed a lot since then. But Alan had good character references. The judge didn't want to wreck his future.'

'I bet he was guilty though. He's a nutter, you can tell. The way the girl said he had raped her and then he acted like nothing had happened. I can just imagine him doing that.'

Rain flowed down the windows as though it was flush-time in a urinal. We sat silently inside our watery cell as I tried to process what Kate had told me. I thought about what might have been happening to Claire at Alan's house and I felt terrible that I hadn't even called the police.

'Would you like to come back to my place for something to eat?' Kate asked.

The invitation took me by surprise. Was Kate taking a holistic Californian approach to my treatment? Was Granola to be part of the cure?

'Thanks, Kate. I'd love to. Maybe I should check with Liz though.'

'Give her a call.'

Kate pulled a mobile phone from her briefcase.

I figured I could eat at Kate's and then go to Puffa later. There'd be no one in the building after ten o'clock. It was just after six, the beginning of the cheap rate and time for the daily broadcast of LIZ FM across the capital. For once our phone wasn't engaged.

'Hi, it's me,' I said. 'What are you up to?'

'Mary's here and we're drinking a bottle of wine. Where are you?' Even through the crappy Cellnet I could tell that Liz had been at the weed as well.

'I'm with Doctor Parker. From the Webster. She's asked me to dinner.'

'That's nice,' Liz said distractedly.

'Well, I thought I might come back later, miss the rush hour. If that's all right with you?'

'No problem. I'm going out myself so I'll see you later. Big-kiss.'

I winced at my wife's patent insincerity. Liz and I hadn't enjoyed a real big kiss in years. Even so I'd have liked her to have put up a token resistance to the idea of me spending an evening with another woman.

'Sorted,' I said to Kate, as though I'd won an important victory. 'What are you going to cook?'

The answer, perhaps inevitably, was spaghetti.

12

Silver Worms

KATE TURNED OFF THE CROMWELL ROAD into a residential area. I kept an eye out for Claire's house but it was getting dark and I was unfamiliar with this part of Kensington. Kate zig-zagged through some side-streets and parked in an avenue lined with plane trees. Patches of bark had flaked off their eczematic trunks.

Kate lived on the second floor of a six-storey house that had been converted into flats. I followed her into her large high-ceilinged sitting-room. The stripped-pine floorboards were dotted with kelims, and bright third-world fabrics covered the chairs and sofas that surrounded a Kashmiri coffee-table. Given Kate's conservative wardrobe, these fashionable ethnic furnishings came as a surprise. I had expected to find the standard-issue coconut matting, photos framed in silver and the odd bowl of pot-pourri dotted about on small, useless occasional tables.

Kate went to get changed and I looked around the room

for clues to her past. A photographic montage of white middle-class teenagers hung on the far wall. I picked Kate out among the young faces clustered at a series of beach barbecues and ski-chalet fondues. Her smile had been much less knowing back then. One of the photographs had been taken a few years later than the others. It showed Kate squinting into the sunset on a beach wearing only a sarong and a bead necklace.

'God, don't look at that! I keep meaning to take it down,' said Kate. She was standing right behind me, barefoot in a pair of corduroys.

'This is a nice place,' I said as she went over to the open-plan kitchen area.

'Thanks. Would you like some wine, Steve? Or there's a beer I think.'

'A beer would be fine. I'm allowed my three units, aren't I?' I was meant to count my drinks on the lithium.

She popped the top off a cold bottle from the back of the fridge and our fingers touched as she handed me the imported German lager. It was a Beck's, just like the one I'd used on Alan in Drummond Street. The label promoted an upcoming art exhibition at the Tate Gallery. In this case all the sugar had turned into advertising.

'Do you live here on your own?' I asked her.

'Crispin lives here. He rents a room. He'll be back from work soon.'

Kate started cooking and I went along the corridor to relieve myself in an overlit bathroom. Patsy Cline struck up in the sitting-room so I had a peek around the flat, safe in the knowledge that any squeaking floorboards would be covered by the music. There were three bedrooms. One of them was unused with cardboard boxes piled high against a cupboard.

The next had to be Crispin's with an old Sonic Youth poster on the wall and a large collection of CDs and video games.

Kate's bedroom was larger with a frilly bedspread and women's clothing strewn across the carpet. The bed was unmade and a pile of books lay on the table beside it. A biscuit-coloured vibrator was wedged between the books and a box of Kleenex. It was an inch or so shorter than Liz's. I turned off the bedroom light and went back to the kitchen area to find Kate chopping some onions at arm's length.

'So do you often ask your patients back for dinner?' I asked her, hoicking myself onto a stool by the pine-topped island unit.

'You're the first one,' she said with a smile. She told me that I was also the first patient she was treating without Dr Mahmood's direct supervision and I guessed that this guinea-pig status accounted for her extra-curricular interest in me.

I asked Kate about her family and discovered that she had one younger sister who was married and lived in New Zealand. Kate said that she had always wanted to be a doctor and had decided to specialize in Psychiatry as a medical student when her mother had begun to suffer from depression. Despite Kate's best efforts her mother was still refusing treatment, blaming her black moods on the weather.

'My mother's the only person I know who gets seasonally adjusted depression three hundred and sixty-five days a year,' Kate said. 'God, I should have called her back! She left a message at the Webster.'

'Call her later,' I said.

'But she's going out for dinner.'

'Then you'd better call her now,' I suggested.

'But I can't face talking to her,' she said with mounting

panic. Even though Kate was putting it on a little, I could see that she was still living in her mother's shadow.

'So call her when you know she's out and leave a message. Say how sorry you are you've missed her.'

It felt odd to be giving her advice for once.

'That's so devious, Steve!'

Kate smiled and took a sip of wine. A key turned in the front door and Crispin came in wearing dripping motorcycle gear. He was younger than I'd expected, a skinny long-haired kid in his early twenties. I suspected that he rode a bike to bolster his masculinity. Kate introduced us and he offered me a sodden hand to wring out over the fired-earth tiles.

'Hiya,' he said without warmth. He had a reedy Manchester accent.

'Hi. How's it going?' I said.

Crispin tossed a lock of ratty hair behind his ear. I couldn't tell if his mildly hostile vibe was due to poor social skills or because he knew that I was one of Kate's patients. Either way I didn't care. I was beginning to feel that my breakdown had been a natural reaction to modern city life and it surprised me that more people didn't flip out. Since I'd left the Webster I had seen madness bubbling away below the surface in nearly every face I passed in the street. I said as much to Kate when Crispin went to dry off.

'People don't have to pretend in a big city,' I said. 'You can see it in their eyes. Have you taken the tube lately?'

'I hate the tube,' said Kate. The onions began to fizz in the frying pan.

'Of course you do!' I said, warming to my theme through the lager. 'Everyone feels crazy down there. So they should, trapped in those silver worms miles underground.'

'Perhaps it's just because I'm mildly claustrophobic,

Steve. And maybe you're just seeing people's pain because it's what you want to see. Because you've been ill yourself.'

'Oh, I get it,' I said, feeling patronized. 'We're talking about a simple case of projection then?'

Kate chuckled at my use of therapy jargon. I watched her wash some lettuce and my thoughts returned to Alan Denton.

'Assuming Alan did rape that student, what do you suppose the chances are that he'd do it again?' I asked her.

'He was found not guilty so that's quite an assumption to make, isn't it?' she said, spin-drying the lettuce leaves in a plastic cyclotron.

'Maybe, but I know he did it. Everything fits.'

I told her what had happened when I'd gone back to get my car from the mews, that I suspected Alan of raping Claire, perhaps even killing her. I suggested that he'd been forced to sack me because I knew too much.

Kate just laughed.

'Oh, come on! That's nonsense!' She dried her hands and fixed me with her professional look. 'You should try to forget about Alan. I know it's hard to take but he sacked you and that's that.' She spoke firmly, drawing a curtain over the subject.

'All right, all right. Perhaps I'm getting a bit carried away,' I conceded. I couldn't expect her to grasp it all at once. Kate went over to the cooker and I followed her.

'But supposing someone was a rapist the urge wouldn't just go away, would it?' I asked.

'Probably not, no. Not without a great deal of work,' she agreed. 'Often the best you can do is to help the patient face up to his problem and develop strategies to contain it. But it's difficult.'

Kate started laying the table and I asked if I could help.

'Ah, the New Man. No, there's nothing to do really.'

She put the spaghetti into the boiling water and I was reminded of the meal I'd cooked for myself after the board meeting. I was reading the copy on a packet of health biscuits when Crispin joined us. He sat on the table wearing a Metallica T-shirt and torn jeans. I noticed he had the same high-caste brand of loafers that Kate favoured and I wondered if she'd bought them for him as a gift.

Crispin opened a bottle of Sauvignon and we ate the pasta while Kate prompted him through an account of the tedious minutiae of his working day, focusing on his attempts to woo a girl called Tricia who worked alongside him behind the counter of an Our Price record shop. The pasta was a little over-cooked but the ragout sauce was good. Kate had put some chilli in it.

'Why don't you ask Tricia out on a date?' Kate asked Crispin. He frowned.

'Oh, come on, why not? What's stopping you?' she teased.

'Leave it out, Kate!' he whined.

'What have you got to lose?' asked Kate. Crispin shot me an angry glance as though I had no business hearing this, but I had the feeling that he and Kate had been through all this before, that they were just acting out a familiar scene. There was something strange between them, something almost incestuous.

'What do you think, Steve? Do you think Crispin should ask Tricia on a date?'

'Go for it, Crispin. It sounds as though she likes you,' I said. I couldn't have cared less either way.

Crispin was a little old to be playing the shy adolescent to Kate's big sister and it made me think about my own relationship with her. I could just imagine Kate as a young girl nursing a series of sick animals until they duly died and broke her heart. I wondered if Crispin and I weren't the new sick rabbits in her hutch. When Crispin finished his food he went straight out to meet some friends in a pub.

'He's lovely, isn't he?' Kate said.

'He's a good bloke,' I said, even though he was a chippy little tosser. 'How did you meet him?' I asked.

'I needed to rent out a room to help with the mortgage so I advertised in the paper for a lodger and he was the first caller.'

'I wouldn't hold your breath over this thing with Tricia,' I said.

'Why do you say that?'

'I think he likes you a lot more.'

'Oh, come on! That's ridiculous,' she said with a smile. She knew I was half-right.

'No, I can see it in the way he looks at you. Before you started talking about Tricia I thought you and Crispin were going out together.'

'We're just friends,' she said flatly.

I felt sure there was more to it but Kate was my psychiatrist and I felt uncomfortable prying into her personal life. It was nearly ten o'clock. I wanted to get over to Puffa so I helped her clear away the dishes. When I said goodbye she graced me with a kiss on the cheek. It felt like another small transgression of doctor–patient protocol.

Breathing the foul air of a tube train as it clattered along the Piccadilly line, I pictured Alan raping the student, raping Claire. Parmesan bubbled in my gorge and made me feel sick. Across the aisle a spectral young junkie was wearing a pair of Chilean workboots that Puffa wholesaled at £39.95.

He nodded out and his head lolled against the shoulder of a Moslem woman whose eyes popped wide in her yashmak. She moved seats and the grey ghost awoke, yawned and checked me over with empty eyes. Above him an advertisement for Dateline promised that 'You too can find love'.

I surfaced at Warren Street and headed for the pedestrian precinct beneath the Euston Tower. A showroom dummy in the window of Laurence Corner army surplus store was modelling this season's rape-wear - black balaclava and combat jacket worn loose over dark-blue nylon track suit.

The wind poured through the concrete canyon sending trash scuttering across the concourse. A dosser lay on a ventilation grille sipping streetlager, watching an empty Disco packet bop around his legs. Drummond Street was deserted except for an old man in a dark suit scavenging in a litter bin. I wondered how long it would be before I joined him.

The night-watchman had been 'let go' as an economy measure. Nobody saw me open the front door of the building with Tony's keys. I climbed the stairs to Puffa, de-activated the burglar alarm, and made my way to Alan's office by the light of the street. Being back in the office brought home just how much I'd lost because of Alan Denton. I let down the venetian blinds in his office, turned on the angle-poise lamp and found his address book next to his diary in the top drawer of the desk.

Sitting in Alan's executive swivel, I scanned the address book for a Claire with a Kensington telephone number. There were plenty of numbers with the right prefixes but none for any Claire. I found only one mention of her name in his diary, ringed and capitalized on a long-gone Tuesday. Undaunted, I took the books and photocopied them. The copies faded to grey at the gutter but were still legible. I put the originals back in Alan's desk and looked in the other drawers. In the third drawer an American hunting knife lay on top of a pile of files. The curved steel blade leered up at me and I put it on the desk while I flipped through the papers. I found nothing of interest.

The bottom drawer was locked. I considered breaking the lock but then I remembered a time when we'd drawn a large amount of cash. Alan had stashed it in the drawer for a few hours, locking it with a key that he'd kept between the leaves of one of the books on the shelf behind his desk. I flicked through a dozen books before a small silver key fell from a copy of *Hambro's 1995 Investment Guide*. As it landed on the carpet tiles I realized I didn't know which pages it had been nestling between. I hoped that Alan didn't know either.

I heard a noise, a clanking sound.

I doused the light and flattened myself behind the door.

To my relief I heard someone descending the concrete staircase we shared with the other offices, someone who must have been working late on the floor above.

I went back to Alan's desk. There were several files in the bottom drawer. I found one marked 'In Deep' but there was nothing inside that threw light on my sacking. I went over and moved the accounts filing cabinet away from the wall. Alan had kept a spare house key taped behind it ever since he'd locked himself out of his house one night. I tore the Banham key loose and put it in my pocket. Then I pushed the filing cabinet back before replacing the desk-key in the middle of the investment guide.

I left Puffa and curled up in the dirty warmth of a tube train to read through the photocopies I'd made. There were four diary entries for the following day. Alan had two business meetings in the afternoon and two evening appointments: 'Trader Vic's 6.00 p.m.' was neatly inscribed with a fountain pen and 'Market Bar 7.30' was scrawled beneath it in Biro. Trader Vic's was the name of the basement bar of the Hilton Hotel on Park Lane and I knew the Market Bar also. It was a designer pub on Portobello Road, a mile or so north of Alan's house. Some months before, Tony and I had taken Gudrun there on her birthday and the management had thrown me out because of a drunken altercation. A snooty rich kid had spilt his drink on Gudrun's sleeve and when he had failed to make a suitable apology I'd felt compelled to deck him.

When I got back to East Putney I found that the front wheel of my mountain bike had been stolen. I left the remains chained to the railings and strode home angrily to find that Liz was still out. There were a couple of empty wine glasses in the sitting-room and I smelt a stale trace of marijuana in the air.

The following morning I woke up alone at nine o'clock and found Liz fast asleep in one of the spare rooms. It looked as if it would rain again. After breakfast I tried all the Kensington telephone numbers in Alan's address book. There were a few answering machines, some no-replies. The people who did pick up the phone told me I had a wrong number when I asked to speak to Claire. I remembered Tony's pathetic efforts to track down his Jim.

Liz came downstairs with puffy eyes and I wondered how long it would be before one of us trod on the other's toes. I offered to make her a cup of coffee.

'That's okay, I'll make it myself,' she said. There was a distance between us, as if we just happened to share a house in an unfunny sitcom.

'No, allow me. Did you have fun last night?' I asked, refilling the cafetière. Judging by the rings round her eyes she'd smoked her way through a kilo of weed.

'I just went over to Mary's. You?'

'Not bad. Doctor Parker cooked spaghetti.'

'That's nice. By the way, I talked to Mum and Dad last night,' said Liz, dislodging some sleep-crystals from the corner of her eye.

My father-in-law Gerald was harmless enough, but I'd never got on with April. As a novice on the nursery slopes of middle-class respectability, I hadn't been good enough for her only daughter. In April's purblind eyes Liz had been destined to marry into the aristocracy.

'I told Dad what Russell said and ran him through the figures. Our income and expenditure,' said Liz.

'What on earth for?' I asked.

Gerald was a retired solicitor whose financial nous had led him to join a Lloyd's insurance syndicate which now faced massive debts. He had helped to set up a registered charity to alleviate the hardship suffered by his fellow Names. When Liz had told me about this I'd offered to send them all a complimentary razor-blade and an EXIT pamphlet.

'Dad thinks we should put the house on the market at a good price and see what happens,' Liz said. 'Have you thought any more about adopting?'

I looked away and pushed down a cuticle.

'It's not the same for you, Steve. You've got all the time in the world.' Liz glanced down at her belly in dismay, as though an egg-timer was literally running out in there. Her lip trembled and I tried to take her in my arms but she pushed me away with tears in her eyes.

'You don't love me!' she cried. 'You didn't even need me when you were in hospital!' She tore a paper towel from the pine dispenser to dry her tears.

'I don't think we can stay together,' she said quietly.

'What was that? Do you want a divorce?' I asked.

In my heart I knew it was the right thing to do, but even though we'd discussed it endlessly in Marriage Guidance her words still came as a shock.

'I don't know what I want. I feel so confused! It's impossible to communicate with you,' she said.

'We're communicating now, aren't we?' I said. Joanna would have been proud of me but Liz just glared and left the room.

Half an hour later I went upstairs and found her meditating, sitting motionless in an armchair feeding a mantra through her head like a spool of Dymo tape. Tony called and asked me to meet him with his keys at a Chinese restaurant in Soho. He sounded angry but he hung up before I could find out why.

Liz came downstairs and informed me that she was going to visit her friend Marla and her husband Carl in Dorset. She planned to stay the night there. Marla was an ex-stylist whose marriage to her music video producer appeared to be holding firm. I said that sounded like a good idea, that we needed our space.

When Liz had left I found my camera and headed for the Underground station. Half-way there I realized that I'd forgotten to take my lithium tablet. I almost turned back for the bottle but I was feeling steadier and didn't feel that I needed the lithium any more. On the poster site opposite the station there was a new poster of a giant Volvo in an Area of Outstanding Natural Beauty. Beneath it a hundred real cars throbbed without moving on the main road, bumper to bumper like a chain of hydrocarbons. The radiator fan of a Ford transit van sucked at the exhaust emissions of a clapped-out BMW. The transit coughed its own leaden puff into the grille of a Honda Civic which in turn exhaled into a Saab with a Baby on Board sticker in its back window. I saw my mono-cycle chained to the railings and made a mental note to buy a new wheel from the shop in Covent Garden.

I arrived at the restaurant at half-past twelve and it took me a minute or so to find Tony. He was sitting at the back of the room looking shifty in a black shroud-like Japanese suit and Persol sunglasses. His face was waxy and shiny, his head a pale bubble sprouting hair as dry as wire. When he lit a cigarette his hand jumped with hangover and I realized that he'd started drinking again.

'Hi, Tone. How are you doing?'

'Steve! Thank God,' he groaned. 'Alan's been going nuts. You left his fucking knife on his desk! He's talking about calling the police. He's been on at me and Gudrun all morning. I can't believe you'd be such a tosser!'

I gasped at my own stupidity and tried to retrieve the situation.

'Calm down, all right?' I said. 'I'm sorry about the knife, but he can't prove a thing. Christ, I didn't even take anything. There's no way he can tie it to you or me.' Nevertheless my carelessness rankled. I blamed it on the lithium.

'But there's no sign of forced entry,' Tony hissed in a stage whisper.

'That doesn't mean anything. There are loads of people who've got keys,' I said.

'No there bloody aren't. The lock was changed, wasn't it?'

'He's got nothing on you though. You didn't even do anything for God's sake.'

'He thinks I've been nosing through his things. And he asked me if I'd seen you,' he said.

139

'What did you tell him?' I asked. Tony's paranoia was contagious.

'What the fuck do you think? Look, have you got the keys?' he asked.

'Chill out, Tone. They're right here.' I handed him the office keys and he slipped them into his pocket, glancing around like a twitchy drug-dealer.

'We shouldn't even be here. If we're seen together and Alan finds out . . .'

'No one's going to see us,' I reassured him. 'Look, since you're obviously off the wagon, why don't we get a bottle of wine?'

Does Dolly Parton sleep on her back? Tony wasted no time ordering a bottle of white.

'I should never have let you have the keys. I don't under-stand what you needed the address book for,' he said.

'I told you, Tone. To find out why Alan sacked me.'

'But it's obvious why Alan sacked you! To get control of the company, you berk! Jesus!'

'Look, I think Alan raped this girl Claire. I found blood on his doorstep and I think he might have killed her.'

'That's the biggest load of fucking crap I've ever heard! If anyone had been murdered it would have been in the papers, wouldn't it? You want to watch it, Steve. I reckon you're going loopy again.'

Tony sucked on his cigarette and blew the smoke out through his nostrils, clouding the table-top with carcinogens. Given his ugly mood there was little point trying to convince him of anything.

'So the new regime didn't work out then, Tone?' I asked. 'The jogging and stuff.'

'Oh, that,' he said, as if it was just a distant memory. 'A

complete waste of time. No, I'm going to give Alcoholics Anonymous a go. I can't do it on my own. There's a meeting tonight.' He looked terrified at the prospect.

'That's good, Tone. I've heard it can really help people.'

'Yeah,' he said, draining his glass of wine as his roast duck arrived. 'I've been seeing a bit of Jim, the bloke I was trying to get on the phone.'

'Really? That's great,' I said.

'I'm going to sort him out with a job in one of the shops.'

'You don't see this as a long-term thing then,' I said.

He looked puzzled and I reminded him that the shops would be closing down in a couple of months.

Tony leaned forward into the overhead spotlight to tell me about love. The beam cast deep shadows around his eyes. With his black suit and pasty complexion, Tony resembled a panda - not a benign bamboo-chewing paterfamilias from Sichuan province but a moulting monochrome flea-factory ravaged by years of underfunded captivity in the inner city squalor of London Zoo.

We champed through our plates of monosodium glutamate and polished off the bottle of wine. Tony downed a large Scotch, paid the bill and asked me to wait for five minutes after he'd left so that no one would see us together on the street. He swayed alarmingly on his way to the door.

I caught a tube to Fulham Broadway and walked to La Paesana past rows of Victorian workmen's cottages that had been gentrified with ruched curtains and brass door-knockers. When I reached the restaurant I was greeted by a beaky young woman in a beige suit and gold earrings.

'I'm so sorry. Is close,' she said, miming heartbreak without much talent.

'That's all right. I just want to speak to the manager,' I said.

'You have an appointment? Is very busy,' she said, glancing back at the half-empty restaurant. Sunlight was falling into the conservatory at the back.

'It's a personal matter. I don't mind waiting. Perhaps I could sit at the bar?' She looked me over and thought about it.

'Mmm, okay. You wait,' she said. 'Who shall I say is?'

'I'm a friend of Alan Denton.'

'Who?' she said, leaning forward and cupping her ear.

'Alan Denton,' I repeated. She went to tell the manager.

I sat on a precarious wicker stool and ordered an espresso to counteract the wine. At the nearest table a paunchy Lothario was feeding spoonfuls of ice-cream to a Sloane woman with an upturned collar and a gold charm-bracelet. I watched the manager moving around from table to table, chatting up the customers and pointedly ignoring me. Eventually he came over and leant an elbow on the bar.

'How can I help you?' he asked. His moustache was drooping and his eyes were bloodshot.

'I'm trying to find someone I met here, a girl,' I said.

He smiled. 'So many girls,' he said with a sweep of his arm.

'I met her here with Alan Denton. Her name's Claire. You know Alan?'

'Alan?' he said, puzzled.

'Alan Denton. With the red hair. We had dinner here a few weeks ago. You know him.'

'Alan. Yes, maybe I know him.'

'How about his friend Claire? Blonde, about twenty-two? You seemed to know her too.'

He rubbed his earlobe and appeared to rack his memory.

'Claire? No, I don't think so. Sorry. Maybe you should ask your friend Alan, no?'

'Well, thanks for your help,' I said. There was no point pushing it.

I caught a tube to Hyde Park Corner and as I stepped off the train I smelt The Smell. Piss and disinfectant, the subway fragrance. On the platform, three tense mid-western tourists were studying a plan of the London Underground as though it was a map of hell. At the top of the escalator two teenage cider-punks were begging from passengers as we emerged from the maw of the inferno. One of the beggars lay on a cardboard tongue and I noticed that he had no legs, an emphatic No Sale for Puffa's designer footwear.

An old dosser with a ragged white beard leaned against the side of a Photo-Me booth holding out a cap. His fingers were shiny beneath the layers of grime. He looked about seventy and his overcoat was tied with a length of greasy rope. The sight of him made me yearn for a pension plan and I wondered why the big insurance companies didn't sponsor these elderly indigents. Was it not this old man's secret function to act as a subliminal whipper-in for the financial services sector?

Having picked my way through the warren beneath Hyde Park Corner, I stepped up into the slightly sweeter air of the roundabout. I skirted the queue of brainwashed tourists outside the Hard Rock Café and walked up Park Lane to the Hilton. Tourists were bearing their luggage in ant-like streams from coach to hotel and back again. It was a quarter to six and I hoped that Alan hadn't arrived early.

I bought some film for my camera from a retail outlet in the Hilton's lobby and descended a curving stairway into the sepulchral gloom of Trader Vic's Boathouse. The subterranean cocktail lounge was spacious, the decor Las Vegas Kon-Tiki. A canoe hung from the bamboo ceiling and an enormous blue marlin was fixed to one wall. A Filipina dressed as a south-sea islander appeared from behind a crude wooden totem pole and showed me to a table formed from a hefty chunk of rainforest. It offered a discreet view of the stairs.

The bar was dimly lit out of consideration for its jet-lagged clientele. On one side of me a shipwrecked Scandinavian was working on the twenty-four-hour breakfast. Beyond him an elderly American lizard sat eviscerating a bowl of King Prawns and nipping at a London Sour. He'd spent too much time in the sun and a liver-spotted wattle wobbled at his throat as he tore at the prawns with cold ferocity. I ordered myself a rum cocktail which arrived in a ceramic coconut. I sipped at it while I waited for Alan to arrive. Across the room a fat man tried to chat up a flashily dressed young woman. He gave up after a while and moved back to his own table. At quarter past six Alan came down the stairs and I felt a spark of hatred.

13

The Gunpowder Trail

I HID MY FACE IN THE MENU and Alan walked right past me. A waitress showed him to a table beyond the bamboo bar-island. He ordered a cocktail and perused some papers from his attaché case. Five minutes later Sally's assistant Julia tottered down the staircase wearing an Armani suit. The hairs stood up on the back of my neck. Julia stopped at the foot of the stairs, squinting into the twilight with her beady eyes. Fortunately Alan waved to her before she saw me and she went straight over to fling her arms round him, kissing him full on the lips.

I wished I'd got that on film because Julia had only recently married a dull plank who worked at Goldman Sachs. However there was no way I could get a picture without using a flash. Julia wriggled her bottom round the Naugahyde curve of the banquette to squeeze up next to Alan. She couldn't keep her hands off him, fussing with his hair and collar. They fell into an animated conversation. I was desperate to hear what they were saying.

I took my cocktail over to a nearby table. It offered a good vantage point, hidden from Alan and Julia by a wooden screen of Polynesian fret-work. I craned my neck but I still couldn't make out what they were saying. They were whispering to each other as if the erotics of their relationship depended on a sense of conspiracy. Julia's hand was kneading Alan's thigh beneath the table.

'Are you waiting for someone?' said a voice behind me. It was the flashy young woman I'd seen with the fat man. She sat next to me and I smelt her pungent body spray.

'Er, no. Just killing some time,' I said.

'Perhaps we could kill it together,' she suggested with a bright smile, stroking the stem of her glass with red fingernails.

'Forget it,' I said. I strained to hear what Alan was saying to Julia.

'There's no need to be unpleasant,' the hooker said with a contemptuous glare. We sat in stony silence for a few minutes.

'What's so special about those two?' she asked, nodding at Alan and Julia.

I wanted to tell her to get lost but I couldn't risk a scene.

'Nothing. Nothing at all,' I said. I moved back to my original table until Alan and Julia finished their drinks and asked for the bill.

I walked quickly to the till, pressed a ten-pound note on the manager and ran up the stairs into bright daylight. The pavement was swarming with Japanese tourists queuing to board a coach which would take them to the next large faceless hotel on their itinerary. I put on my sunglasses and pretended to photograph some of the Hilton's architectural features. Alan emerged blinking into the glare with his arm round Julia. I got some good shots of them, and I got some better ones when they headed over to the taxi rank and deep-kissed.

When I zoomed in with the camera it was as though I was standing right next to them. I could almost hear their tongues and lips at work as they exchanged a good pint of saliva. Julia's eyes were clamped shut but Alan's were open, just going through the motions. He lifted his wrist to read the time off his Rolex behind her back. Alan broke away and the cosmetically bleached moustache on Julia's upper lip glittered like a phosphorescent caterpillar. Alan said something to her and she pulled a sad face before she climbed into a cab. Alan waved her off and took the next one in the line. I watched him head off north in the direction of the Market Bar.

I caught a tube to South Kensington and walked to Alan's place beneath a darkening sky. There was a pub on the corner of Alan's mews called the Earl Spencer, a small neo-Elizabethan tavern. Its bowed windows were glazed with orange 'hand-blown' panes. I went inside and ordered a Scotch from an unfriendly diminutive publican. There were only three other customers in the pub, a couple of trysting office-workers and a thin woman in her sixties with dyed hair drinking shorts. Dusty horse brasses hung on the walls between decorative wooden beams. Atmosphere came courtesy of the Muzak corporation.

I downed my drink and walked out into the cobbled cul-de-sac to gaze in at several rosy domestic vignettes of owner-occupiers eating meals and watching television. There was a vintage car showroom half-way down the mews and the grille of a Silver Ghost loomed out of the darkness. Alan's little house had a blue-and-orange Neighbourhood Watch sticker behind the glass. The downstairs lights were on. Alan's BMW was parked by his front door and just for the hell of it I scratched a sine wave along the door panels with the Banham key from the back of the filing cabinet.

The gap between the curtains gave me a restricted view of Alan's sitting-room. It was a mess by his standards. There was a newspaper on the pale sofa and I could see some dirty dishes stacked in the open-plan kitchen at the back, illuminated by low-level strip lighting. I looked at my watch. It was seven forty-five. I rang the doorbell and there was no reply. If Alan had switched on a burglar alarm I knew I'd have to run for it but I remembered that he hadn't primed one when he'd taken us out to dinner.

I looked up and down the mews, turned the Banham key in the lock and opened the door. No alarm sounded and I felt the thrill of burglary, blood tapping at my temples as my senses keyed up. I went to the drinks cabinet for another belt of Scotch.

I climbed the stairs and went into the main bedroom. It looked different but I couldn't tell if this was because the position of the bed had been changed or just the result of the deep shadows cast by the light from the street. I drew the curtains and turned on the bedside light. The pale green bedspread looked brand new but I couldn't be sure that it hadn't been there before. I searched the fitted wardrobe and found only clothes on hangers and a stack of laundered shirts.

There were some Durex Elite condoms in the drawer of the bedside table. Beneath an old copy of *Esquire* I found a curled tube of KY jelly and some white powder in a small origami envelope. The powder tasted sour and rubbery. It didn't surprise me that Alan had a taste for cocaine, the mark of the successful yuppy. I lifted the bedspread and found deep drawers in the frame of the bed.

The first was full of sheets and blankets but the second contained some top-shelf porn magazines and a Helmut Newton photo-book. At the back I found a pair of handcuffs and a Zorro mask along with some lengths of black silk rope – the bondage enthusiast's starter-kit, the Lego bricks of S&M. It was tame stuff compared to the equipment Tony had round at his place but it offered an intriguing glimpse of Alan's head.

I checked the time and headed for the study. The bureau was stacked full of personal papers, bank statements and stock certificates. I flipped through them with jittery fingers and discovered from an estate agent's letter that Alan owned two flats in Hackney which he rented to tenants on short-term lets. In addition, he held over two hundred thousand pounds in various investments. I felt a pang of envy.

I searched the small drawers at the back of the bureau and found his passport. Sickeningly, Alan had filled in his occupation as 'Entrepreneur'. I was looking through a loose pile of papers for Claire's address or phone number when I heard a car pull up outside. I went to the window and peeked through the curtains. It was only a woman getting out of a Mazda but I decided to leave the house. If Alan did happen to return there was no way out other than the front door.

I turned off the lights and was heading down the stairs when a key turned in the lock. I shot back upstairs and hid behind the fitted wardrobe in the spare room. The front door slammed shut. The sour taste of Scotch rose in my throat and I struggled to control spasms of panic. A pipe clanked on its mounting as the kitchen tap was turned on. I cursed my stupidity and heard Alan's muffled voice below. I realized he was talking on the telephone. The bedroom phone pinged when he hung up. There was no sound but my breath stop-starting.

Then I heard him coming up the stairs. My heart tried to punch its way out through my ribs. I held a lung-full of air hard against them. There was a heavy glass ashtray on the bedside table four feet from where I stood. I visualized myself picking it up and smashing it into Alan's face.

The landing light went on. I tensed, ready to make my move. Alan passed right by the spare-room door. I saw his shadow travel across the carpet. He went into the master bedroom. I could hear him moving about on the other side of the plasterboard wall. Had I put everything back? Would I have to make a break for it? My mind threw up a hundred bad possibilities. Fear clawed its way through my guts.

There was a knock on the front door and I guessed that he'd called the police, that they'd come to arrest me. I'd have to make a clean breast of it. Plead insanity. There was another knock and he went downstairs to answer it.

'I'm just coming!' Alan shouted. 'It was down the back of the sofa.'

The lights went out and I heard him leave. I slid down the wall, my heart pounding. A car drove off.

I waited for five minutes before I let myself out. Once I was in the street I began to run, laughing hysterically as panic rippled out of me in great sheets. I'd got away with it and I felt too high to go home. I went to a pub and called Kate. It was Saturday night and I'd expected her to be out but she picked up the phone and asked me to come over for a drink. She opened the door in a white towelling dressing-gown.

'Are you sure this is all right? If it's not convenient I'll come back another time,' I said. She seemed distracted and I noticed a bottle of red wine on the coffee table that was two-thirds empty.

'No, no. Stay. I'm just vegging out. Get yourself a drink.' I fetched a glass from the cupboard and poured myself some wine. The television flickered with the sound turned low. A hijacked jet glimmered through the heat-haze of a desert runway. The weather was good over there, the sky a deep cobalt blue.

'Is Crispin around?' I asked.

'He's gone off for the weekend. We had a row about money.'

'Sounds like me and Liz,' I said. I meant it as a joke but it came out wrong and Kate gave me an odd look. On the news a woman was being bundled into a courtroom to face charges of abducting a baby from a supermarket in Leeds.

'Crispin owes me rent and he said he's going to move into Tricia's flat,' Kate said, taking a sip of wine.

'Oh, yeah?'

'It doesn't really bother me. You can't see how a man and a woman can share a flat and just be friends, can you, Steve?' She was a little fractious from the alcohol.

'They can be friends up to a point, sure.'

'And then of course it has to develop into something physical?' She laughed caustically.

'Probably,' I said, just to see where it would lead us.

'That's so pathetic. Really screwed-up male thinking.'

Kate went over to the kitchen area and opened another bottle of wine.

'Male thinking? I agree men are pretty screwed-up but then so are women,' I said.

'Oh, but I'd say the problem starts with men! Most of you have a ridiculous attitude to love.'

'It depends what you want,' I said with a smile.

Kate poured herself a big glass of Cabernet Sauvignon and smiled back. 'But you have no choice about "what you want", do you? You see some little airhead and you can't take your eyes off her!'

'So do women have a choice? They turn twenty-eight

without having a kid and their ovaries start screaming.' Her eyes widened and I knew I'd hit a nerve.

'Screaming?'

'They want to be fertilized. And they get hysterical about it,' I said.

'Bullshit! I've got till I'm forty to have a child!'

'You really want to be fifty when your kid's ten?' I asked.

'No, but I'm not going to rush it before I find the right partner.'

'Most women do though, don't they? It's really just a game of musical chairs. The big biologist stops the music and you just reproduce with whoever you happen to be with at the time. And you tell yourself you're in love with the jerk. That's what my mum did. She was never in love with my dad but she had two of his kids before he buggered off. What's that if not a pathetic idea of love?'

'It isn't mine,' said Kate. 'I don't confuse love with sex.'

I thought of the two-speed vibrator in her bedroom. At the Webster Kate had all the answers but now she was talking as much rubbish as me. I didn't want to get any further into the mine-field of gender politics and wondered how I could pick my way back out without losing any limbs.

Kate went over to the CD player and put on an Isley Brothers track. She started dancing to it and I could see that she had quite a buzz on from the wine. I watched her until she beckoned me to join her. I held her as she moved in my arms. My cock hardened and when she felt it against her thigh she laughed and broke away.

I stood there feeling stupid, wondering if she'd set me up or if it had just happened that way. On the television the police were exhuming the third body from a garden in Belgravia. I sat down and Kate refilled my wine glass.

'You're not sulking, are you?' she asked.

'Is that a professional question?'

'Hey, come on! I was only teasing.'

'Yeah, well, I'd best be going,' I said.

'I'm sorry, okay? Look, you can stay here if you like. The spare bed's made up and everything.' Her offer surprised me and I thought it over. I had plans to check up on Alan the next day and the prospect of a trip back to my empty house was depressing.

'Why not? That'd be great,' I said with a smile. I even wondered if my luck was in.

We watched an old Hammer horror film and I waited in vain for Kate to make a move. In the end I said goodnight and went to bed in the spare room.

I couldn't sleep. The flats had been poorly converted and I could hear the film's soundtrack through the cardboard door. After a while a couple started making love directly above my head: just the timeless to-and-fro of human copulation. Then the vocal track kicked in with some call-and-response, a woman's low moans and the man's grunts. The bedsprings squeaked faster as they took it up to the crescendo.

'I'm coming!' the woman squealed.

'Yesss!' yelled the man as if he'd kicked a ball into the back of the net. Some cats fought each other in the gardens in the street and then all was quiet save for the background hum of the main road. I'd just about nodded off when Kate came into the room.

'Steve? Are you awake? I can't get to sleep. Can I get in with you, just for a cuddle?'

I rubbed my eyes and by the light from the door I saw that she was wearing a short white nightdress which glowed silver against her darker skin.

'Sure,' I mumbled, moving across the small double bed to make room for her. She slipped under the duvet and lay down with her back to me. I put a fraternal arm round her. Kate smelt as sweet as Claire had. Although she lay quite still, her breathing was fast and uneven. I nudged her tit with my forearm and when she didn't push it away I got a lazy erection which snuggled happily against her rump. When she felt it she caught her breath, turned round and put her mouth on mine. We deep-kissed, judo-wrestling with our tongues until they threatened to snap their mooring cords. Kate threw a leg over me. I felt her body heat up and soften, her hips widen against my thigh. We kissed slowly and then Kate pulled her lips away with a wanton smile. She licked me all over my face and dragged my hand across her breasts, pushing it down her body, guiding my fingers to her clitoris.

'That feels good,' Kate whispered, spreading her thighs. She slipped the tip of her tongue into my ear as she found my cock, squeezing and buffing it with the palm of her hand. She slid down my body. I felt the soft weight of her breasts against the tops of my thighs. She put my cock in her mouth and began to suck it. I grasped her leg and dragged it up across my chest. Kate nestled herself down on my face and I licked her like a dog, her wetness all over my face. She smelt faintly of cumin. In the pale moonlight I could see that she was an unnatural blonde with brown pubic hair. I put a finger inside her and flicked her clitoris with my tongue.

Kate removed my cock from her mouth for a moment. 'That's great, just there,' she said. She sucked at my cock, cupping my balls with one hand. I thought I was going to come then and there. I grabbed her round bottom and tried to steer her astride me but she leant over to produce a condom from beneath the pillow.

'Hang on,' she said, on auto pilot as she tore the packet open and rolled the rubber onto me. Her jaw was slack and her lips glistened with spit. I saw the red glint of a Mates wrapper on the sheet. Before the thought of Richard Branson could jeopardize my erection, Kate lowered herself onto me with a series of tiny yelps.

'Oh God,' she moaned. She threw her head back, her bare throat a pale triangle in the half-light. She swivelled her hips and the moonlight caught a thin line of hair running like a gunpowder trail from her navel to her mons. I stroked her breasts and she put a hard bullet of nipple to my mouth. Then she sat up to pitch back and forth. When Kate started moving faster, I pulled her down onto me. I was worried I was about to come. I tried to think about Richard Branson.

'Fuck me!' she moaned.

'I am,' I gasped. I bucked up against her, trying to make a crab with my knees at ninety degrees. She grabbed a handful of my stomach and rode me like a jockey.

'Oh God, oh God . . . You're coming, Steve, aren't you? I can feel it . . . Oh God. I want you to yell when you come, okay?'

I spurted and roared as the spasm ran through me and out into the Mates. Kate lay down beside me. I felt for her clitoris but she pushed my hand away gently. I hoped my shout had woken the footballer upstairs.

'Mmm. I think I'll be able to go to sleep now,' she said, kissing my lips and removing the rubber bag from my cock.

'Where are you going?' I asked as she stood up.

'To get rid of this,' she said with a smile, holding up the sac as if it was a dead mouse.

I fell asleep and woke in the early hours with my arm trapped beneath her shoulder. I didn't know who she was until

I recognized the curve of my psychiatrist's cheek beneath the pile of blonde hair. Panic gripped me, the panic a fox feels when the trap snaps shut, the blind panic that enables him to bite through his trapped leg to lope off on the other three. I had a hangover and I just lay there in the darkness, prey once more to my Inner Torquemada. We shouldn't have done it. Kate was my psychiatrist. I was married. After a while I eased my arm out from beneath her with diamond-cutter caution. I wondered how Kate would be feeling about what we'd done when the wine had worn off.

I finally fell asleep again. When I woke in the morning I looked around the unfamiliar room and she wasn't there. Outside cotton-wool clouds were blowing across a baby-blue sky. I dozed until Kate came into the room.

'How are you feeling?' she asked with a sheepish grin.

'Never better. How about you?'

'Terrible. Appalling. I've had to take two Nurofen.' She closed her eyes and massaged her temples.

'I always have this effect on women. Don't worry, it'll pass,' I said.

'Oh, God, no. I had a great time. It's just that I never drink that much. I must have had a whole bottle of wine. Would you like some tea?'

I had a shower and joined her in the kitchen.

'So do you often sleep with your patients?' I asked.

Kate smiled ruefully.

'We didn't exactly sleep together, Steve. You snore so much I had to go back to my own bed.' She was trying to keep it light but I noticed that she'd drawn blood picking at one of her thumbs.

'You know what I mean,' I said.

'I don't make a habit of it, no. It's against the rules.' She poured me a cup of tea with an unsteady hand.

'Well, who's to know? It's between us and no one else,' I said.

'Good,' she said. 'I'm going to have a bath. Help yourself to cereal or whatever. I'm having lunch with my parents and I've got to leave soon.'

I wondered if this was just an excuse to get rid of me. In the cold light of day I didn't feel bad that we'd made love. On the contrary I felt alive again. In bed with Liz I usually imagined some disembodied invigilator hovering around keeping score on how loving and considerate I was being. With Kate I'd had fun. I ate some cereal and she came back wearing a denim skirt.

'You know, you're much less uptight in real life,' I said.

'What, you think I act uptight at work?' she asked.

'No, not exactly. Just more in control.'

'So would you be if you worked with a bunch of lunatics.'

I got up from the table and held my stomach in as I crossed the room to go and get dressed.

'You don't need to do that, Steve. You've got the body of a Greek god,' she said.

It was the first compliment my physique had received in years, even if it was drenched with irony. I dressed in my stale clothes and returned to the kitchen area.

'Is Crispin back?' I asked her. She was eating muesli.

'No. I told you he's away. Why?' she asked, fat-free milk dribbling down her chin.

'Isn't that his crash-helmet in the hall?'

'It's mine,' she said, wiping her chin with the sleeve of her robe. She explained that she owned a moped which she seldom used. When I asked her if I could borrow it for the weekend she gave me the keys without a moment's hesitation. Her spontaneous kindness warmed my heart.

Kate reminded me to take my lithium and I lied that I already had. I'd left the pills at home but I wasn't worried: I was feeling really good for the first time in ages and I didn't want to blunt my senses. We left the flat together and kissed goodbye in the street before Kate drove off in the Audi. I put on her crash-helmet. It was a tight fit, snapping a few more hairs loose from their follicles as I squeezed it onto my head.

The moped ripped through the still air as I rode to Alan's mews with the sun playing its English summer game of peek-a-boo behind the clouds. Alan's car was still outside his house, the scratch I'd made along its flank resplendent in the sun-shine. Since it was still early, I drove to South Kensington to have my film of Alan and Julia developed at a one-hour Photo-lab.

I bought a paper and went back to Alan's mews. The sun re-emerged from behind a cloud. The Sunday streets had been washed clean by the rain and cars gleamed as if they were brand new. The Earl Spencer was offering Morning Coffee so I locked the helmet to the moped and went inside. It was empty except for the pink-faced publican who was riding out the recession in an alcoholic haze. Nasty, British and short, he made little attempt at small talk this early in the day. I sat in a window seat from where I could observe Alan's front door and drank a stale Rombouts filter coffee, gazing out into the street through the 'hand-blown' orange panes. It was like looking at the world through the bottom of a pint of bitter and the effect was heightened by the reek of stale beer in the pub. After half an hour Alan came out of his house and walked up the mews, banana-shaped through the distorted fish-eye pane. He passed the window and I followed him onto the street.

As soon as I saw Alan my mood darkened. My hatred wiped away the mellow vibe I'd shared with Kate. I knew then that I wanted to kill him, to strangle him and see his teeth bite through the pink of his tongue, the blood glaze his teeth and bubble over his chin as his earliest memories gurgled out of him to be lost for ever.

14

A Walk in the Park

I STALKED *ALAN ONTO* GLOUCESTER *ROAD* and he entered a smart foodstore, the kind of place where the outrageous mark-up on a pint of milk is computed from market research into the gullibility, laziness and surplus income of its target clientele. I loitered by a futon shop nearby and watched the bright reflected traffic move across its plate-glass window. Bracketing my eyes I made out thin Japanese mattresses on wooden pallets, sad souvenirs of the eighties. The futon trade had slowed to snail-pace. Soon the legend 'SALE Last Few Days' would be poorly executed in whitewash on the inside of the window by a bored sales assistant, perhaps one letter painted back-to-front, the chore nonetheless a welcome diversion from the excruciating boredom of watching dust accrue on the keys of a silent till.

'Hello, Steve. What are you doing here?' It was Alan's voice, directly behind me.

My nerves yanked tight as a parachute harness. Had I just imagined it?

I turned round into blinding sunlight and saw the silhouette of a man.

'Who is it?' I stammered.

'Hey, relax. It's only me. Alan.' He put a hand on my shoulder and I flinched. Across the street two policemen sat in their Rover getting younger by the day.

'Christ, you gave me a fright!' I said. I tried to laugh it off but the muscles in my neck were locked tight as bolts.

Alan had seen me following him. He'd doubled back to catch me and the police-children knew I'd broken into his house.

'I'm sorry if I alarmed you,' said Alan. He seemed relaxed and amused. 'How are you? Liz told me that you'd left hospital.' His sentences came out of his mouth as disconnected units and turned round in my head like luggage on an airport carousel, none of it mine.

'Yes. That's right,' I said. Alan sucked on the straw of a fruit juice carton and his composure compounded my own discomfort.

'You've been following me, haven't you?' said Alan, but his lips didn't move.

It was just a voice in my head, my Inner Ventriloquist.

'What brings you over here, Steve? I thought you'd be home mowing the lawn on a nice day like this,' he said, his lips again synched to the soundtrack. He was taking a good look at me. I felt he could see right into my mind.

'I've been to see my therapist,' I said.

'On a Sunday?' he said, raising an eyebrow.

'It was the only time she had free.' Alan's face was so close to my own that his freckles swam before my eyes. The cut on

161

his cheek had healed to leave a pink arc two inches long that bowed up at the corner like the ghost of a smile.

'Have you ever slept on one?' Alan asked.

'What?' I asked. Had he seen me with Kate?

'A futon. You were looking at the futons, weren't you?'

'Oh. Yeah, I've got a bad back.' Across the street the policemen jumped out of their car and flagged down a black motorist.

'I wouldn't bother. They're terribly uncomfortable. Where are you heading, boss?'

'I was on my way to the tube, going home.'

I wondered if it sounded as phoney to him as it did to me. Alan suggested that we might get a coffee in Kensington Gardens. I was at a loss for a suitable excuse. I tagged along like a zombie and when we passed a coffee-shop I wondered why Alan was so keen to lead me into the park.

'The therapy sounds like a good idea,' he said. 'I suppose it's quite normal after a breakdown. Who are you seeing? Someone good?' Alan drained his box of juice and lobbed the carton into a litter bin without breaking stride. It was hard work keeping up with his pace in the heat.

'A doctor from the Webster,' I wheezed as we overtook an Arab in a white ankle-length shirt. 'She just checks my medication and then we have a chat. I won't have to go for long.'

'What medication are you on?' he asked.

'Lithium. It's not a drug really, just a salt-type thing.'

'Oh, yes. I've heard of it.'

'By the way, I feel bad about that scar on your cheek. I wanted to write or something.'

'Don't be silly. You weren't to blame. Anyway I'm told

the scar adds character,' he said with a grin, jutting his jaw like a Spitfire pilot.

We crossed into the park by Kensington Palace and I wondered when Princess Diana was going to show up for Group at the Webster with a mobile phone and a handbag full of chocolates. Bees sucked at flowers, pensioners sat still as reptiles on slatted benches and single men lay on the grass with their beer-guts cinched by brightly coloured briefs, allowing florid melanomas to blush across their flesh. We left the path and headed across the dry grass, the bald earth black beneath the sparse blades.

'Watch out! Dog shit,' said Alan, indicating an ochre turd.

I side-stepped it to little purpose. There wasn't a single spoonful of soil in the whole park that hadn't passed through a dog's bowel at some point. Two girls in cut-offs were heading towards us and Alan smiled at them as they passed us.

We walked on in silence and Alan led us into a leafy arbour. I slowed my pace, enjoying the cool shade. Alan walked ahead and half-way along the path he turned and glared at me, spotlit by a sunbeam which pierced the green canopy above us. His teeth were clenched so tightly that I could see the muscles of his jaw poking through his cheek.

We stood facing each other for a moment. I was convinced that he had brought me into the park to kill me, that he was working himself up in order to attack. I'd be just another statistic, another mental patient discharged to die in the community. No one would ever know that Alan was responsible.

I tensed to defend myself. Did he have a knife? My stomach shrank from the thought.

163

A woman appeared behind Alan, pulling a brown Labrador in our direction.

'What's the matter, Steve? Are you out of breath or something?' Alan asked.

My heart dropped down a gear or two. 'No, I'm fine. Let's get this coffee. Where's the café?' I asked.

'Not far,' he said.

We entered an area of flower beds criss-crossed by Tarmac paths along which torpid au-pairs pushed their baby-buggies. Alan took us past a regiment of Fuji film tulips that were so bright that they drained all the colour from their surroundings. A radio whispered an account of Wimbledon, the commentator muted lest he offend the rain-god.

I had a sense of foreboding, an airy feeling in my chest. My skin tingled as though a hundred silverfish were crawling over it. We walked past a dead tree-stump with some charmless fairies carved into the trunk and entered a children's playground full of toddlers and their minders.

A little blond boy in a navy-blue blazer was being pushed on a swing by his Filipina house-slave. 'Higher! I want to go higher!' the boy commanded. Alan headed towards a wooden structure which housed a refreshment booth but it was padlocked. A sign explained that it was closed for two weeks.

'That's a drag,' said Alan.

'I'd better go,' I said.

'We could get something to eat if you've got time.'

'I dunno.' I was uneasy but I figured I would be safe in a crowded restaurant and I hoped I might discover something out about Claire.

'Haven't you got things to do yourself?' I asked him.

'Absolutely nothing,' he said. 'How does pasta grab you?'

I shrugged and we headed across the grass towards Kensington. Above us a jet laid its vapour trail across the sky like a line of Alan's cocaine.

Pasta Pasta Pasta was a fast-turnover restaurant in a corner site just off the High Street. The dingy interior was depressing on such a sunny day. A baby-sick smell of fresh Parmesan almost made me gag as we passed the service station. We sat down and Alan ordered a bottle of wine from the waitress.

We broke bread sticks, perused the menu and picked our pasta. A white English family sat on one side of us and on the other a middle-aged tourist couple ate in total silence. They reminded me of my own marriage.

The wine arrived and Alan toasted my health. 'Here's to our friendship,' he said. 'By the way, how are you getting on with Tony?'

'Fuck Tony,' I said. 'I don't want anything to do with him. Or Julia. I reckon she had a lot to do with getting me sacked. I hate her.'

'She's certainly one of the least spiritual people I've ever met,' said Alan.

That made me laugh. He was hardly Krishnamurti himself.

'Tony's in a bad way,' Alan said. 'He was arrested for drunk-driving yesterday.'

'You're kidding.'

'Well, it was bound to happen sooner or later. His lawyer had the case postponed for a month but I don't think Tony can really contest it. He was way over the limit. He got drunk at lunch and ran a red light.'

I remembered Tony weaving badly on his way out of the Chinese restaurant.

'You've got to be crazy to drive drunk these days,' I said. 'The police are really cracking down.'

'But you do it yourself, Steve!' Alan laughed.

'Me? That's a joke!' I said. Had he forgotten that he'd arranged for the Shōgun to be repossessed?

'Well, you must have been over the limit the night we went out to dinner with Liz,' he said.

I tensed, taking a sip of wine before I replied. 'Liz drove me home,' I said warily.

'Really? But your car wasn't there when I got up in the morning, was it?'

I choked on a mouthful of linguine. To my horror I realized that Alan had known of my return to the mews from the beginning.

'I picked it up early so I wouldn't get a clamp,' I mumbled.

'Before seven? Well, whatever you say, boss,' he laughed. 'But it sounds to me like you're in denial.'

I slumped in my seat. Alan had been ten steps ahead of me all the way along. There was no chance that he would let anything slip about Claire's whereabouts in the circumstances. We'd reached a temporary stalemate. When Alan insisted on paying the bill I put up only a token resistance.

I left him on Gloucester Road and headed for the photo-lab to collect my prints. The encounter had left me feeling despondent but the photographs went some way to restoring my spirits. They were better than I could have expected and included several clear shots of Alan and Julia cannibalizing each other in Park Lane. I had more than I needed.

Everything led back to Claire and I decided to see if I could find her house again. I used Kate's moped to comb the streets between Kensington High Street and the King's Road but it had been dark and I'd been drunk when we'd dropped Claire off that night. There were plenty of large houses with semi-circular drives. None of them jogged my memory. At one point I came across a wedding convoy of black limousines near Sloane Square with two more suckers riding the oblivion express at the head of the column. I wished them luck. At that very minute the royal red helicopter thwacked overhead, transporting The Man Who Would Be Tampon across London like a bird of ill omen. Unable to find Claire's house, I returned the moped to Kate's place. At Gloucester Road underground station the people on the platform seemed strangely artificial - unfeeling carbon statues, showroom dummies. I had the feeling that if I were to push one of them onto the electrified track, none of the others would bat an eyelid.

At East Putney I discovered that, in addition to the front wheel, the saddle of my mountain bike had now been stolen to leave a mutilated stump. I was livid. The skeleton was being picked clean and I'd only ever ridden the bike once. Soon just the padlock would be left, chained as a memento to the battered street furniture.

I needed a drink and stopped for a vodka in a grim thirties boozer at the end of a row of shops that had been cut adrift at the edge of a housing estate. The shops read like a list of idle pleasures - Tobacconist, Off Licence, Bookmaker's and Video rental store. There was Sky TV in the pub and the bar area was awash with Premier League football shirts. I pushed my way to the bar through a group of Crystal Palace supporters drinking their sugary pints of Wife-beater. I bought my vodka and sat by a bleary window that gave onto a world of concrete and tarmac. A sixties church spire bristled as sharp as a drawing pin on a teacher's chair, waiting for God to come back and take his seat.

I necked another vodka and left the pub for the leafy middle-class boulevards. I was trudging the long deserted avenue that skirted the golf course when the sun dropped behind a dark band of cloud and the shadows disappeared from the street. There were no playing children to give a purpose to the quiet bulk of the houses, only the whisper of a television set and the hissing pulse of an automatic lawn-sprinkler. The air was close and the street felt sad and empty. As I walked my mind wandered down melancholy violet groves of its own imagining.

I thought I heard someone following me.

When I looked round there was nobody to be seen, just the long road curving back towards the high street. As I walked on I became convinced that I could hear footsteps hitting the pavement a split-second after my own. I spun round and saw something disappear behind a tree. I crept back silently along the grass verge only to find that there was nothing there.

When I reached my house Mary Marighela's ageing Range Rover was parked alongside Liz's Punto in the driveway. Liz always liked to turn up the volume when the neighbours were away and disco music was pounding from inside the house. I recognized the track as Gloria Gaynor's 'I Will Survive', the spurned woman's anthem. I froze, horrified that Liz had somehow found out about my night with Kate.

'Go on now, go! Walk out the door!' yelled Gloria, belting out the soundtrack to a billion broken hearts. There was nobody around downstairs. I moved through to the back of the house as Gloria snatched victory from the jaws of defeat on the stereo in the sitting-room. The French windows were open onto the garden.

Liz and Mary were dancing around on the lawn, throwing disco shapes to the music. Mary was singing along with Gloria, using Liz's old purple plastic bong as a microphone.

Sofa-cushions were strewn on the grass and an empty bottle of Absolut vodka lay on its side. A large zip-loc bag of weed, several fashion magazines and chocolate wrappers were scattered on the grass. When the song ended Mary huddled down to re-light the bong and Liz looked round to see me watching them from the doorway.

'Steve!' she cried. Mary saw me too and they fell about laughing. I stood there feeling foolish.

'I'm sorry, Steve, it's just your face!' cried Liz. 'You look like you've seen a ghost!' It wasn't so far from the truth. I hadn't seen Liz that happy for years and I wondered at the transformation. I asked after Marla and Carl and Liz said that they were fine. Apparently they'd bought a Vietnamese pot-bellied pig.

I went to get myself a beer from the kitchen and returned to the garden where the women lay sprawled on the cushions. Gloria had made way for Sylvester's 'Mighty Real' and Liz had thankfully reduced the volume. Mary sucked smoke through the bong-water and Liz was flicking through a copy of *Vogue*. She held up a photograph of a bony pubescent model wearing a ball gown in a derelict building.

'It's lucky she's got big feet or she'd fall through that crack in the floorboards,' Liz giggled.

'Straight into an eating disorder clinic,' said Mary through a billowing cloud of smoke.

I swigged at my beer, feeling light-headed. 'Guess who I had lunch with today? Alan Denton,' I said. Liz sat up, startled. 'Yeah, I went up to town and I bumped into him in Kensington.'

'Really?' said Liz. 'What did you talk about?'

'Finding me a job,' I said. 'I thought maybe he could help with some contacts.'

'Great, Steve. That's really positive,' said Liz, relaxing a little. 'Steve wanted to kill Alan last week,' she said to Mary.

'I don't blame him,' said Mary, cross-legged in her halter-top.

'I can't afford to hold grudges, Liz. We need money,' I said.

Liz's shoulders slumped at the reminder of our troubles.

'I could really use a swim right now,' she said, glancing over at the empty pool. An aerosol line of bright green algae ran around its pale blue rim, iridescent in the evening light. It was going to cost two grand to replace the pump and I wondered if it was too late to cancel the contractor. Liz took some grass from the plastic bag and rolled a pure one-skin joint.

'D'you want some?' she asked me, proffering the wonky paper twist.

'You must be joking! You know what it does to me,' I said.

'That was because you were depressed. Things are different now.'

Maybe Liz was right, I thought, maybe things had changed. I was feeling reckless from the alcohol and I'd already taken two deep drags on the joint before Mary told me it came from California.

'What? What was that?' I asked, panic gripping my neck. I'd assumed it was the usual home-grown Liz scored from the guy at the health-food shop.

'A friend brought it back from San Francisco,' said Mary. 'They grow it all day and night with ultra-violet lamps in these huge factories. In the country. It's all high tech, like the wine and the silicone.'

'I know what it's like, Mary. I've smoked it before,' I said, getting to my feet. I felt dizzy.

'Just relax, Steve. You'll be fine,' said Liz.

I lay back down on a cushion and it felt as though my skin was being tightened like a drum across my face. Mary went through some t'ai chi moves down by the fence and I chatted to Liz as the rush intensified.

Liz told me that Mary had rowed with Lenny because Mary was missing Jonah and Lenny wanted to keep him in California for another week. Mary was particularly upset because Jonah had grown fond of Casey, Lenny's new rock-chick girlfriend.

It was probably the effect of the grass but I figured that if Liz and I divorced it wouldn't be the end of the world. At least we hadn't infected a kid with our problems. I thought about Tony Mold, pushing his triplets round the sad Sunday park with all the other divorced dads before heading back to a lonely flat to write out an alimony cheque, guzzle a solo take-away and ruin Kleenex over some ropy weather-man. I felt no guilt about sleeping with Kate.

The full moon began to rise through the trees and I wondered if Liz was sleeping with someone else too. The idea didn't bother me unduly. Liz read a magazine and I watched Mary making graceful shapes at the end of the garden. Then she segued into some Jeet Kune Do moves, chopping and kicking at an imaginary opponent. The odds favoured Lenny.

When the sun had disappeared, the three of us went inside to embark on the stoned preparation of an elaborate meal. A leg of lamb was roasting in the Aga and the smell caused saliva to spring forth at the back of my mouth. Liz set me to work on a bag of organic Brussels sprouts. They were so riddled with mould that I had to peel off half the leaves before carving an X into the sheared stalk. I dutifully prepared a pile of pale green dum-dum bullets. Mary sat beside me peeling carrots and cutting them into thin strips the length of a filter cigarette.

Liz skinned some peppers, removing the seeds before laying the red tongues in a dish like vegetarian fillet steaks. It was a tricky job, inconvenience food. I opened a bottle of sparkling wine and we ate a first course of rocket salad and shaved Parmesan. The wine gave the Parmesan a disagreeable taste of soft iron.

'This is delicious,' I lied, sucking the end of a rocket leaf into my mouth.

Liz removed the lamb from the oven and asked me to carve. As soon as I cut into the meat I could tell it needed another hour. It was red and fibrous, still breathing as I neared the bone. Liz said there was something wrong with the Aga and I tried not to think how much it would cost to repair. There was nothing to do but drink and smoke dope until the lamb was ready. Mary recharged the purple bong and started talking about astrology. I recalled that the previous Christmas she'd maintained that the Star of Bethlehem had been a UFO, a fact as incontrovertible in her mind as the occult provenance of crop-circles.

'I only wish I'd known more about the stars before I married Lenny,' she said. 'I'm Leo and he's Capricorn you know? We never stood a chance,' she said.

'Why don't Leos get along with Capricorns?' Liz asked, taking a pull on the bong.

'Leo's a fire sign, Capricorn is earth. They're opposite each other on the chart. Not at all compatible,' said Mary. I'd always thought the main problem had been Lenny's chronic drug habit.

'Which signs are meant to be compatible then?' I asked.

'Well, you're Gemini, right? You should be compatible with Leo,' said Mary.

'The rising sign's important though, isn't it?' asked Liz, clearly unable to imagine me living in domestic harmony with anybody.

'Oh, sure. It's all highly complex. You have to have your chart done,' Mary said, trying to hold in a lungful of smoke as she spoke. In consequence she sounded like a third-rate ventriloquist.

'I heard that the star signs were originally designed to fit the Persian calendar, and their year was much longer than ours,' I said.

'So what?' said Mary, not getting it.

'So they had to shoehorn it in to fit with ours. Apparently there's even a thirteenth star sign no one ever talks about, so it's all out of kilter,' I explained.

'It's more than out of kilter,' said Liz, her eyes glowing red from the dope. 'I know the guy who does the horoscopes for *Mode* and he just buys up old magazines from a street market and rewrites them.'

'Everyone knows newspaper horoscopes are rubbish. That's not what I'm talking about. You have to have your chart done properly,' said Mary.

'So you think the stars are up there moving us all around like chess-pieces? Do you really think they could be bothered?' I asked, lighting up another of her Marlboro Lights. The marijuana was wearing off and I felt flat and morose.

'The stars affect the tides, don't they? Why not us? We're mostly water after all,' said Mary.

'Do you know what's up there, Mary? Nothing,' I said. 'Too much of nothing.'

'God, you're so negative! You should try and get in touch with your spiritual side.'

I saw the pepper mill standing over on the sideboard and I was glad that it wasn't pulsing with cosmic energy, glad that I'd left my 'spiritual side' behind. I even wondered if I should start taking my lithium tablets again as I was due for another group session at the Webster the following day. Mary lit the bong and I took a hit. The cool smoke went straight to my head.

By the time the lamb was ready the courgettes-with-caraway seed had turned beige in the warming oven but no one minded. We ate fast with drugged hunger and when Liz had finished she reached across for Mary's grass.

'This stuff's too much without tobacco. Have we got any more cigarettes?' Liz asked.

'There should be some in my jacket. I left it in the hall,' I said, unable to move from the table. Liz went to get them and I asked Mary how her training was going.

'Pretty good. I've got a competition coming up and I'm in the gym three hours a day while Jonah's away. I've been practising some new stuff. This is "Monkey Grabbing the Peach".'

Mary stood up, threw an overarm punch into space and retracted it in one liquid movement.

'Wow, that's incredible,' I said.

Liz came back into the kitchen holding my photographs of Alan and Julia. I realized to my horror that I'd left them in my jacket.

'What are these, Steve?' Liz asked unevenly. Her face was washing-powder white.

'Just some old photos,' I stammered.

'That's bullshit, Steve! You've only just had them developed!' she cried. 'There's today's date on the packet!'

Liz threw the photographs on the table and burst into tears. When I tried to comfort her she fled into the garden and Mary followed her.

Stunned, I looked through the photographs. The kissing couple were clearly unaware that I had been photographing them, and I guessed that Liz was angry with me for spying on Alan and for lying about it so dismally. I cleared away the plates like a robot and Mary came back inside. I asked her if it would help if I apologized to Liz. I was woefully stoned from the bong.

'Don't worry, Steve. Liz'll be all right. She's just really stressed out at the moment. Incidentally, who is this woman?' Mary asked, picking up the prints.

'That's Julia, Sally's assistant. She was with Alan.'

'I can see that,' said Mary. 'But why on earth did you take pictures of them kissing?'

'I was just fooling around, that's all,' I said.

I went outside and found Liz sitting on the step, staring at the full moon. I sat next to her without speaking and she put a sisterly arm through mine. I apologized to her for lying about the photographs. My body felt as if it was made out of lead.

'It's not just the photographs, Steve. It's everything. I need to be on my own for a bit. I'm going to stay over at Mary's place tonight.'

She smiled emptily and I wondered if it was finally all over between us, if this was the big black full stop, the anti-moon.

15

Ash Monday

LIZ LEFT WITH MARY. The next morning I woke up alone, feeling abandoned and miserable. The Marlboro horses had stampeded through my chest leaving hoof-prints all over my lungs and a horseshoe twisted round my throat, tight as the tie on a bag of rubbish. Like a coalmine, my lungs were facing imminent closure. It took a considerable effort just to get out of bed. I dozed, picturing the Black Smoker on the ocean floor from which life on earth had originated, a Balkan Sobranie discarded by a litterbug god. I wished he'd stubbed it out properly and spared us all the aggravation.

The kitchen was bright with sunlight but it only served to pick out the dust on the shelves and on the top of the fridge. I took a lithium tablet and summoned the will to call Julia at In Deep.

'Steve! It's such good news that you're better! I've been thinking about you a lot. We all have,' she said.

She sounded surprised when I asked if we could meet to discuss my employment prospects.

'If you really think I can help, then, of course . . .'

'Is there any chance we could meet some time today?' I asked.

'Gosh, that's going to be difficult.'

'I know it's short notice but I've got the bit between my teeth. Just for half an hour. I need to pick your brains.'

'Well, I guess I could manage it. Two-thirty?'

'Good. But do you mind if we don't meet at the office? How about the English Muffin on the Piazza?'

'Fine. Two-thirty then. Ciao,' she said.

I called Tony on his mobile but it was switched off and I didn't want to call him through the Puffa switchboard. I brooded all morning, fighting the urge to call Liz at Mary's house. I put on a suit for my meeting with Julia and took a tube to Covent Garden.

On the Piazza a couple of young street entertainers wearing black body stockings and Dr Martens were throwing each other around on a blue plastic mat. A coachload of Austrian tourists gazed on, unblinking as a herd of cattle. I was lucky to find a free pavement table at the English Muffin. The air was hot and sticky. Although the shops on the Piazza bustled with punters, most of them were just window-shopping.

A backpacker stopped right in front of my table to consult a fold-out map of central London. His ice cream dripped from the cone to form another pale pink Serpentine in Hyde Park. The Canadian maple leaf was sewn onto the back of his nylon pack. He turned to ask me for directions to Trafalgar Square, stressing the final syllable of Trafalgar, and I gave him a complex set of instructions designed to leave him stranded in an urban no-man's-land to the east of Aldwych. I made him repeat each twist and turn of the route until I was sure he'd memorized it.

He was thanking me profusely when I saw Julia clicking across the cobbles in a white silk shirt. She was wearing her engagement ring, a five-grand rock. Dollar signs must have dinged up in her eyes when the plank had put it on her finger.

'Steve, darling! You look wonderful. It's so good to see you. God, it must have been awful, being in hospital and everything.' She sat down and ordered a Perrier water.

'Thanks, Julia. I'm a lot better now thanks.'

'Do they know what caused it? Your breakdown, I mean?' she asked, blinking with concern.

'Oh, pressures at work, that kind of thing.' A mother dragged a screaming child out of a book shop and twisted his ear.

'So you're looking for a new job? That's great.' She smiled and her mask of white make-up cracked in the heat.

'Yeah. But I'm also trying to work out what happened to my last one. I can't quite grasp the chain of events, you see. I thought Alan wanted to dump Tony but then it seems he changed his mind at the last minute. It doesn't make sense.'

'It was a business decision, Steve. That's all. I really don't think there's any point in going into it again, do you?' She pursed her lips but I knew how much it was costing her to suppress her natural urge to dish the dirt.

'Please, Julia. It's important for me to know what really happened. Surely you can understand that?'

'But I don't know the details. All I can tell you is that Sally and I were very pleased that Alan wanted to buy into the company.' She lit a Kent cigarette with a Cartier lighter. Her plum lipstick had begun to melt and bleed into tiny tributaries around her mouth.

'Yeah,' I said, 'but if he'd already bought Tony's shares

then Alan could do as he pleased. He could have sacked Tony at the board meeting without my agreement.'

'I imagine Alan had given Tony his word that he could stay on if he sold him his shares.'

'His word! What's Alan's word worth?' I spluttered.

Julia sat forward. 'Look, I understand that you're angry, Steve, but we're here to talk about your future. I haven't got much time and I honestly have no idea what was going through Alan's mind, okay?'

'Like hell you don't!' I flipped the photos from Trader Vic's on the table in front of her.

She squinted at them. When she saw herself clinched with Alan on a Mayfair street her lips puckered into a shocked 'O'.

'Where did you get these? You have no right! I can't believe you'd do this!' she squealed. An Italian tourist at the next table turned round to give me a disapproving look and I glared back at him.

'Believe it, Julia. But don't worry, I'm not going to flash them around. I just want you to tell me what really happened.' She flushed, venomous.

'You disgusting little pervert! This is blackmail!' She got up to go and I laid a heavy hand on her wrist, reeling off her husband's full name and their address in Surrey. It had the desired effect.

'Oh, gosh,' she said and started to sniffle. Then an idea bubbled up in her head. 'But what's to say you didn't take these last year or the year before?'

I picked up one of the photos and held it up to her. 'When did you buy the Armani suit?' She scanned the photo for a way out and then sagged back in defeat.

'Okay, what do you want? Money?' she asked wearily, as if she was actually sick of the stuff. I almost felt sorry for her in her power-clothes, clothes she could ill afford on what Sally would be paying her. I guessed she'd only married the plank at the bank in order to upgrade her wardrobe.

'I just want you to answer some questions. If you tell me the truth I'll give you the photos.' I could see that she was relieved.

'*And* the negatives?' she asked.

'And the negatives.'

'How do I know you haven't made another set of prints?'

'Trust me, I haven't. All I want is information and it won't cost you a penny,' I said.

Julia shrugged.

'When did you start seeing Alan?' I asked. She took a gulp of Perrier and pumped it south.

'Just the last few months. We were working together and it just sort of happened. It was very strange, very wonderful for both of us. There hasn't been anyone else. Not since my marriage.' Julia had been married for less than a year but I let it pass.

'When did Alan tell you he wanted to keep Tony and drop me?' I asked.

'God, he planned to get rid of you all along! He wanted you out and he used Tony to do it. He had it all worked out.'

'I don't understand! I thought I was doing a great job with the wholesale business.' Despite her predicament Julia smiled in the knowledge that she'd scored a direct hit. I knew she was telling the truth. My theory about Claire started to crumble.

'So what? Look, Steve, Alan wants the company for himself. You were a hindrance, surplus to requirements. And he thought you were becoming erratic and unstable. It turned out he was right, didn't it?' she said with a sneer. I sat there unable to speak. 'You're a shit, Steve. A creepy little nutcase and I hope I never see you again.'

She got up to leave. I handed her the photos and the negatives without a murmur.

'I hope you fucking die,' she said.

I sat rooted to my seat, unable to move. The rest of the world fell away. The noise, the shoppers, the buildings disappeared down a tunnel. I'd lost my job, my marriage, my sanity. I felt faint. Everything was fucked up and I was alone. My idiotic obsession with Claire had blinded me to the simple truth that Alan wanted power. I'd got it all wrong from the very beginning.

Eventually a waitress asked me to leave. I stood up feeling dazed. I was meant to go to Group but I wandered the streets in despair, insubstantial as a ghost. Finding myself near Kate's flat at six o'clock, I rang her bell to find she hadn't yet returned from the Webster. I still had the key to her moped so I drove over to the pub at the end of Alan's mews and started drinking lager. I wanted to see Alan one more time just to look him in the eye and tell him that I knew he'd double-crossed me.

I didn't expect Alan to come home for an hour or more but before I'd taken a sip of my third pint he walked into the pub and marched up to where I was sitting.

'What the hell are you doing here, Steve?' he said, standing over the table. I spilt some beer.

'I'm having a drink, Alan. What do you think I'm doing?' I glanced at the publican who was wiping the counter. Alan couldn't try anything. 'Why don't you sit down,' I said.

'I got your little note this morning and if you really think

I'm going to pay you fifty grand you're off your fucking head,' he said, trying to keep his voice low.

'What are you talking about. What note?' I asked.

'Don't give me that shit! Blackmail. Julia tells me you tried something like this on her this afternoon.'

'You think I'm trying to blackmail you because you've been fucking Julia? Get a life!' It was absurd.

'Don't get clever with me, you fucking psycho! You know exactly what I'm talking about! You've been following me. I saw you on that bloody moped the other day for Christ's sake!' The publican was staring at us but Alan was oblivious, twitching like a robot with a glitch in its circuitry.

'I'm just waiting to see my therapist. I told you she lives round here.'

'Shut up! I went to La Paesana last night and Luigi told me you'd even been down there asking questions about me.'

'Why should I want to ask questions about you? It must have been someone else. Maybe it was the police,' I said.

'Bullshit. Luigi described you perfectly. And someone's stolen my house key from the office. I bet you've got it on you right now, haven't you?' His knuckles were white and I was uncomfortably aware of the Banham key in my jacket pocket. 'Blackmail's a crime too, Steve, and if I go down I'm taking you with me. You just keep your fucking mouth shut. We've got each other by the balls on this.'

'Is that right?' I said and smiled.

He'd done something that was going to put him in jail and I was exultant. It wasn't just greed. Alan was bad from deep inside and it coiled up in his eyes as I watched. His face changed shape the way it had done outside Puffa, as if something had taken over the controls and rearranged his physiognomy to suit its dark design. I expected Alan to explode into violence, to run amok at any moment.

My hand inched towards the Canada Dry ashtray on the table between us. Alan leant forward and grabbed my arm roughly.

'Give it a break,' I said. 'I'm still convalescing.'

Something clicked behind his eyes.

'Shit, you've broken into my house, haven't you? You've been in my bloody house! That's how you found out about it, isn't it?'

Alan got up and ran into the mews. I followed him outside, put on the helmet and started the moped. I wanted to get away from there before he came back. I braked to turn left onto Gloucester Road but the moped just kept going, out of control.

The brakes didn't respond, the pedal flapped uselessly. I sailed across the road in a wide arc into the path of an oncoming car.

The moped slid from under me and everything went into slow-motion. I had time to read a sign in the window of an Off Licence - Carlsberg retailing at 89p a can.

I hit the tarmac, taking the impact on my hip and my forearm.

Tyres squealed. I braced myself for a sudden bone-crushing, flesh-tearing thud. It didn't come. I opened my eyes and looked round to see the nose of a maroon Ford Mondeo just two feet from my face. There was a smell of burning rubber.

I got up and limped to the side of the road to sit on the kerb. A junior executive got out of the Mondeo and wheeled the moped over to me.

'You all right, mate? Nothing broken?' he asked in a south-London accent, pushing his Ray-Bans back on his forehead.

'I don't think so.'

'Christ, you're lucky I went for the ABS option or you'd be brown bread by now,' he said. 'Brakes, was it? Looked like your brakes.'

I limped around a bit and the pain didn't get any worse. I'd torn a flap of skin off the heel of my hand and there was an MTV-friendly rip in the knee of my 501s. When I put my fingers into the hole there was thankfully no blood to be found. The moped's fairing was cracked, the handlebars were bent out of shape and a length of brake cable hung loose from the rear wheel.

I inspected the cable and saw that it had been snipped in two, a shear cut. I followed the length of the front brake cable and found that it had also been sabotaged.

It had been no accident.

Alan had seen the moped outside the pub and cut the cables. I was lucky to be alive. I caught a cab back to Kate's place, cursing myself for being so careless. My mind was spinning too fast to think straight. I waited for Kate on the steps of her building. Fifteen minutes later she drove up in the Audi.

'Steve! Where have you been? I've been so worried! You missed Group and then Alan Denton called me at the clinic. He says you've been following him around, spying on him. You smell of drink too. How much have you had?' She noticed my bleeding hand. 'Jesus, what happened?'

'I fell off your moped,' I said. 'Alan cut the brake cables. He accused me of blackmailing him.'

'Blackmailing him? About what?'

'I'm not sure. But he just tried to kill me, Kate.'

'Don't be so stupid!' she scoffed. 'You're drunk.'

We climbed the stairs to her flat and she went to the bathroom for some disinfectant and a plaster.

'I only had a pint, I swear. How did Alan know how to get hold of you?'

'That's no great mystery. He just phoned the Webster and asked to speak to your doctor. When did you start following him?' She took my hand to disinfect the cut.

'I haven't been following him. I bumped into him a couple of times, that's all.' The disinfectant made me wince.

'You've got to tell me the truth, Steve,' Kate said, nailing me with her professional look as she applied the plaster.

'I was just having a drink in a pub near Alan's house. He came in and accused me of blackmailing him! He thinks that I sent him a note demanding fifty grand to keep quiet. I think it's got something to do with that night in the mews. He knows I went back there to get my car.'

Kate looked disappointed. 'You haven't been taking your lithium, have you?' she asked.

'Of course I have. Do you think I want another break-down?' I said. 'We have to report this to the police. Alan tried to kill me just now!'

'It can wait until tomorrow. Look, it may just be the shock of falling off the moped, but I think there's a possibility that you're becoming manic.'

I went pale at the prospect, terrified that Kate was going to section me.

'I'm going to give you something to calm you down,' she said. I recognized her no-nonsense tone from the Webster. 'And you've got to stop obsessing about Alan.'

'I promise,' I said, a pair of fingers crossed in my pocket as

185

a childhood reflex. It had been a mistake to stop taking the lithium. I needed to be calm and grounded when I made my report at the police station. As it was, I was spinning from the encounters with Julia and Alan.

I swallowed Kate's pill and was surprised when she put her arms around me, kissing me on the lips. Kate hadn't alluded to our night together and I'd thought she wanted to forget about it. She put a couple of frozen pizzas in the oven and we canoodled on the sofa while they heated up.

'How did Alan sound on the phone?' I asked.

'Listen, that's enough about Alan, okay?'

The pill gave me a soft woozy feeling, a rubbery glow that was by no means unpleasant. When the pizzas were ready we sat with them on our laps in front of the television but I was still too wound up to eat.

'Where's your appetite?' Kate asked.

She put her pizza-crust aside and straddled me on the sofa, pinning my arms to my side with her knees while she force-fed me a mouthful of pizza. She shifted her weight onto my crotch and the pressure made me hard.

'That's better,' she said, putting the pizza aside. She unzipped my fly and took my cock in her hand. I swallowed the pizza and pulled her mouth down onto mine.

'Steady,' she said.

Kate stood up and led me along the corridor by my cock, pulling me into her bedroom. I stripped, watching as she peeled off her tights, unbuttoned her shirt and took off her bra. My heart was pounding and my cock throbbed, bouncing up like a dowser's wand with each heartbeat. We rolled around on the bed, using our hands and our mouths on each other. Kate gripped my cock and I put two fingers inside her. She reached over for a condom and rolled it onto me with feverish urgency.

Neither of us could wait. Kate was panting and I took her on the side of the bed. She slammed herself against my thrusts, her eyes wild and unfocused. All too soon I felt a wave rise unexpectedly inside me. I couldn't hold back. My cock spurted like a crop-sprinkler. I was horrified that it had happened so fast. Kate was twitching beneath me with an unsatisfied lust.

'Shit,' I said.

'Never mind,' she said, pulling me into her arms. We kissed and she stroked my chest. I slid down to the floor and kissed her pussy. It smelt rich and heady like plankton but I could taste a hint of the condom's spermicidal lubricant. I licked at Kate's clitoris and stroked her until she began to writhe and moan. After a while my cock came back to life.

We ended up making love on the floor. Kate adjusted the angle of her hips to suit her better and placed my own fingers between us to rub against her clitoris. I began to get carpet burns on my knees so I lifted her onto the bed. We fell into a steady rhythm and I wondered what I could be doing to help her come. Kate rolled over to straddle me, riding back and forth along my cock. Finally, she started to tremble.

'Oh, God, I'm coming,' she moaned. 'Are you coming? Tell me you're coming, Steve!'

I gasped in agreement.

She went to work on her orgasm and I felt waves of red heat coming off her skin as her nervous, vascular and muscular systems built towards her climax. The muscles in her pelvis contracted as she came, bringing on my own weak orgasm seconds later. Kate sighed with contentment and we lay on the bed and dozed for a while.

When I knew she was asleep I crept along to the sitting room and phoned home. Liz was out and I left a message that I was staying at Tony's place. I left one for Tony asking him to cover for me, reminding him that I'd done the same for him a hundred times when he'd been married. Then I got back into bed with my psychiatrist.

The next day Kate went to work. We enjoyed a long goodbye kiss against an eczema-tree in the street and I felt reasonably clear-headed. I told her that I had to go home, but I promised that I would come to the Webster for Group at two o'clock. When she'd driven off I went back to the moped and wheeled it to Kensington Police Station at the top of Earl's Court Road. A cop eyed me with suspicion as I parked the moped on a solo motorcycle bay. I felt a vestigial twinge of police para- noia as I approached the blue lantern and entered the station. At the desk I informed a white-haired sergeant that Alan Denton had tried to kill me the previous evening.

The sergeant raised his eyebrows and led me to an inter- view room. I sat impatiently on a battered chair while he entered my name and address on an incident sheet. On the table stood a tape recorder that looked as if it had come second-hand from a language school. The sergeant didn't switch it on.

I told him about Alan's sabotage, about his accusation of blackmail and the violent commotion that I'd overheard when I'd gone back to collect my car from his house. He heard me out with a look of bored disbelief.

'Did you actually see Mr Denton cut the brake cables, sir?' he asked.

'Of course not! Do you really think I'd have driven the moped if I'd known the brakes had been tampered with?' The sergeant was clearly slow in the head from banging it against his promotion ceiling.

'How would you describe your relationship with Mr Denton, sir?' he asked.

'We used to work together but I'm no longer with the company,' I said.

He sighed and asked me for the registration number of my moped.

I explained that it didn't belong to me, that I was just borrowing it. He asked me who actually owned it and I gave him Kate's name and address. When he asked me to describe my relationship with Dr Parker, I told him that she was my psychiatrist at the Webster Clinic in Marylebone.

'I see, sir. Are you receiving treatment from Doctor Parker?'

'As a matter of fact I am, yes. As an outpatient.' His eyes twinkled mirthlessly.

'Thank you for coming in to see us, sir. I'm going to make a note of this interview and file it. And if anything else comes to light, you be sure and come and tell us, all right?'

'But don't you want to have a look at the moped? Do some forensic tests?'

'I don't think so, sir. No. That'll be all for now.'

I could hardly believe it. He stood up and opened the door for me, allowing himself a smile as he ushered me back to the reception area. I sat on my fury and pushed the moped to a nearby garage. At least the Cypriot mechanic was in no two minds about what had happened to the brake cables.

'You're quite bloody right, mate. They've been clipped straight through. The outer casing and all,' he said. 'Bloody vandals.' He said he could fix it the following day. I used the pay phone in the office to call Tony on his mobile.

'Tone, it's Steve. Can you talk?' I asked him.

'Yeah. There's only me and Gudrun here. We've lost the Paraguayan deal and it looks bad. Sally might even pull the plug. Alan was freaking out and now he's taken the rest of the day off.'

'What reason did he give?' I asked. Something was happening. Alan had never missed a single day's work.

'I don't know, but Gudrun said he phoned his bank and arranged to draw a load of cash from his private account. And so much for your crackpot theory that he murdered that girl Claire. She's a blonde chick, really young, right?'

'Yeah? And?' Adrenalin flooded the back of my neck.

'She was here an hour ago. Alan's taken her out to lunch.'

'D'you know where they went?'

'I've got no idea. But Claire seemed fairly animated for a stiff.'

'Maybe he told Gudrun. Why don't you ask her?'

'No way, Steve.'

'If you don't I'll ring her myself.'

'Hang on.' I heard him call through to Reception. 'Steve? Are you still there?'

'Tell me,' I said.

'Gudrun booked them a table at the Fish Plaice. Near Leicester Square. For one o'clock. Listen, Steve, don't . . .'

I hung up. I knew the restaurant. It was ten to one. I took a tube to the West End. I bought a plaid shirt, dark glasses and a black Smurf cap with NYC embroidered on the front from a shop in the Trocadero Centre, threw my flight jacket in a litter bin and took up position in a Wendyburger franchise from where I could see the door of the Fish Plaice.

I couldn't risk a look inside the Fish Plaice and struggle to contain my curiosity. At two o'clock I succumbed to the dubious pleasure of a cheeseburger. The cheese looked and tasted like a slice of Vapona fly-killer. I was chewing the burger when Alan came out of the Fish Plaice wearing a leather jacket. He held the door open behind him. I choked on a mouthful of dead cow as a blonde girl followed him out of the door wearing a man's raincoat. It was Claire. My mind fish-tailed across the highway. Was she the blackmailer? Neither of them were smiling and Claire looked miserable.

16

Hot Dog

I DROPPED THE CHEESEBURGER INTO A GREEN LITTER-BIN sponsored by BFI Wastecare and followed Alan and Claire along Panton Street. Two hundred starlings changed direction as one above the trees as they entered Leicester Square. Alan put a hand on Claire's shoulder but she kept her own hands in her pockets. They walked up to the entrance of the Prince William Cinema and went inside beneath a sixty-foot billboard advertising *Jurassic Park: The Producer's Cut*. The film had been re-released with ten minutes of previously unseen dinosaur action to coincide with the school holidays and an upcoming film festival.

I slipped in through the push-bar doors. Alan and Claire were crossing the vast expanse of nylon carpeting on which the cinema chain's red and blue logo repeated itself like a computer virus. Alan bought tickets and they disappeared into the auditorium. I went over to the ticket booth. A Sikh in a lime-green bow-tie asked if he could help me.

'I'm with the couple who just bought tickets. The red-haired guy and the girl in the raincoat. Do you know where they're sitting?' I asked.

'The seats aren't numbered for the afternoon performance, but your friends bought tickets for the stalls. The usher will show you.'

I bought myself a ticket and walked over to the pink neon frenzy of the refreshment booth. Still hungry, I scanned the health-free fare on offer in the kiosk. Bright orange frankfurters revolved on steel rollers beneath an infra-red lamp like test-tubes in a chemical weapons laboratory. I ordered a hot dog and a chocolate-taste milkshake to sort out my blood-sugar level. The saleslady smiled at me, adjusted her ludicrous paper hat and picked a hot white bun from the metal spike of an electrified iron maiden. Into this she inserted a furter to form the hot dog. On the wall behind her hung a diploma from a Salesforce Initiative Development course that the Puffa shop staff had attended with no discernible effect on our sales figures. I paid and bit through the plasti-bap, puncturing the orange sheath to release the hot pig slurry compressed within. Despite the scarlet ketchup it tasted ugly. I guzzled the thing and felt it come to rest like a doodle-bug in my upper digestive tract as I made my way to the auditorium.

Just as I reached the swing doors Claire came out and bumped straight into me, spilling my shake. I looked down and mumbled an apology as I brushed past her into the red half-light of the auditorium. I prayed that she hadn't recognized me.

A catatonic usher tore my ticket, indicated the block of seats below the aisle, and I peered into the gloom looking for Alan. When my eyes had adjusted I saw that he was sitting fifteen feet in front of me, just five rows down. He didn't look round as I sloped away to the side of the auditorium with the Smurf cap pulled low over my eyes.

The cinema was nearly empty, dotted with a few lonely adults killing a dull Tuesday afternoon. Spoilt for choice, I picked a seat in the back row of Alan's section, right up against the barrier, some twenty feet from him. I sat down on spongy velour and looked up at the ceiling which sparkled with a thousand tiny lights. Claire returned with a dustbin of popcorn and Alan put his arm along the back of her seat.

I wished I'd bought a Cola instead of the milkshake, something capable of cutting through the residue of grease left in my mouth by the frankfurter. I gurgled up the vestiges of the half-litre shake and felt the first twinge of indigestion. A plangent Carpenters' tune washed the auditorium: 'Rainy Days and Mondays'. I listened to poor bulimic Karen, wasting away somewhere out in the ether.

I felt sick. Perhaps like Karen and Maria I had 'a problem around food'. The house lights dimmed, the curtain rose in rayon ruches and I saw Alan shift in his seat to get comfortable for the film. The trailers were followed by advertisements for the season's new emetic liqueurs and then the lights came up again as the speakers exhorted us to purchase more refreshments. I felt awful. Like a drug mule on a long-haul flight, I had the feeling that something terrible might be about to happen in my stomach.

The lights dimmed for the main feature and soon the film was zipping through a bewildering array of locations. I was too nervous, too curious about Alan and Claire to follow the plot. I made a plan to follow Claire when she left the cinema and effect a chance encounter with her on the street. After a while I felt the need to relieve myself so I walked like an

Egyptian down the narrow row and out onto the main aisle towards the purple pool of a TOILETS light.

When I got back to my seat a baby dinosaur was hatching from an egg only to be fondled by Richard Attenborough. I hoped that in some parallel universe a baby 'Dickie' was at that very moment being delivered into the sharp claws of a Tyrannosaurus Rex. I looked over and saw Alan and Claire staring at the screen, utterly engrossed in the film.

I closed my eyes to think things through and the after-image of Alan's profile was etched on my retina. Claire was the key and I felt that if I pressed her she would tell me what I needed to know. A long chase sequence ensued on screen and I found myself gripped by the stream of images. As Laura Dern faced death-by-dinosaur I glanced over to where Alan and Claire were sitting.

They were no longer there.

I jerked up in my seat and panicked.

I rushed out to look for them in the foyer. A manager in a lime green blazer was arranging a pile of promotional material by the glass doors, and I asked him if anyone had left the cinema since the beginning of the performance. He shook his head. I raced back into the auditorium and climbed up into the circle, thinking that Alan and Claire might have sneaked up into better seats. I was nearing the back of the auditorium when a torch clicked on, the beam hitting my aching belly like a laser gun.

'You have a ticket?' asked a disembodied female voice. It was an usher. When I showed her my stub she clucked her tongue and herded me back down to the cheap seats, illuminating the steps with her torch. I scanned the stalls frantically as we descended the stairway.

Then I saw Claire moving along one of the front rows, clearly silhouetted against the screen. She sat down and I felt a huge sense of relief. If Alan had walked out and left her to watch the film on her own, so much the better.

The dinosaurs rampaged as I took my seat but I kept an eye on Claire. I couldn't afford to lose her again. The film's plot was just a paper-clip holding the special effects sequences together. My stomach ached and I shifted in my seat, imagining the orange frankfurter wriggling through my guts like a day-glo pot-holer. Someone passed along the aisle directly behind me but when I looked round there was no one there. The film dragged on and my head began to throb. I needed one of Tony's Solpadeine tablets. My skin felt hot and prickly. I wondered if I'd picked up a virus. My forehead was boiling. When I sat forward, my hand brushed the seat and encountered a blob of molten chewing-gum glued to the velour. Beads of sweat broke out on my face as the frankfurter began to jog along the tow-path of my alimentary canal.

My legs itched in my jeans and I shivered, cold sweat freezing on the front of my T-shirt. My body-temperature had gone haywire but I determined to tough it out until the film was over. A lava-lamp bubbled in my stomach. I was desperate for fresh air but I couldn't risk losing Claire. I saw that Alan had re-joined her. Squirming in my seat, I was convinced that I'd been poisoned by the frankfurter. New symptoms fell into place like the pieces of a jigsaw puzzle. A nauseous spasm supported my diagnosis and an unbearable thirst confirmed it. In fact this raging thirst soon supplanted all my other symptoms. Like a dehydrated E-head in a night-club lavatory, my blotting-paper tongue probed my mouth for moisture. I glanced at the luminous dial of my watch.

The film couldn't go on for much longer.

The thirst was unbearable and I was soaked with sweat. I thought I was about to faint. I had to get a drink of water right away.

I stood up gingerly and a wave of nausea threatened to capsize me. It was even worse than I'd expected. Using the backs of the seats for support, I edged down the row. My shirt was gummy on my back as I made it out into the aisle on jelly-legs. I reached the EXIT and shuffled down the steps into the foyer, heading for the refreshment kiosk where the sales-lady sat reading *Hello!* magazine. I navigated towards her across the sea-swell of carpet and asked her for a glass of water.

'Sorry, we don't do water. Lemonade?' she said. I swayed slightly and leaned on the counter.

'Are you all right?' the sales-lady asked. My eyes were pulling in and out of focus. My flesh felt like wet cold putty.

'I'm fine. Just a touch of flu. I'll take a giant lemonade, please.' I was shivering. She picked up a metal hose, pressed a numbered button on the head and squirted clear liquid into a paper bucket.

'Here you go. Are you sure you don't want to sit down?' she asked. I shook my head as she handed me the litre of 7Up. I needed both hands in order to drink it.

'That'll be one pound forty,' she said. I paid, swallowed another mouthful and turned to go. When she saw my back the saleslady screamed. I spun round as the cinema manager ran towards me in his lime-green blazer.

'Hey! What's happening here?' he asked, grabbing me by the shoulder.

'Look at his back, Shafraz! He's covered in blood! It's all down his legs too, look!' shrieked the saleslady, trapped behind the counter. She was already reaching for the phone as Shafraz turned me round.

'Call an ambulance, Denise. Quick!' he urged.

She tapped out three nines on the wall phone.

Mute with terror I probed my lumbar region. It was wet and sticky. When I drew my hand away it was covered with dark treacly blood. It glistened, brown beneath the pink neon light. I passed out.

I came round in a hospital bed, groggy and rubber-mouthed with sedatives. My left hand was attached to Liz, my right to a bag of transparent drip. The plastic tube disappeared beneath a gauze bandage on the back of my hand. A tiny green plastic tap protruded from the dressing. The sac of clear liquid had drawn up a thin plume of my blood along the tube to drift in suspension like slow-motion cigarette smoke, as though a blob of ectoplasm was slowly sucking my lifeblood away. I sat bolt upright and Liz settled me back down on the pillows. There was something on my neck, a foam-rubber neck-support like the one Alan had worn on his visit to the Webster.

'It's okay, Steve. It's all over. You're safe,' said Liz, trying to mask her own anxiety with a wobbly smile. She had dark rings around her eyes and it even looked as if she'd dressed in a hurry for once. Yin and Yang cleaved together on her T-shirt like a pair of co-dependent teardrops.

'What's that in there?' I asked, pointing to the sac.

'It's just glucose and antibiotics, that's all. Try not to move about. You thrashed around and jogged the needle,' she said. Liz was so tense that she sounded almost bad-tempered. 'They're going to change the bag in a minute. It's nothing serious. You're going to be fine. I'm just so glad you're safe.'

'What happened, Liz? What the fuck happened to me?'

'You were attacked in the cinema. Someone cut the back of your neck with a razor-blade. And you lost an awful lot of blood, nearly three pints.' Liz bit down hard on her lip as if she planned to shed some of her own in sympathy.

'Jesus,' I said, feeling the back of my neck. I slid my fingers up beneath the back of the support and made out a long row of stitches through the gauze just below my hairline.

'Do the police know who did it?'

'Not yet. I know it's horrible but you're all right now. They gave you a blood transfusion. You can go home tomorrow probably, maybe the day after.' I could see the strain in her eyes. 'I can't believe anyone would do this, just attack you like that. It's totally insane. The doctor said you were really lucky.'

'I don't feel so lucky right now. And I don't understand how come I didn't feel anything when it happened.'

'The doctor said you wouldn't feel it much necessarily. It was clean like a paper cut and it wasn't that deep. It looks like he did a good job with the stitches. Very neat.'

'How many stitches?'

'About fifteen, I guess. Very small though. I had a look when they changed the dressing.'

'Great,' I said. I felt the stitches again, visualizing them as a row of black flies feeding on the wound, sipping at a secondary mouth.

'Try and rest, Steve.'

'Where am I?' I asked. For an awful moment I thought I was back in the Webster.

'Torville Ward, St Thomas's,' said Liz. The room was small and there was an empty bed squeezed in next to mine. The window gave onto the Thames and across the water the Houses of Parliament shone pink and tangerine in the evening light. I turned back to Liz and noticed that she was sporting a new black DKNY handbag. Donna Karan wasn't known for her competitive pricing policy and it irritated me that Liz had been wasting our dwindling funds.

'I like the new bag,' I said.

'It is nice, isn't it?' Liz said. 'But don't fret, we haven't got to worry about money for a while. Dad's given me some shares to sell.'

This surprised me. I didn't think Gerald had any shares left after the Lloyd's fiasco. There had even been talk of selling his six-bedroom Georgian spread in Hampshire. I started to question Liz about the shares but she cut me off angrily.

'What were you doing in that cinema, Steve? You were sniffing about after Alan, weren't you? The police questioned him.'

The mention of Alan's name brought it all back to me. Each detail pricked through the sedatives like a new tooth.

'Has he been arrested yet?' I asked.

'Of course not, but the police are making his life hell. They went round to his house and interviewed him again this morning. He rang me up to find out how you were. He sounded really upset. It was embarrassing. He said you've been pestering him again. I thought you'd stopped all that.'

'But Alan's guilty! He did this!'

'Oh, that's nonsense!'

At that moment Tony walked into the room and Liz stood up to greet him. She tried to be civil to Tony but they didn't like each other. The atmosphere was sticky with small talk. We discussed the gruesome nature of the attack and the increasingly violent nature of city life. I didn't bring up Alan's name again because I didn't want to antagonize Liz. I was disappointed that he wasn't yet behind bars and I wanted a chance to tell the police what had happened. I could hardly wait to see the look on Liz and Tony's faces when they heard that Alan had been charged, when they discovered that I'd been right about him all along.

Liz made her excuses and left. Tony stayed on to regale me with an account of his own problems with the law.

'Friday was the pits, Steve. I was breathalysed just after I left you. They took me to Bow Street and stuck me in a cell to wait for a blood test. I'd refused to piss, you see. I knew they'd have to get a doctor in if I asked for a blood test and I'd have a bit more time to sober up.' Tony winced at the iniquity of it all.

'Then what?' I asked.

'So I was in the cell and knew I'd got to exercise like a bastard, really sweat the booze out. So I started running on the spot, did a few press-ups. I thought I was going to blow a valve. Then I did some sit-ups and a curtain of blood came down across my eyeballs, like at the beginning of a Bond film. And I bloody passed out, didn't I? Woke up with the doctor standing over me. He took some blood and I was way over the limit. My lawyer managed to put off the case till next month but I'm going to lose my licence. No question. Then Alan drove me home and gave me a load of grief in the car. And when I got into the flat I found that Jim had made off with the CD, the telly and five hundred quid in cash. I felt like sticking my head in the oven. I would have if it hadn't been a microwave.'

'You're looking a lot better, Tone. Have you started jogging again?'

'God, no. It's all down to AA. I really hit rock bottom with this driving thing. I've been to four meetings now.'

Tony beamed with the zeal of the new convert and told me how he'd come to recognize his drinking as a disease over which he had no control.

'It's like I'm seeing everything from a new perspective. It's really incredible. You should see for yourself.'

'Me? Do you think I'm an alcoholic?' I asked. It was the least of my problems.

'That's for you to decide. I wouldn't want to be judgmental, but I don't think it would do you any harm to come to a meeting.'

He treated me to a smug little smile. I wanted to tell him to get lost but I stopped myself in time. Any display of anger at this point would merely indicate the depth of my denial.

'Maybe so, Tone. Maybe so,' I said. He gave me a packet of Marlboro and a little Alcoholics Anonymous pamphlet.

'It takes you through the Twelve Steps of the recovery programme. Enjoy.'

'Only twelve? You're going to need at least thirty-nine, Tone. By the way, I was right about Alan being a violent psychopath.'

'You're not saying that he did this now, are you?'

'Time will tell, Tone. Time will tell.'

Tony gave me a condescending smile and left to attend his fifth AA meeting. I wondered when the police would arrive to interview me.

That night a frail old man was wheeled into my room and lifted onto the other bed. He snored loudly, practising for his death rattle. In the middle of the night I woke to hear him making a dreadful choking sound and I rang the buzzer above my bed. A nurse took one look at him and ran off to get a teenage doctor. The doctor began to whump down on his chest. The nurse tried to give him air but his tank didn't work and she had to drag one over from beside my bed. When the cardiac team arrived the old man was already dead. After they'd wheeled him off to the mortuary two nurses scrubbed his mattress down for what seemed like an hour. One of them gave me a sleeping-pill the size of an M&M but I didn't sleep again that night. I couldn't help wondering if the old man would have lived if he had been on a private ward.

The following morning a nurse changed my dressing and introduced me to Dr Miller, a psychiatrist in his late twenties with designer stubble and a saxophone badge on the lapel of his second-hand jacket. Miller told me that he'd managed to obtain my notes from the Webster and that he'd prescribed lithium and a tranquillizer for shock. A blood test had shown that my lithium level was very low and he asked me when I'd stopped taking it. I told him that I might have forgotten once or twice. He gave me a little lecture on the importance of taking medicine as directed. When he told me that the police wanted to talk to me I said I was more than ready to oblige.

I lunched on lukewarm lasagne and two detectives came to see me that afternoon, young Kindergarten Cops in suits and ties. The taller one, DC Robson, told me that they were treating the attack as Attempted Murder. I liked the sound of that. It would mean a long sentence for Alan when a jury convicted him.

I explained how I'd gone to the West End and followed Alan Denton and Claire to the cinema. Then Robson asked me how I'd known that Alan was going to have lunch at the Fish Plaice. I told him that Tony Mold had told me.

'Did you speak to anyone else at the cinema, sir?' asked Robson. He looked a little like Christian Slater. I shook my head and he frowned.

'We interviewed the clerk in the ticket booth and he said that you'd told him you were with some friends. Who were these friends?' he asked.

'Oh, I see. No, I only said that I was with Alan and Claire

so he'd tell me where they were sitting. I wanted to be able to keep an eye on them. I wanted to talk to Claire on her own and find out what was going on.'

'Would that be Claire Vogel, Mr Cork?' asked the short cop with the buzz-cut.

'I don't know her last name but she's blonde, about twenty-two,' I said. Robson looked over to the buzz-cut who nodded.

Robson asked me why I had been so keen to talk to Claire and I told them the whole story. I left nothing out and it took quite some time. They had more patience than the sergeant at Kensington but they made fewer notes than I would have liked and only really began to pay attention when I described my movements in the cinema. When I'd finished Robson uncrossed his legs and sat forward.

'Did you notice anyone else moving around in the auditorium, Mr Cork?' he asked.

'Only Alan. I told you he moved seats. There were very few people watching the film.'

'Can you think of anyone else who might want to cause you harm? In your private life, perhaps?' he asked.

'Look,' I said. 'I know you have to be thorough but it's obvious that Alan Denton did it. You've got to arrest him!'

Robson cleared his throat and graced me with a supercilious smile. He had the imaginative reach of a Polo mint. I appealed to the buzz-cut who assured me that they would be taking the investigation very seriously, that they'd talked to people as they left the cinema, and had accounted for most of the audience against a list of the cheques and credit card slips held by the cinema box-office for the performance in question.

'But I've told you what happened!' I cried. 'It was Alan Denton! He thinks I'm blackmailing him! Can't you see that? Do you think I did this to myself?'

'No, sir. Nobody's suggesting that,' Robson said. 'According to the doctor there's no way your wound could have been self-inflicted. Bear with us, sir. We've made a note of your suspicions but since you didn't actually see your assailant we have to follow up all the possible leads. This is a very serious offence and I suggest that you leave the investigation to us, Mr Cork. We'd like to interview you again. We'll be in touch through Doctor Miller.'

They left and I felt that the whole wide world was against me. The police hadn't taken me seriously on account of my mental problems. To Robson and his sidekick I was just a nutter who'd happened to be in the wrong place at the wrong time. I could just imagine what Miller had told them about me.

A nurse brought me a bunch of tiger-lilies and ran some London tap water into a pink plastic jug. The card read: 'Get well soon. Love from all at Puffa.' It was Alan's sick joke. I dozed, hopeless and depressed, and then Kate came into the room. I lit up and opened my arms to her.

'How's your neck?' she asked sharply.

'I'll survive, just about,' I said, expecting more sympathy. I thought she would give me a kiss but she just pulled up a chair by the bed, folded her arms and glared at me.

'You're a real jerk, Steve. You lied to me. You let me down.'

She spoke with cold fury. I knew from my marriage that attack was the only form of defence in such circumstances.

'Hold on! You make it sound like this is all my fault! I've

just been attacked by a maniac, haven't I? I've got a great gash in the back of my neck and I lost a lot of blood. An awful lot. I nearly died!'

'You expect me to feel sorry for you?' Kate snapped. 'If you'd gone home like you said this wouldn't have happened. But not taking your pills and lying about it, then telling the police Alan attacked you? What the hell do you think you're doing?'

'Alan tried to kill me again! I followed him to the cinema. He was there with Claire, the girl I told you about!'

'Of course. The girl. But I thought that Alan was meant to have murdered her? None of it adds up. Listen, Steve, the police rang me. They wanted to know about your mental state, about your obsession with Alan.'

I started to protest and she looked away, seething.

'You've broken my trust,' she said.

'I've never lied to you, Kate,' I said gravely. I had to win her back. She was the one person I felt I could count on.

'Really? And when did you stop taking your lithium?' she asked with a look of withering contempt.

'Lithium? What makes you think I stopped taking my lithium?' I asked.

'Oh, cut the crap! Doctor Miller took a blood sample, remember? Look at me, Steve.' She gripped my hand. 'I'm going to give it to you straight. Once more and only once more. You've confabulated this whole thing about Alan to explain why you were sacked. And now you're using it to explain away your bad luck with the moped and this thing in the cinema. Get it?'

My spirit collapsed. Kate was intelligent, she knew how my mind worked and I felt something for her, maybe even love. But she didn't believe me any more than the police had.

'Have I gone mad again? You've got to help me!' I implored her. 'Are you really saying two psychos tried to kill me on two consecutive days?' I was in despair and Kate put her arms around me.

'Calm down, Steve. I don't think you're particularly manic, but I am convinced you have a paranoid fixation about Alan.' She held me while I mewled on her breast.

'Do you hate me?' I asked her. I felt wretched, beyond hope. The more vigorously I tried to convince her of Alan's culpability, the more I confirmed her diagnosis.

'Of course I don't hate you. I'm just angry because you lied to me,' Kate said sadly. She told me that she had to go back to the Webster and that she'd come back later if she could.

I was devastated when she left. No one believed me. No one was on my side. I was a gang of one.

17

Polaroid

From the moment you handle the
Polaroid ProCam, you'll see that it is in
a class of its own - and every inch the
tough, durable work tool that you need
for business use.

And we're not just saying that.
We guarantee it.

POLAROID®

DR MILLER CAME TO SEE ME later that afternoon and kept
trying to chip away at my case against Alan. The whole dreary
litany was dragged out for re-appraisal: my low self-esteem,
my anger at my absent father, the effect of redundancy on my
self-image. Dr Miller even implied that I had sabotaged the
moped myself in order to implicate Alan. I didn't have the
energy to argue but it sickened me that Alan was free while I
was trapped on the end of a drip. Miller told me that he
wanted to keep me in hospital for a few days to make sure of
my lithium level. Then he gave me a pill and watched to make

sure that I swallowed it. When he left I dozed fitfully until something disturbed me.

Claire was standing in the doorway watching me. I thought I was hallucinating.

I shut my eyes and re-opened them. She was still there. It was no dream.

I clutched the bedclothes, half-expecting Alan to walk in behind her.

Claire looked frightened, younger than I remembered. Her jacket was soaked and her hair was plastered to the side of her face. I stared at her goggle-eyed as the shock subsided. Dirty rain was hissing at the window.

'Hello? Mr Cork? Are you all right? We met with Alan Denton. Do you remember me?'

Claire took a few steps into the room and I sat up, wide awake. Her shoulders were hunched up around her ears as if she was trying to shrink back to her childhood.

'Of course I remember you. Why don't you sit down?' I asked softly. She perched on the edge of a chair.

'I'm sorry to barge in like this but the police told me you were here. I've got to talk to you. I was in the cinema when you were attacked, you see.'

'What would you like to talk to me about?' I asked.

'The police interviewed me about what happened in the cinema,' she said. 'Is your neck still very painful?'

'It's better, thanks. What did the police say?' I was scared to blink in case she disappeared.

'They stopped us in the foyer when we left the cinema and asked if we knew you. Then they took me to the manager's office on my own and asked me about you and Alan.' She kept glancing at the door as if the police were going to reappear any second. She was plainly terrified to be in my room.

'And what did you tell them?' I asked. Claire lit a cigarette and it wobbled on her lips, an adult prop. She took a deep drag and it seemed to steady her nerves. This scared little girl was nothing like the fantasy that I'd conjured up in my brain.

'I told them I'd met you with Alan once, that's all. But they want to interview me again and I have to know if it's true you've been blackmailing him. He said you were but then this morning he agreed that he might have been wrong.' Her frown cut a deep furrow on her brow. It was the only line on her face.

'You're asking me if I'm blackmailing Alan? Of course I'm not! I don't even know what he's being blackmailed about. Do you?'

'Not paying tax or something. Apparently he was given a lot of money when he sold a company and he never declared it. He says you broke into his house and found proof, a letter from a Swiss bank that he should have torn up. And then you asked him for fifty thousand pounds or you'd tell the police.'

She looked at me accusingly. I was stunned, struck by the absurdity of the situation.

'Ha! What a joke! You're telling me this is all about tax evasion?' I laughed so hard I nearly burst my stitches.

'What's so funny?' she asked, scandalized by my laughter. 'Alan could go to prison if they find out.' She glared at me with youth's deadly seriousness.

'Of course he could go to prison! People on welfare have to survive for a week on what he spends on an expense account lunch every day! And I'd thought he was being blackmailed for raping you.'

'For raping me? Why would you think that?' she asked, shocked at the very idea.

'You remember the night we met at the restaurant? Well,

I went back to the mews later on to get my car and I heard someone being beaten up in the house. And your Mini was parked outside.'

'That's right. I went over to see him. He did hit me a couple of times, actually. At first we thought he might have broken my collar-bone. We even went to the hospital for an X-ray. But Alan would never rape anyone. It's just that he's so incredibly jealous that he loses control. If I even look at another man he goes crazy,' she said, unable to disguise her wonder that she could provoke such feelings. 'And you know how it was in the restaurant,' she added.

'He was jealous in the restaurant? But there was nothing going on between us. I was there with my wife,' I protested.

'It had nothing to do with you,' she said. 'I was having a drink with an old boyfriend at the bar. I had no idea that Alan was going to be there.' My vanity lay punctured, puckered.

'What happened in the cinema, Claire? Please, you have to tell me.'

She sat there fidgeting and I could tell that her mind was pulling two ways. Claire was a mixed-up young woman, desperate to tell someone but loath to betray Alan. She twisted the laces of her trainers round her finger, looking about fifteen again. Then her story came out in a rush.

'I saw you in the foyer when I went out for popcorn and I told Alan. He'd been in a terrible mood at lunch saying you were blackmailing him and how despicable and cowardly you were. He went to the loo half-way through the film. He was away for ages so when the police stopped us in the lobby and told us you'd been attacked I knew he was responsible. When we got home he swore me to secrecy and said you'd deserved it. But then this morning he found another note in the letter-box.'

'Another blackmail note?'

'Yes. Asking for another fifty thousand pounds. And I knew you were still in hospital so you couldn't have delivered it. I told him that it couldn't have been you, but he was so upset that he wouldn't listen.'

'Why don't you tell the police all this?' I asked.

'I'm frightened about what they'd do to him. I really love him.'

'You've got to tell the police. He'll attack somebody else, Claire.'

'No he won't! You don't understand him. How could you? He seems so self-assured but underneath he's desperately insecure. He only attacked you because he thought you were blackmailing him. He just went mad for a few minutes.'

'That's no excuse though, is it? And what do you think he was doing walking around with a razor blade in his pocket?'

'The police said they're treating it as Attempted Murder. It would be the end of him, don't you see? He'd kill himself rather than go to prison.' Her eyes pleaded with me. She looked half-crazy herself.

'It was bloody nearly the end of me! He nearly killed me! Doesn't that mean anything to you? What kind of Moral Philosophy are they teaching you these days? I thought you were taking a degree in the subject.' Claire sniffed back a sob and stood up angrily.

'But you're all right now, aren't you? And how do I know for sure that you're not blackmailing him?' she snapped. 'Alan said that you might have an accomplice. He says you're psychotic.' She went over to the window and stood watching the rain clouds apply some hydropathy to the Houses of Parliament.

'Alan's the one who's psychotic,' I said. I was terrified that she'd run off but to my relief she slumped back down in the chair. She looked exhausted.

'Oh, God! What am I meant to do now?' she wailed, rubbing at her eyes.

'Come on, you know you've got to tell the police. It's why you came here, why you're telling me all this.'

'I should go. I'm sorry I came,' she said. She took a ragged scrap of tissue from her pocket and dabbed at her nose.

'The police won't blame you. You only protected Alan because of how you feel about him. Because you thought I was blackmailing him. They'll understand that.'

In fact I thought there was a good chance they'd prosecute her as an accessory because she'd fingered me for Alan in the cinema.

'I doubt that Alan would go to prison anyway,' I said. 'He needs help, Claire. Professional help that you can't give him.'

'Oh, that's rubbish! Of course I can help him! And I couldn't care less about what happens to me! Can't you see that? Have you never really loved someone?'

She looked at me with wild eyes, as if she was auditioning for the lead in a remake of *Wuthering Heights*, but her words struck a chord. There had been a time when I'd loved Liz like that.

Claire began to weep. I wanted to comfort her but I couldn't move because of the drip in my arm. I wanted to tell her that romantic love is just a con-trick, a biological ruse that temporarily blinds people to the truth of each other's failings.

'I understand how you feel, Claire. I really do. But it's gone too far. You have to tell the police,' I said.

'I've got to go. I need time to think.' She was trembling, big-eyed like Bambi in the forest, with her head tucked into her shoulder.

'No. Look, you're still in a state of shock. Let me call a nurse.' I tried to find the buzzer above my head. As soon as I reached for it Claire looked up in terror and flew out through the door.

I called out to her but she was already gone, running down the corridor.

I couldn't afford to lose her.

Without thinking I tore the drip from my arm and rushed out after her in my hospital gown and headed for the lifts. The doors were closing on one of them. I caught a glimpse of Claire's frightened face among the other passengers.

I raced barefoot across the linoleum and stabbed at the call button to open the doors. It was no use. I watched helplessly as the lift twinkled down through the numbers displayed above the door and came to rest at G. I swore and pounded the wall with my fist.

I was desperate. I'd lost Claire and she was the only person who could put Alan behind bars. The shock of her sudden departure left me reeling. Light-headed and shaky, I tottered back to my room.

Most of Torville Ward had been closed down because of a shortage of staff and I managed to get back into bed without being noticed. I tried to think things through. I pressed the buzzer for a nurse and told her that my drip had come loose in my sleep. When she had refitted it I asked her for the pay phone and she wheeled it up to my bed on a trolley.

I called West End Central police station and asked for DC Robson. Fifty pence later he came onto the line. As soon as I mentioned Claire's visit he cut me off abruptly, saying that he would be coming in to see me the next day and that I could tell him about it then.

When I remonstrated with him he simply hung up the phone.

I cursed into the mouthpiece. Because of what he'd heard from Kate and Dr Miller, Robson didn't believe a word I told him. At least the cop with the buzz-cut had given me Claire's last name. I rang directory enquiries and asked for the number of a Vogel somewhere in Kensington. I didn't know the initial but apparently there was only one Vogel listed in the area. I asked for the name of the street and was told that it was Tregunter Road. Then a robot voice gave me the telephone number and I jotted it down.

Kate walked in as I put down the phone and kissed me.

'Are you all right?' she asked. 'I'm sorry if I was hard on you earlier, Steve. I was angry, but I had no right to take it out on you.'

'Forget it,' I said. Her hand was warm in mine. I knew she was my only hope. I told her about Claire's visit and saw her kindly smile morph into a sceptical grimace.

'Oh, Steve! How do you expect me to take any of this seriously? Let's postpone this conversation until Doctor Miller's happy with your lithium level.'

'Look, Kate. Maybe I am off my rocker. Let's assume I am, but if Alan really did attack me then this girl's life's in danger. He must know she'll tell the police. She's already cracking up under the strain. I phoned Robson and told him she was here but he thinks I'm crazy because of what you told him. Doctor Miller thinks I've got a paranoid obsession about Alan too.'

'I think Doctor Miller's made a sound diagnosis,' she said.

'But he only thinks that because of what you told him! In the end it's down to you, Kate. Listen, I know I was wrong about Alan raping Claire. But she was here and she knows that Alan attacked me in the cinema. She can prove it!'

'Oh, come on, Steve.' Kate was losing her patience.

'I beg you! I've got Claire's phone number. All you've got to do is call her and tell her you're a friend of mine, that you want to talk about what happened in the cinema. It'll be easier for her to tell you than the police. Please, Kate, just one phone call. It's not much to ask. Even if I really am nuts it won't do any harm. If you feel anything at all for me.'

'Oh, spare us!' Kate said with a laugh.

I begged her and begged her. I even threatened to discharge myself from hospital if she didn't do as I asked. That seemed to clinch it. Kate agreed to make the call on condition that I promised to stay put and take my pills.

'I knew you'd do it!' I cried. I thought about the future and imagined running across white sand holding her hand. 'Kate, I love you,' I said.

'Steve, you're full of shit,' she replied, dialling Claire's number on the pay phone. 'She'll think I'm a fool. Which I am.'

Claire was out but Kate left her name and number on an answering machine, asking Claire to call her back. I wrote down Alan's home number and gave it to Kate, suggesting that she might phone there later if Claire didn't call back.

'Are you happy now?' she asked,

I pulled her towards me. We soul-kissed and I felt the tension melt in my neck. Kate looked round at the open door. She closed it and came back to sit on the chair beside the bed. She pulled back the bedclothes and dragged the hem of my hospital gown up towards my navel. The fabric brushed over my stiffening cock. The door had an observation panel made of reinforced glass. Kate hadn't noticed this feature. If anyone walked past in the corridor they would be able to see into the room.

'Kate,' I said.

'Doctor to you.'

She leant forward and took me in her mouth. She was looking up at me with my cock in her mouth, maintaining eye contact, and her gaze made me moan out loud. Then Kate rubbed her face all over my wet cock and balls, nuzzling them, lapping at them with her tongue. Her hair tickled my belly.

I tried to prolong the moment by concentrating on the transparent bag that was dripping glucose into my arm. At that moment Kate began to suck at my glans as if it was a lollipop, as if she was trying to suck the sweet liquid from the bag right through my body and out via my penis.

It was too much. I couldn't pull back from the brink.

A bomb detonated deep in my abdomen and my body reared up like the desert floor in a subterranean test explosion. I looked up to see Kate wiping her mouth with a tissue.

'I love you,' I said.

'Aren't you confusing love with sex?' she asked with a gentle mocking smile.

'Sometimes they're the same thing,' I said.

Kate raised an eyebrow at my uncharacteristic rush of positivity. Nevertheless the feeling stayed with me. I wasn't sure that Kate and I were really that lucky but I knew that I felt good as I held her. Before she left I made her promise to call me as soon as she'd heard from Claire.

I buzzed and asked the nurse to wake me if anyone telephoned. Eventually I drifted off to sleep after dining on catering food. I woke up at nine-thirty the following morning to find that the glucose drip had been removed while I was asleep. When I finally got hold of the phone-trolley I found that Kate had already left home.

I called her at the Webster but the receptionist said she hadn't arrived.

'When do you expect her?' I asked.

'She was due in at ten, but there's a train strike and the traffic's perfectly frightful.'

It was almost ten-thirty. When I called back an hour later Kate still hadn't shown up and I began to get worried about her. I tried Liz at home but she was out so I called Tony on his mobile. It gobbled the units on the LCD display as if I was connected to a Chat-back line in Rotorua.

'It's Steve. Is Alan in the office?'

'I wouldn't know. I'm still at home in bed. Alan's off with flu and I'm fucked if I'm going in.'

'Look, Tone, you've got to come over and get me out of here. And bring some clothes for me to wear.' Most of my blood-soaked clothing had been taken by the police as evidence.

'Why can't Liz pick you up?' Tony whined.

'Liz is busy and I've got to get out right now. How soon can you make it?'

Tony groaned. 'An hour maybe?' he said. I reminded him about the clothes.

Dr Miller came by on his rounds and told me that DC Robson would be coming to see me at six. I asked Miller how long he intended to keep me in hospital and he told me that he wanted to move me to the psychiatric ward for a few days until my lithium level had stabilized.

I shaved and waited for Tony. He arrived around lunch-time and gave me the green Adidas track suit he'd bought for jogging purposes. The track suit was far too small for me, as tight as a body stocking. Tony told me that I looked like the Jolly Green Giant run to seed. He cackled uncontrollably and I guessed that he'd already had a drink. As if to confirm my suspicions, he pulled a bottle of Jameson's whiskey from his Nike bag and poured a slug the size of a small porpoise down his throat.

'Leave it out,' I said. 'You've got to drive.'

'You know what they said at AA? "One drink's too many and a thousand's not enough." Never a truer word, Steve.'

'What's that then? The thousand and third? Have a look and see if there's anyone official in the corridor. Doctors or nurses.'

'Why? Are you bunking out?' he asked with an idiot grin.

'Something like that.'

We made it to the car park and I crawled into Tony's Porsche.

'Are you sure you're all right to drive, Tone?' I asked. He'd had trouble negotiating the hospital's swing doors.

'Course. 'Less you want to?'

'What, with this thing on my neck? Just take it slowly and head towards the Old Brompton Road.'

I told Tony about Alan and Claire, not caring if he believed me as long as he kept driving. Facing an inevitable twelve-month ban, Tony had little left to lose, and treated the streets of central London as an arcade game. My foot stabbed at an imaginary brake pedal as we lurched towards the wheels of a container lorry. Tony overtook and undertook without recourse to the indicator lights, drunk to a point where he feared no more than a cartoon explosion and the appearance of the words GAME OVER flashing upon the screen. Thankfully we made it to Tregunter Road in one piece. I recognized Claire's house, but there was no sign of her Mini. Tony pulled into the semi-circular drive and I rang the bell. A uniformed Filipina house-slave opened it six inches, the full extent of the brass security chain, and I asked to speak to Claire.

'Claire not here. Sorry,' she said with a mechanized smile.

'Do you know when she'll be back?' I asked.

'Don't know. No one home.'

I climbed back into the car and asked Tony to drive to Alan's place. On the way I called the Webster again on Tony's mobile phone. Kate still hadn't arrived. I was worried sick about her and tried to still the horrible pictures in my head with a mouthful of Tony's whiskey. Alan's car wasn't in the mews but I knocked on the front door and called his name through the letter-box. A grey-haired gent in a cardigan came up behind me.

'Can I help you?' he asked, bristling with suspicion.

'No, I don't think you can,' I said.

The busybody walked off towards the main road, glancing back over his shoulder. Tony was propped against the battered Porsche in a motorcycle jacket, sipping at a whiskey bottle. I realized that my tight green track suit, cracked trainers and foam-rubber neck-brace were equally unlikely to inspire confidence in an owner-occupier. I waited for the man to turn the corner, tore open the plastic bag that contained my personal effects and tried the front-door key that I'd taken from Alan's office. He hadn't found the time to change the lock since my last visit and the door swung open. Tony staggered over and grabbed my arm.

'Steve! What are you doing? Alan's in there for fuck's sake! I told you he's got flu. You can't go fucking breaking in!'

'Never you mind, Tone. Alan's not here,' I said, pulling myself free of his grip. 'You wait in the car. I'm going inside.'

'You're fucked up, Steve! You can't do this!'

I stepped inside and Tony scuttled back to the Porsche. I closed the door behind me.

The place was a mess by anyone's standards. By Alan's standards it was Hiroshima. Tinfoil take away cartons and dirty plates littered the coffee table. Clothes were strewn around on the floor. When I called his name there was no reply. I picked up an ornamental poker from the grate as a precaution and made my way upstairs.

The house was deserted. The bureau in the study was open and the floor was covered with hundreds of bank statement sheets as if someone had played fifty-two pick-up with five years' supply.

The bed in the master bedroom was unmade and there was a familiar smell in the room, a scent that I couldn't quite place. I pulled the drawer out from the bed frame and found that the handcuffs and the cords were gone. I remembered the cocaine in the bedside table and thought that Tony could use some to sober up. When I opened the drawer I found a stack of Polaroids.

There was a shot of Claire standing on the bed wearing only black stockings and the Zorro mask, her skin bleached by the Polaroid's flash. Another showed her kneeling naked on the bathroom floor with her hands cuffed around the base of the lavatory, her face pressed against the cold porcelain.

I flicked through a few more before I saw a shot of Liz.

She was naked, pouting at the camera with her hips canted in a modelling pose.

In the next she was lying face-up on the bed, blindfolded

221

with her wrists tied to the bed posts above her head. Her legs were held apart by a three-foot rod strapped between her ankles. Alan had stood over her, looking down to take the photograph.

I threw up some National Health Service cuisine onto the carpet. Then I went downstairs and swallowed a tumbler of vodka.

'What's wrong?' Tone asked.

I got into the car and showed him a Polaroid of Liz with a necklace of Alan's sperm glittering on her breasts. Behind her was the dim but unmistakable outline of the button-back headboard in our bedroom in Roehampton.

'Fucking hell, Steve! It's Liz, isn't it?'

'Take me home,' I said.

18

Hug a Tree

I WAS IN A STATE OF SHOCK, stunned by Liz's betrayal. Tony drunk-drove us towards Roehampton, weaving a wobbly line through the lava-flow of lunch-time traffic. I gnawed at my knuckle. If Liz had slept with anyone but Alan I wouldn't have cared, and it hurt me all the more to realize how easy it must have been for him to get my wife into bed. I looked through the Polaroids until Tony took them away from me.

We arrived at the house and there was no sign of Liz's Punto. I went inside and called out to Liz but she wasn't home. I used the phone in the hall to phone the Webster. Kate still hadn't shown up and I knew in my guts that something was badly wrong. The receptionist took my number and promised that she would ask Dr Parker to call me as soon as she arrived. The drawer in the hall table had been pulled open. I went through to the sitting-room and found that the French windows were open onto the garden.

Tony called to me from the front of the house.

'Hey, Steve! Come here!' he yelled. He'd opened the garage doors and Alan's blue BMW was parked inside. Tony was standing next to it.

'I think there's someone in here,' he said, ashen-faced.

It was gloomy inside the garage and I couldn't see anything. Dread chilled my bones and my teeth chattered in my head.

I stood rooted to the spot, peering into the darkness at the back of the garage. Cold sweat pumped out through my pores.

'Where?' I asked Tony. My voice sounded high and remote.

'In the boot. Listen.'

I approached the BMW and heard an urgent muffled groan from inside.

'It's locked,' said Tony.

We tried to force it open with a screwdriver but it was no use.

'Wait here,' I said. 'There's a crowbar in the garden shed.'

I padded along the side of the house past the trellis-work, my heart thudding. A solitary tuft of cloud was moving in the blue sky and its shadow sped across the golf course, momentarily darkening three tiny Airfix figures as they made their putts on the green of the fourteenth hole.

As I turned the corner I tripped on a coil of garden hose. The lime-green pipe was meant to retract of its own accord but the spring had worn out earlier in the year and I hadn't got round to replacing it.

I got back on my feet, skirted the drained pool and made my way across the lawn towards the garden shed, my senses on red alert.

Leaves rustled in the soft breeze. The sun shone brightly and I was blinded for a second as I walked into the shadow cast by the shed. The key to the shed was hidden under the wooden door. I crouched down and put my hand beneath it to feel around. The concrete floor was cold and damp to my touch as I scrabbled blindly for the key. When I found it I stood up to undo the grey corroded padlock. The mechanism was stiff and I struggled with it to no effect. The key wouldn't turn.

The door was new and solid enough to deter the opportunist thief. There was no way that I could kick it open. I had a tin of Three-in-one oil in my tool-box which I kept in the laundry room. A few drops would free up the padlock. I slipped back into the house through the French windows.

I was passing through the kitchen on my way to the laundry room when I saw a sweater thrown carelessly over the back of a chair. It was blue and nautical with a zip up the front. I'd never seen it before but I guessed that it might have belonged to Mary. Lenny had been into yachts. I took a belt of Scotch from the bottle on the sideboard to steady my nerves and headed into the laundry room. Then I heard someone moving about at the front of the house.

'Tony?' I called out. He couldn't hear me.

I picked up the tin of oil and went back out into the garden for the crowbar. I crossed the lawn to the shed and up-ended the padlock to pour a few drops of oil down the keyhole. It took a little time but the key finally turned in the padlock and the hoop rasped open, raising gooseflesh on my arms.

The shed was dank. I took the crowbar from its rusty nail and got out of there. It felt good to have the crowbar in my hand as I headed back towards the garage. I couldn't see Tony. A bird chirruped somewhere to my right.

As I passed the hedge Alan stepped out from behind it swinging a golf putter at my stomach.

The shaft struck me across my soft gut.

I went down as the breath whistled out of me. I tried to call out to Tony but no words came.

Alan swung at my head, his face wooden.

I took the second blow on my forearm. The pain shot through me like a lightning bolt. I tried to scrabble away on my hands and knees. Then the back of my head exploded.

A light flashed on and off. I opened my eyes. Pain hammered at the back of my skull. I found myself hugging the birch tree in the garden. When I tried to move away from it I found that my wrists were tied together on the other side of the trunk.

Another wave put me under again. When I came round I saw Tony lying face down on the grass some ten feet from me. There was blood all over his face. His hands and feet were bound with electric flex and he had a dishcloth stuffed in his mouth. I turned and saw Alan dragging Kate round the side of the house by her hair.

The sight of her was annihilating. My heartstrings snapped.

I yelled out but no sound came.

I struggled to break away from the tree in a frenzy, oblivious to the pain as the cord cut into my wrists. I jerked at the cord, feeling hot blood trickle down my fingers. It was useless.

Kate was handcuffed, her shirt torn. Her legs were tied together with the black rope from Alan's bedroom and she was squealing through a gag. I guessed that it had been her muffled groan that Tony and I had heard in the boot of the car.

On the golf course two men in bright kiddy-coloured clothes were pulling their trolleys along the fairway two hundreds yards from where I stood. One of them was wearing a yellow V-neck with a blue-and-white diamond pattern on the front, while the other was sporting a pair of plaid trousers.

I tried to shout out to them but there was something in my mouth that muffled my voice and smelt of petrol.

Alan laid Kate out face down at right angles to Tony and went into the house muttering to himself. He re-emerged with a wooden driver, swinging it in front of him like a scythe and humming the refrain from a rap song I couldn't quite place. His face was swollen, contorted and demonic.

'I haven't played golf for years!' Alan said, chuckling like a cocktail party bore.

He smiled at me with wide shining eyes. Primitive fear climbed my spine, clamping my vertebrae hand over hand. Alan had the look of madness, schizoid and mesmeric, a look that I'd glimpsed on his face before. He walked over to stand in front of Tony and looked at me again. I tried not to catch his eye.

'Would you like a game, boss? What do you say? Well, we'll play in a minute or two. I just want to practise my swing with Tony first. How's your neck by the way?'

Alan came towards me. I tried to shrink away. He removed my neck support to run a proprietorial finger along the line of my stitches.

'Not bad, though I say so myself. A sliced white oaf.' He smirked and turned back to Tony. I felt guilty relief wash through me.

Alan put my neck support on Tony back-to-front, forcing Tony's jaw forward on the grass. Then he knelt down and stood a matchbox directly in front of Tony's chin. Alan picked up the club and prepared to tee off, bending his knees and rolling his shoulders.

Alan took a swing and the club head flew over the top of the matchbox, whistling down centimetres from Tony's nose. Tony whimpered through the gag and tried to wriggle backwards.

Alan swung the club and missed again.

'For God's sake, Tony! You put me off! Keep your eye on the ball!'

Tony began to cry and Alan took a couple of steps back to sort out his swing. He seemed satisfied after three practice strokes and addressed the matchbox once more. Tony's eyes were screwed shut. His legs were twitching in terror.

Alan stooped down and placed the matchbox closer to Tony's face, barely two inches from his jutting chin.

Alan swung again. Tony flinched as the club came down. It clipped the matchbox which skittered a few feet across the grass. Alan groaned in dismay and kicked Tony in the ribs.

'Come on, Tony! Teamwork! We're in this together. You have to keep still!'

Alan retrieved the matchbox and placed it even closer to Tony's chin.

Alan stood over the matchbox, closing his eyes while he regained his composure. Then he adjusted his grip and raised the club in the air. Sunlight glinted on the steel shaft.

The club whooshed down and hit Tony full on the jaw with a terrible dull crack. When I looked again Tony's face was turned away from me and he was writhing in agony on the grass.

'Fuck it,' said Alan. 'You should have kept your eye on the ball, you dumb faggot. Didn't I tell you that? Now who's next? Steve or the doctor?'

I looked at Kate and her pupils were spaced with fear. I noticed that her bare shoulder was covered with red marks that looked like cigarette burns.

I ached for her.

She was only three feet from Tony and his face was right in front of her. I struggled to free myself but the knot was fast. Alan attached the support to Kate's neck. Then he placed the matchbox in front of her face. He swung the club and missed by a mile.

'Shit, I think it's my grip. What do you think, doctor? Do I need a glove?' Alan turned on his heel and went back inside the house.

As soon as he was out of sight Kate began to roll away across the grass in blind terror. I groaned to try and get her attention. She was heading for the deep end of the empty swimming pool, rolling quickly down a shallow slope.

There was nothing I could do. When Kate hit the concrete apron that surrounded the pool she caught sight of the blue void just in time and braked the roll with her elbow only inches from the edge. I sent up a prayer of thanks to the jets that were queuing in the sky to make their descent at Heathrow.

Tony was struggling to free himself and his crimson jaw flapped as he wrenched at the flex which bound his wrists.

Alan came back into the garden wearing my golfing glove. He jogged over to Kate and swore at her, grunting as he dragged her back towards Tony. Then he turned her onto her stomach and stood the matchbox in front of her face once more.

Alan picked up the club and swung.

He hit it well. The matchbox sailed through the air and he went to collect it with a spring in his step. Then he removed the gag from Kate's face and she screamed.

Alan kicked the side of her head and I felt the impact in my heart.

'Sshh! Don't be a spoilsport, doctor. You've given me trouble enough already. If you make a noise we'll all have to go inside and play another game,' Alan said. I hoped that the neighbours had heard Kate's scream but then I remembered that they were away.

'Now are you ready to tell me where my money is?' Alan asked her.

Kate was crying. 'I've told you I don't know anything about it!' she sobbed.

'Oh, please! Steve couldn't have done it on his own. He's been in hospital, hasn't he? Don't make me angry, doctor. You'll put me off my swing.'

He put the gag back on her and swung wildly at the matchbox. The club missed her face. When he untied her gag again Kate was too frightened to speak. She just lay there shaking with her eyes closed making little animal noises. Alan replaced the gag and mussed her hair with a show of affection.

Then he turned towards me.

'Well, it looks like it's your turn, boss. What's your handicap?' He walked over to me with the driver and the matchbox. 'Maybe we'll try something else though. What d'you say?'

He dropped the driver on the lawn.

'How about some more fun with a razor blade? Perhaps we could try a little cosmetic surgery? Or maybe a new game

230

altogether. Human Torch perhaps, burn off some fat?' I gasped and inhaled petrol fumes from the rag in my mouth.

Alan struck several matches together. They flared palely in the sunlight. Cupping the flame he lit the rag and it flashed white in my face. The heat was incredible and I smelt my own flesh burning before he whipped the rag from my mouth. He stamped it out on the grass in a fit of laughter. I screamed and Alan punched me in the ribs.

'Okay, boss. Time to talk before I lose my patience. Where's my money?' he asked. My face felt as if it was still being blowtorched.

'I don't know about any money!' I cried in agony.

Alan pinched the blistered flesh of my cheek. The pain was shattering. He put a hand over my mouth to stifle my scream.

'Where's Liz?' I wailed.

'Liz is enjoying a pleasant day shopping. She's in a good mood because she's finally filed for divorce. And because I fucked her twice last night. Now where's my money?' he asked.

'I haven't a clue!'

'Oh, come on, boss. You had my front-door key in your pocket. And look what I found in your bedroom!' He held a crumpled letter under my nose. I'd never seen it before. I glimpsed the logo of a Swiss bank at the top of the page.

Alan snatched the letter away and lit it with a match. Black wisps fluttered away on the breeze.

'There goes your proof, boss. It took me quite a while to find it,' said Alan. 'I had to search the whole house. Because of you I've had to waste a lot of time down here. I've grown very tired of your wife and now I want my fifty grand back. Did you really think I'd let this go on and on? You and the doctor were too greedy. You should have got the message in the cinema.'

'Me and Kate?' I asked. He was jumping to conclusions the way I had over Claire.

'Yes, you and Kate, the young lovers. Don't try and play the fool with me! I know you're crazy but you're not that far gone. The doctor even had my home phone number in her pocket, and do you think I don't know what you get up to in your sessions? I saw you kissing outside her flat for God's sake!'

He punched me in the face.

I came round dripping with water. Alan was spraying me with the garden hose.

'Shall I do the roses while I'm at it?' he asked. 'I've always had green fingers.'

I tried to pull myself together, to hold back the fear. 'If you just walk away from here you'll only get a few years but if you keep this up you're going to kill someone and then it's life,' I said, shaking.

'You think I care about killing you?' he screeched. 'I had to kill the girl I love because of you two!'

His words iced my blood. If he'd already killed Claire then he had nothing to lose. I glanced over to the golf course, hoping that someone had heard him.

Alan slapped my raw face.

'Look at me, you piece of shit! Do you really think I care about killing you? You mean nothing to me! Nothing!' he yelled.

He was raging. I knew that I had to try and keep him talking at any cost. Our only hope was that Liz would come back or that the organic meat van would make a delivery.

232

'Does prison mean anything to you?' I asked him.

'Ha! I don't imagine the police'll have much trouble putting two and two together.'

I was puzzled and Alan laughed.

'Liz told me that you haven't been taking your medicine, boss. Apparently you're meant to be spending another week in hospital so that makes you an escaped mental patient, doesn't it?'

'You want the police to think I killed Claire? Forget it. What motive could I have?'

'You were obsessed with her. You even told Robson about your rape fantasy. And you've already proved that you're capable of psychotic violence in front of witnesses.' His eyes sparkled and he took a razor-blade from his shirt pocket. I pretended not to notice as he unwrapped it, folding the paper along one edge as a grip.

'But what about Kate and Tony?' I stammered.

'Your partner who betrayed you and your psychiatrist-lover? Two more of your victims. No, it'll be an easy case to crack, even for DC Robson. You killed them all in a psychotic frenzy, set fire to your house and then killed yourself, overcome with remorse. We'll keep it simple.'

It was just possible that he would get away with it. Behind him I saw Tony kicking against his bonds, making some progress.

'Enough of this,' Alan snapped, jerking the cord that tied my bleeding wrists. 'Are you ready to cell me where the money is?' He held the razor-blade to my throat.

'What do you need the money for?' I asked through clenched teeth.

'Because the police could trace it back to me through the

serial numbers. I had to draw it through my London bank, you see. You didn't give me enough time to get it from Geneva. That was stupid.'

He slapped my face again. I had double-vision for a few seconds.

'Where's the cash? It's here somewhere, isn't it? It's not in Kate's flat, I know that. It was a stroke of luck that she came back while I was looking for it. Were you two planning to fly away together? The loony and the shrink, it's really quite . . .'

Tony was up and running, his hands still tied behind his back, zig-zagging towards the side of the house, his slack jaw a bloody wattle swinging from side-to-side at each step.

Alan grabbed the driver and took off in pursuit. Tony slipped on the flagstones and Alan was on him, swinging the club at his body. Tony jerked about on the ground, helpless as the club rained down on him. I screamed for help at the top of my lungs and Alan rushed over to smash the club into my ribs. I doubled up, starved of oxygen.

'You piece of shit!' Alan snarled.

I gagged for air, each tiny breath an agony. Tony lay still. I prayed he wasn't dead, that Liz would come back and raise the alarm. The pain in my ribs was excruciating but I was desperate to keep Alan talking.

'You can't get away with this. Even if you do find the money,' I croaked, curled up at the base of the tree. 'You can kill the others but how are you going to kill me? Suicide's a hard one to fake.'

'Your body will be burnt to a crisp, boss. It'll look like you just threw yourself into the flames. I'm going to have to kill you first of course, but I'll do it in a way that's undetectable.'

'How?'

Alan pulled a spool of wire from the pocket of his Stüssy trousers. He crouched down to show it to me with a smug grin.

'I've sharpened the end of this piano wire and I'm going to stick it through your nipple and push it down into your heart. And I'll make sure that I don't scratch any of your ribs on the way in either,' he informed me. He pinched the blistered flesh of my cheek and gave it a twist. The pain pushed me into hysteria.

'I think I remember that one from Quincy ME,' I said, scraping together some mock-bravado as I eyeballed the needling point of the wire. 'And the bloke got caught.' I staggered to my feet.

'That was television, boss. Nobody cares that much in real life,' said Alan.

He stuffed the burnt rag back in my mouth. I glanced at Kate. She winked at me and that wink was the most beautiful thing I'd ever seen. Life was precious and my heart went out to her. I felt a ludicrous surge of happiness, a spiralling lunatic bliss that lasted until Alan hit me in the face again.

He carried Kate into the house, an unwilling bride across the threshold. Then he came back for Tony. I heard an electric cart on the golf course and turned to see a young groundsman with Robert Plant hair purring along not a hundred yards away. He looked over in my direction and waved, probably under the impression that I was hugging the tree to express my oneness with nature. He drove on oblivious and I cursed the New Age.

Alan came out again, cut me loose and led me into the house. Each step jolted my rib. There was no way I could make a run for it.

Tony and Kate were sitting up side-by-side on the zebra-skin sofa like a couple of interviewees on breakfast television. Tony was in bad shape but at least he was breathing. The driver had cleaved his lower lip in two and it was splayed to reveal splintered teeth beneath the blood-soaked dishcloth. Alan put me in the director's chair and tied me to it with flex he'd cut from the desk lamp.

'You all chat quietly among yourselves. I'll be back in a minute,' he said. Kate and I communed helplessly with our eyes until Alan returned, dragging Claire through the French windows. Her body was stiff and it bumped as he pulled it over the sill.

Claire was wrapped in her mackintosh. Her eyes were closed and her lips were worm-coloured. Alan laid her pale dead body on the Conran carpet, a Hans Bellmer doll bent and twisted to the shape of his BMW's boot. Her chin was tucked into her collar-bone and it looked to me as if her neck had been broken. I felt sick. Kate and Tony were transfixed, staring at the corpse in horror. Alan stood over Claire's body with his hands on his hips, breathing hard. I was surprised to see that tears were streaming down his face.

'Look what you made me do!' he shrieked at me. 'You repellent little shit! She was going to go to the police because of you!'

He stepped towards me and began to hit me in the face with his fists.

When I regained consciousness Alan had left the room again. Tiny points of light swarmed before my eyes and I'd lost my peripheral vision. My head had swollen out like a water melon. Kate was whimpering and her tears ran into the gag that bisected her cheeks.

The director's chair was light. I tried to stand up and walk it across the carpet but the beating had wrecked my sense of balance. I fell sideways and couldn't get up again. Claire's trainers were in my line of vision, pigeon-toed and inert.

Alan came back with a can of petrol. He was wearing a pair of yellow washing-up gloves.

'Just for the forensics,' he said. 'Oh, dear, boss. Did we have a tumble?' Alan stood me up in the chair and emptied the petrol around the room. He went to refill the can and when he came back he saved the last gallon to splash over the three of us.

'I hereby designate this room a no-smoking zone,' he said with a chuckle. 'Now we've got things to talk about, boss.' He removed the rag from my mouth and sat down in the armchair.

'I'm not going to play games anymore. There's no time. I'm going to have to kill Tony and the doctor before I set this place off. And I'm going to have to kill you too. That isn't negotiable. You had the letter from my bank hidden in your bedroom so I know you've got the money. What I propose is this: if you tell me where you've hidden it I'll make it easy on all of you. What do you say?' he said.

'Fuck you!' I cried and spat at him.

Alan smiled and turned Kate onto her stomach. Her knees slipped down to the floor and he pulled up her skirt. Tony tried to stand but Alan just elbowed him in the stomach. He flopped forward gagging for breath, his shirtfront soaked with blood from his pulverized jaw.

'It's up to you, boss. I feel like fucking the doctor here and I can't decide whether or not to kill her first.'

Alan went over and picked up a bone-handled corkscrew from the drinks trolley. He scratched and prodded Kate's bare buttocks with the twirling tip. Pee gushed down the back of her legs and smelt of ammonia. My mind raced around for an angle.

'What do you say, boss?' He yanked Kate's head back and mashed his lips against hers. Then he slapped her buttocks hard and pinched the welt.

'Let's see what the good doctor would prefer,' Alan said, untying her gag.

'Give him the money, Steve! Just give it to him!' she cried hysterically. Alan replaced the gag.

'You see? I knew you had it. Where is it? In the mattress?'

Everything fell into place in a flash of lucidity. Alan had found the letter in our bedroom, and I knew who'd been blackmailing him. Liz must have come across the letter in his house and somehow deduced that it was proof of tax evasion. Maybe Alan had even boasted to her about it. When Liz had seen the photos of Alan and Julia she'd known how to exact her revenge. So much for the shares from her father.

I considered telling Alan that Liz had seen the Trader Vic's photos, letting him work it out for himself. But then he'd have had no reason to keep the rest of us alive.

'All right, I'll tell you,' I said. 'The money's in the attic. There's a recess behind the old dresser.'

It was bullshit but I reckoned it would keep him busy for another ten minutes while I thought of something else.

'Are you telling the truth, boss? If you're not I'm going to come back and turn the doctor inside out,' said Alan.

I heard a car on the gravel outside. Alan leapt from his chair to stuff the rag back in my mouth. He turned on the CD player and the Happy Mondays came over the speakers as he left the room heading for the front door. I heard Liz call out

'Tony?' and then a loud thump. I imagined the worst and the remains of my spirit collapsed.

Kate and Tony turned their backs to each other on the sofa and Kate picked blindly at the complex knot that bound Tony's wrists. I could see that it was hopeless.

Then Mary Marighela walked in through the French windows smoking a joint, her eyes widening in surprise at the little bondage party.

Kate, Tony and I jigged around in a kind of sedentary tarantella, wild with delight. I hadn't heard a car. Mary had walked over from her place across the golf course.

To my horror our saviour appeared to be stoned off her head, waving the joint around like a censer. I expected a crumb of burning hash to blow us all to death at any second and so did Kate and Tony. Three pairs of eyes were trained on the smouldering tip. Sweat poured down my face, stinging my scorched skin.

'What's going on, Steve? What's that smell?'

Alan backed in from the hall, dragging Liz into the room.

'What the fuck's going on?' asked Mary.

Alan dropped Liz and sprang at Mary, going for her throat with the washing-up gloves.

Mary side-stepped just in time but his lunge had taken her by surprise. She stumbled across the floor.

Alan wheeled on Mary as she tried to regain her balance. She tripped over Claire's corpse and fell to the floor. The joint fell from her mouth and I braced myself for the explosion. Luckily it landed on one of the few dry patches of carpet.

Alan leapt at her but she rolled to the side and scrabbled to her feet. Mary adopted a martial arts stance, knees bent, playing an imaginary clarinet with her hands. Alan manoeuvred for an advantage and glanced around for a weapon.

Mary shadowed Alan's moves warily as they circled the coffee-table.

Alan saw the lava-lamp bubbling on a speaker cabinet and made a grab for it. Mary read his mind and kicked it from his hand with her loafer, following through to chop at his shoulder with the side of her hand.

Alan jumped back like a scalded cat.

'That hurt, you fucking hippy bitch!' he snarled. He winced as he tried to move his left arm.

Mary leapt onto the coffee table and kicked at his head but she slipped on a copy of *The Face* and crashed to the floor. Alan upended the table on top of her. The edge of the table caught her a glancing blow on the shoulder. Alan rushed over to finish her off.

Somehow Mary got a foot up into his stomach and pivoted him on top of Kate. Tony managed to throw himself across Alan. It gave Mary time to get up and drive her fist into Alan's face. Then her forearm smashed into him like a piston. She pulled Alan off the sofa and kicked him in the abdomen.

Alan lay groaning on the ground and Mary stood over him striking Jeet Kune Do poses. I willed her to get on with it, to finish him off. When he tried to grab her legs she stamped down on the side of his neck. Alan stopped moving.

Mary checked that Liz was breathing and untied me. Freed, I ripped the scorched rag from my mouth and went to Kate. I released her and held her in my arms while Mary attended to Tony.

Alan stirred on the carpet.

I grabbed the lava-lamp and smashed it to pieces against the side of his head. Hot red wax and water sprayed from the plastic casing in psychedelic swirls. I kicked him until Mary restrained me.

'Calm, calm, calm,' she muttered, over and over like a mantra.

A week later I was still in the local hospital. I had a broken rib and my head was bandaged with a gauze turban. I had a sore lump on my skull the size of a golfball. My face was one huge blister and there was a plaster cast on my fractured arm. I'd also broken my big toe kicking Alan. It throbbed all the time and kept me awake at night.

Kate had been transferred to Charing Cross Hospital and was still in Intensive Care. She had a chip of bone lodged against her brain and the doctors couldn't decide whether to operate. Like a good atheist I said my prayers for her every hour. I was desperate to see her.

Liz had suffered only mild concussion and had gone home to convalesce with her parents. The police interviewed me briefly, telling me that Alan had been charged with Claire's murder.

Tony was going to be fine but his jaw had needed to be rebuilt and his remaining teeth were wired together, making conversation impossible. A remorseful Jim had been in to see him the previous day and had apologized for stealing the stuff from his flat. He'd brought along a bottle of Absolut vodka and Tony had sucked up half of it through a Biro tube before a nurse had intervened. A large bottle of hair tonic had also been confiscated from the cupboard in his bedside table. Nobody was quite sure how he had obtained it.

That afternoon Mary came to see me. She gave me

another healing crystal and I thanked her for saving my life. I was happy to see her, happy to be alive. We discussed the news about Alan and joked about the fight.

'You were better than Cynthia Rothrock back there,' I said. 'The way you kicked Alan in the neck, it was straight out of *Enter the Dragon*.'

'Compared to a sixteen-stone rock star on a cocaine binge, Alan was a pushover,' she replied. I laughed and my rib stabbed me.

'Liz feels really bad about all this. She feels responsible for what happened to Claire and now there's this thing with Doctor Parker,' she said.

'Kate's going to be fine,' I said. I couldn't allow myself to think otherwise.

'I know, but it's been really hard on Liz. She only tried the blackmail as a prank, you know. When it worked out so easily she just kept going. Alan had really hurt her,' Mary said. 'There's something else you should know, Steve. Something important. Liz is pregnant.'

'Liz is pregnant?' My mind went into heavy rotation. 'What do you mean, she's pregnant?' Mary looked stricken.

'The doctors did a test when she was here. It's a routine thing.'

'How pregnant?' I asked.

'You mean how long?'

'Yeah, how long?'

'I don't know. Seven weeks, I think.'

It could just possibly have been mine but of course it was far more likely to be Alan's. When Mary left I pondered the ramifications of what she'd told me. I figured that Liz would try and have the baby even if it had been fathered by Adolf Hitler.

Liz came to see me the following day. As soon as she came into the room I detected the glow of reproduction in her complexion. She asked after my condition and a tear came to her eye.

'I feel terrible, Steve. I'm so sorry. This is all my fault,' she said.

'That's ridiculous,' I said. 'I'm as much to blame as you are.'

We talked about Claire's death and about the charges against Alan.

'I never expected that the blackmail would work,' Liz said. 'I just wanted to pay Alan back, to hurt him. Can you understand that?'

'Of course I can. I've felt the same way ever since he fired me.'

'Mary told you about the baby, didn't she?'

'What are you going to do? It is Alan's, isn't it?'

'Oh, God, I don't know. Probably. It must have happened around the time you came out of the Webster. But the fact that I'm pregnant doesn't change things. I still think we should go ahead and get a divorce.'

'I agree. I'm in love with Kate Parker,' I said. Liz blinked.

'Really? Your psychiatrist? I thought you'd had an affair with Julia,' she said. Nothing could diminish the secret radiance in Liz's womb. 'Listen, Steve, the police want to interview me again. Did you tell them about the blackmail money?'

'No, they just asked me about what happened at the house. Don't tell them a thing. You've got the money hidden, haven't you?'

'Yes, I've got it hidden.'

'Where?'

'In the attic.'

'You're kidding!'

'What's so funny? Do you want it? You should have it.'

'You keep the money. For the baby,' I said.

'It's strange, isn't it? You were right about Alan all along.'

'I was wrong about everything else.'

'Life goes on, Steve,' she said with a Mona Lisa smile.

It was the kind of thing you tell a kid when its pet's just died. We bade each other farewell, two shipwreck survivors drifting apart on a choppy sea. I hoped that I wouldn't live to regret my magnanimity. Liz could still take me to the cleaners in a divorce court.

Three days later a nurse told me they were going to operate on Kate. The doctors didn't want me to leave my bed but they couldn't stop me. I took a taxi to Charing Cross Hospital in Hammersmith.

The sky was dark over Putney and rain was falling softly on the city. I looked at the clock on the waiting room wall and wondered when Kate would be going up to the operating theatre on the fourteenth floor. The strip light on the ceiling began to blink and strobe. I pulled a chair from the wall and placed it beneath the light fixture. If I could correct the fault, Kate was going to be all right. I stepped up and tapped the metal casing. The sooty tube righted itself and its cold glow filled the room once more.

I needed to see Kate again, to hold her hand before she went under the knife. When I reached the nurses' station on Ten South the rockabilly nurse told me that she had already been taken upstairs. Anxiety dried my mouth. I went to the washroom and ran the cold tap. I imagined the liquid rope threading itself through seven people: Kate, me, Liz, Tony, Mary, Alan and Claire, drawing us together like a string of cultured pearls. I cupped my hands and closed my eyes and drank from the tap.